Ruthless

Knight

Book 2

(Legendary Bastards of the Crown)

By

Elizabeth Rose

RoseScribe Media Inc.
Cover created by Elizabeth Rose Krejcik
Edited by Scott Moreland

ISBN – 13: 978-1542982788
ISBN – 10: 1542982782

Books by Elizabeth Rose:

♛ **(Legacy of the Blade Series)**
♛ Prequel
♛ Lord of the Blade – Book 1
♛ Lady Renegade – Book 2
♛ Lord of Illusion – Book 3
♛ Lady of the Mist – Book 4

♔ **(Daughters of the Dagger Series)**
♔ Prequel
♔ Ruby – Book 1
♔ Sapphire – Book 2
♔ Amber – Book 3
♔ Amethyst – Book 4

♜ **(MadMan MacKeefe Series)**
♜ Onyx – Book 1
♜ Aidan – Book 2
♜ Ian – Book 3

❊ **(Elemental Series)**
❊ The Dragon and the DreamWalker: Book 1, Fire
❊ The Duke and the Dryad: Book 2, Earth
❊ The Sword and the Sylph: Book 3, Air
❊ The Sheik and the Siren: Book 4, Water

♘ **(Greek Myth Fantasy)**
♘ Kyros' Secret
♘ The Oracle of Delphi
♘ Thief of Olympus
♘ The Pandora Curse

♙ **(Barons of the Cinque Ports Series)**
♙ The Baron's Quest
♙ The Baron's Bounty
♙ The Baron's Destiny

✢ **(Tarnished Saints Series)**
✢ Tarnished Saints Christmas Prequel
✢ Doubting Thomas – Book 1
✢ Luring Levi – Book 2
✢ Judging Judas – Book 3
✢ Seducing Zeb – Book 4
✢ Saving Simon – Book 5
✢ Wrangling James – Book 6
✢ Praising Pete – Book 7
✢ Teaching Philip – Book 8
✢ Loving John – Book 9
✢ Playing Nate – Book 10
✢ Igniting Andrew – Book 11
✢ Taming Thad – Book 12

♕ **(Legendary Bastards of the Crown Series)**
♕ Restless Sea Lord – Book 1
♕ Ruthless Knight – Book 2
♕ Reckless Highlander – Book 3

☆ **Cowboys of the Old West Series**
☆ **Tangled Tales Series**

And More!
Visit http://elizabethrosenovels.com

To My Readers:

It is best to read the series in order so no surprises will be ruined. However, each book also stands alone.

The books in the Legendary Bastards of the Crown series are:

Destiny's Kiss – Series Prequel
Restless Sea Lord – Book 1
Ruthless Knight – Book 2
Reckless Highlander – Book 3

Elizabeth Rose

Prologue

Whitehaven, England 1366

From betrayal and deceit, a legend is put to rest.

Rowen, the triplet brother of Rook and Reed Douglas, died the day he was wed.

Or at least that was the way it transpired in the minds of his two very angry brothers.

"I dinna care if he's our brathair, I'm goin' to kill him for betrayin' us." Reed drew his sword from his scabbard. Rook's hand shot out and grabbed his wrist to stop him.

"Nay. Now is not the time or place." Rook glanced back at their brother in the distance as they had, first watched his wedding and, now, his knighting from their position behind the rocks. Rowen knelt before their father with his head bowed as Lady Cordelia, his new wife, stood at his side.

"The bluidy bastard is kneelin' at the king's feet and pledgin' his allegiance to our enemy!" spat Reed, pulling out of Rook's grip. "Let me kill him now and be done with it."

"Stop being so reckless, Reed, and use your head. If we move in now with all Edward's men to protect him, we're as good as dead. And don't forget, all three of us are bastards," Rook reminded him in a low voice. "Rowen doesn't deserve wealth and riches, and especially not being knighted." Rook's body tensed at the mere thought of his brother becoming a knight. Rook had been training for years on his own. His secret fantasy of someday being a knight had pushed him forward although he knew it would never happen. He'd stolen weapons and chain mail and all he could from the dead soldiers after their battles to aid him in his progress. But even after all this, he was still only a bandit and a recluse hiding away in the dark and dreary catacombs, while his brother collected a bounty that Rook had always coveted. Aye, he found himself wanting to kill their brother as well.

Having discovered at the young age of twelve that King Edward had sired them and then wanted them killed, the brothers held animosity toward their father. The boys' lives were saved. They were then raised in Scotland by their late mother's sister and husband. They were separated on the terrible night of Burnt Candlemas. King Edward and his men had plowed through Scotland, killing, pillaging, and burning everything. The triplets held no love in their heart for the man who caused so many deaths and devastated their land. Or so it used to be. Now, Rook didn't know what was running through Rowen's daft head.

"We've worked too hard for the last three years stealin' from Edward tryin' to make him miserable," said Reed. "Now, with Rowen's new alliance, our reputation of bein' the Demon Thief is over."

"Aye," agreed Rook, his eyes focused on his brother being knighted as he spoke. "It will be hard to continue our raids on the king with Rowen working against us now. He'll be wise to our ways. We'll never take Edward by surprise again."

"With everythin' we've taken from Edward through the years, it doesna compare to what Rowen has just gained."

"Nay, it doesn't." Rook's gut twisted, seeing his brother collecting the bounties of being the first-born triplet. At one time Edward wanted to save only the first-born and kill the other brothers since they were triplets. Triplets were said to be spawned by the devil. Everyone believed in the superstition that twins and triplets were cursed. "Now the king has taken even more from us than we could ever have imagined. He's taken our brother."

"Och, Rook, dinna be a fool. Rowen gave himself to the wretched man of his own choosin'."

"I know," agreed Rook with a slight nod of his head. "He traded us for a wife, land, riches, and a title." It was everything Rook wanted in life and would never have. Even if Rowen had been born first, he didn't deserve any of what he'd gotten from the alliance. "I hate him as much as you do right now."

Rowen had been stolen and raised by pirates that night so long ago when the brothers were separated. Reed had made it to the Highlands and found Ross, the man they'd thought was their father. Rook, on that horrible night, had been swept away to safety in the catacombs by a concerned monk. And in the catacombs he'd resided from that day, starting in Scotland and ending up at Lanercost Priory across the border where he now ruled over the dead.

"He betrayed us!" Reed's fist clenched over the hilt of his sword. "He even gave up command of the Sea Mirage to get what he wanted."

"He was a fool to trade the fastest ship on the sea for a

girl!" spat Rook. "You will never see me turning into a milksop at the hands of a woman."

"What are we goin' to do?" asked Reed. His jaw twitched as much as his fingers, as he was always ready for a fight.

"We wait," said Rook calmly. He'd learned to hide his feelings through the years, letting them churn inside instead of reacting recklessly like Reed. Then again, Reed was always the oddball of the three of them with the way he dressed and spoke like a Scot when they were truly English.

"I hereby dub thee Sir Rowen of Whitehaven," announced King Edward, tapping Rowen on each shoulder with his blade. The crowd cheered and clapped in response. Then Rowen's eyes lifted and he spotted them standing there. But neither Rook nor Reed did a thing to acknowledge their brother.

"We wait for the right time. Then the Demon Thief will continue to make our dear old father pay for wanting us dead," Rook vowed under his breath. "And next time, Rowen will pay as well."

Rook's raven squawked and landed on his outstretched arm. Reed's bird, a red kite, circled the sky overhead. Rowen's sea hawk swooped past them, settling on a branch nearby. They'd once been a team of brothers. They were triplets – each with the same face but with different hair color. They'd once had such a tight bond that no one could break them apart. But not anymore. Now their brother had pledged his allegiance to their enemy. And in doing so, he'd made an enemy of himself.

"Let's go," said Rook, turning to leave, feeling fire pushing through his veins.

"What about our brathair?" asked Reed, sheathing his

sword.

Rook glanced back over his shoulder, once more, to see the traitor who he'd once loved.

"We have no brother other than each other," said Rook. He turned his back on Rowen, the same way his brother had turned his back on them. "We will never mention Rowen's name again. Do you understand? He is dead to us. Dead, I say!"

"Aye." Reed spat on the ground and turned away as well.

Then Rook headed back to his domain in the bowels of the ruins of Lanercost Priory where he would continue to live – amongst the dead.

Chapter 1

Two months later

Rook sat atop his horse and waited in the thicket, watching silently along with Reed and their men as the king's horse-drawn covered wagon came down the well-traveled road. They'd waited for what seemed like forever for their chance to raid again, and now the legendary Demon Thief would strike once more. But this time, it would be without Rowen at their side.

"Now?" whispered Reed, being as impatient as always, sitting atop the horse that Brother Everad usually used. Some of Rook's hired mercenaries had horses, but not the villagers who fought with him. All the Scots were on foot. Rook only had the two horses that he'd stolen after raids.

"Not yet," Rook whispered back, holding his hand in the air, ready to give the signal to attack. Thunder rumbled overhead and rain pelted down like arrows from the sky. Rook felt it in his bones that this wasn't a good omen.

He looked over to the loyal monk, Brother Everad. The monk had been with Rook since the day he'd saved the man's life so long ago. Even though he was a man of the cloth, he always traveled with him on the raids and fought as well. With a dagger gripped in each hand, he looked upward and blessed himself.

Lightning flashed across a blackened sky as the wagon clattered over the bumpy, wet road. A man led the traveling party, but Rook couldn't see his face since the man had the hood of his cloak pulled low. A troop of a dozen royal guards led the way down the road with another dozen soldiers at the rear. He had no idea what was in the covered cart but hoped it was gold and jewels. The men had become restless lately. If he didn't throw them a bone soon, he was going to lose his small army.

"I only see a few dozen men," said Reed. "We should be able to take them easily, even if Brody and his crew refused to help us fight."

Rook felt disgusted by the amount of loyalty Rowen's first mate showed him, even after the betrayal. Sure, Brody was captain of the Sea Mirage now, but they were pirates! Pirates were meant to pillage and steal. It was a way of life – of survival. He wondered how much his traitorous brother paid them to back out of the raid.

Rook's raven cawed from the treetops. Reed's red kite let out a cry as well. The man at the front of the group stiffened his back at the sound. Rook only hoped he hadn't been alerted.

"Now!" cried Rook, dropping his hand, charging his horse down to the road at a fast run as he led the way. With sword drawn, he rushed toward the wagon with Reed and the raiders right behind him.

"It's the Demon Thief!" one of the guards called out, causing all the soldiers to draw their weapons. Swords clashed in battle as lightning split the sky overhead. They made their way to the wagon easily, but what they found inside was the last thing he wanted to see. There were trunks and barrels of the king's riches under the tarp, but that wasn't all they found.

"It's a trap!" Reed shouted. Another dozen soldiers jumped out from inside the wagon and began to fight. They should have learned their lesson the last time this happened. Now, they were outnumbered. Damn Rowen for putting them in this position! Any of the lives lost here today would be his brother's fault.

Men fought from horseback and also on foot. It wasn't long before bodies fell all around them, broken and bloodied. Before they knew it, the man under the cape at the front of the group rode toward them with his sword drawn. With a cry of a sea hawk from overhead, Rook knew it was his brother, Rowen.

"Stop!" shouted Rowen, lowering his hood to show his identity. "Call off your men and no one else has to die."

"Nay! Never," shouted Rook, taking down a soldier.

"Damn ye, Rowen. How could ye do this to us?" asked Reed, off his horse now and fighting two men at once like a madman.

"I'm not the one doing anything," Rowen answered. "I'm only escorting the king's shipment. You're the fools who decided to try to steal it. Did you honestly think you'd get away with it now that the king is aware of your game? You should have learned your lesson from the last failed raid."

The rain pelted down relentlessly, making it harder to fight. Rook's horse slipped on the muddy road and, before he knew it, he landed prone on his back on the ground.

Rowen was off his horse immediately, holding the tip of

his sword to Rook's throat. "Just say the word and this could all be over," said Rowen. His blue eyes stared down at Rook as he spoke. "Give yourself up and I'll try to convince Edward to align with you, as well."

"Ye bastard!" shouted Reed, jumping through the air and taking Rowen down with him. "We'll ne'er align with the English king." Rook sprang to his feet and, this time, held the tip of his sword to Rowen's throat.

"I should kill you for betraying us," snarled Rook, tempted to push the tip of the blade just a little farther.

Reed held off more soldiers as Rook glared down at his brother.

"Then what are you waiting for?" Rowen challenged him. "Kill me if it'll make you feel better. But you know as well as I that if you had been in my position, you would have made the same choices."

He was right. That thought bothered Rook to no end. It was also the only thing that kept him from pushing his blade through his brother's neck.

"You betrayed your own flesh and blood! And now you fight against us for the king."

"I'm a knight now and have pledged my allegiance to our father," Rowen answered.

"He's no' our faither!" shouted Reed, still fighting like a madman.

"I want to talk with you both. I need to explain things. Give me a chance," pleaded Rowen.

"It's too late for talking," said Rook. "And I don't give second chances."

"Rook, we canna hold them off much longer," came Reed's call for help. "We've lost too many men, and the ones that are left are all wounded."

"Call off your men," Rook challenged Rowen.

A look of despair came over Rowen's face and he shook his head slightly. "I can't do that, I'm sorry. Please leave now before you're killed."

A soldier jumped out of the shadows and swung at Rook. Rook jumped out of the way but wasn't fast enough. The edge of the soldier's sword came down and nicked his leg. Rowen grabbed his blade and jumped to his feet stepping in between them. "This one's mine," he told the soldier, taking Rook by the collar and flinging him across the ground. Rook landed on his injured leg and let out a shout.

"Get the hell out of here already. I won't tell you again!" Rowen warned him, then headed back toward the cart.

Reed ran over with the rest of the men following close behind. Rook spied a good dozen of their men dead on the ground and the others were bloody and injured.

"Rook, ye're wounded," said Reed, reaching out and helping Rook to his feet.

"My lord, let me help you." Brother Everad hurried to his side, putting his arm around Rook to help him walk.

"We dinna have a chance against so many," Reed told him. "We'll lead the soldiers toward the coast while ye head back to the catacombs."

"I'll never forgive him for this," said Rook, leaning on the monk as he reluctantly headed toward their horses that had wandered into the woods.

Looking over his shoulder as he limped away, he saw Rowen watching him. Several of his soldiers started after him, but Rowen stopped them.

"They're no threat to us anymore," said Rowen. "Now gather our dead and put them in the cart. Let's get the hell out of this rain."

Chapter 2

Lady Calliope Duval opened the door of the villager's hut to see the downpour of rain outside.

"Oh, my," she said, realizing she would now have to hurry back to Naward Castle and be soaked in doing so. She'd sneaked out to begin with, hoping her uncle, Lord Ovid, wouldn't notice she'd gone. She'd left through the postern gate with a bag of goods tied to her back, not even taking a horse for fear the guards atop the battlements would see her leave.

"My lady, I can't thank you enough for what you do for us." The woodcutter's wife held her baby in her arms while her four other young children stayed at her side. She was a plump woman with dark hair and had a very kind face. Calliopc had brought hcr coin as wcll as brcad and meat. She'd left the same at four more of the villagers' houses as well. The villagers, or serfs, weren't allowed to hunt in the royal forest even though it was filled with more deer and other game than the castle occupants could eat. Her uncle had hung two men just this past year for poaching.

When Calliope's late father was Lord of Naward, things

were different. He'd always made sure the villagers were treated fairly and were warm and fed.

"It's the least I can do to help you feed all your children. And I'll make certain when the weather gets colder that you have enough wood to burn as well." With Ida's husband being a woodcutter, one would think they'd have plenty of wood. But her uncle didn't allow wood from his forest to be burned in their little huts. It was actually the king's forest, but he'd been granted the right to hunt and use wood since he was noble.

"Hank has had to take up fighting with the Demon Thief in order to keep us from starving," the woman said. "It doesn't bring in much money, but we need everything he can get. Your uncle has raised our taxes three times in the past year. We've had to sell most of the livestock just to pay the rent. We barely have enough pigs and chickens left to feed us through the winter."

"I understand," she said, staring out the door at the rain. The cruck-framed house was one simple room where up to eight peasants lived. Its walls were made of wattle and daub, or a woven lattice of sticks, filled in with straw mixed with clay, dirt, and manure. The roof was thatched and the windows opened with simple shutters to keep out the cold. She remembered visiting the village as a child. The huts always smelled of smoke from the cook fire, but now there wasn't much cooking or burning of wood happening. The coldness of the dirt floor covered with straw sent a shiver up her spine. "Don't worry; I won't say a word to anyone that the villagers are helping that man."

"Men," Ida corrected her. "It is no longer a secret that the Demon Thief is three men - the bastard triplets of King Edward. And now that one of them has married and paid his allegiance to the king, there are only two of the brothers left to go on the raids."

Calliope's head turned and her brows dipped. Most the information she had was given to her by the villagers. Her uncle barely ever spoke to her and kept her locked inside the castle like a prisoner. She couldn't remember the last time she'd been outside the castle gates without having to sneak out on her own. Besides the villagers, the only other person who ever told her anything about life beyond the castle walls was Wardell. He was the king's messenger and a friend she'd grown up with. He came to the castle often. She'd seen him just yesterday, but her uncle had sent him away before he could tell her much of anything.

Her eyes darted over to the ruins of Lanercost Priory in the distance. Looming before her was the crumbling ruins of tall stone arches. The place was said to be haunted. No one ever went near there anymore. No one except the Demon Thief. She'd never seen the Demon Thief, but knew one of the bastard triplets lived like a rat in the dark and dreary catacombs of the priory. Like a lord of the Underworld, he ruled over the dead.

"They're out raiding at this very minute," said Ida. "I worry about Hank every time he leaves. If anything happens to him, I don't know how I'll survive without him."

Shouting was heard. Calliope saw two serfs carrying someone, coming toward the hut through the rain.

"Hank?" Ida put down her baby; her eyes transfixed on the two wounded men as they dragged a dead man along with them. "Hank! God, no!" She darted out into the rain and threw herself down in the mud, holding the head of her dead husband on her lap. The woman rocked back and forth crying.

Her children started to run to her, but Calliope reached out and stopped them, pulling them back into the house. "You stay here," she said. "Your mother will return shortly."

The men dragged Hank's dead body inside, leaving him on the floor. The children looked down at their dead father and started crying.

"What happened?" Calliope asked the man she recognized as Hank's brother, Tom.

"We were ambushed," said Tom, sinking atop a chair. He was bruised and bleeding. Calliope ran to the washstand to get a wet rag to aid the men.

"There were too many of them. Without Rowen and his men, we had no chance," said the other man named Horace. These men were vassals of her uncle and had been fined more than once when her uncle accused them of taking too many of his crops. They both had wives and children to support as well.

"Tell me what happened," said Calliope, cleaning first one man's wounds and then the other.

"Rowen was there," said Horace. "The brothers were fighting and almost killed each other."

"Who killed my Hank?" asked Ida, hugging her husband to her chest, not wanting to let him go.

"It was one of the king's guards," said Tom. "They had men hiding in the wagon. We were doomed from the start."

Ida wailed again and the children continued to cry. Calliope's heart broke for these poor people.

Realizing nightfall was setting in, she needed to get back to the castle before her uncle discovered she was gone. It was a good hour's walk and, in the storm, it was going to take even longer.

"I've brought food and coin," Calliope told the men. "I

wish I could stay to help, but I need to return to the castle before I'm missed." She gently helped Ida to her feet. "Ida, Hank is gone now, but your children need you." She guided the woman to her children and then looked back to the men. "Will you bury Hank for her?"

"I'll take care of my brother," said Tom.

"Someone needs to stay with Ida and the children tonight."

"I'll bring my family here and we'll all stay together," offered Horace.

"Good," she answered with a nod, trying to stay strong. These unfortunate people had lost so much that she felt as if she needed to do more to help them. "I'm going to talk to my uncle and see if I can convince him to help you."

"Nay," said Tom with a shake of his head. "We don't want him to know we're helping the Demon Thief or he'll imprison us. It's bad enough that when he finds out Hank has died, he's going to charge Ida a fine to continue farming the land."

Calliope looked out the door, focusing on the priory once again. A sudden fear ran through her that more had died than were mentioned. "Did Brother Everad raid with you today?" she asked, feeling her heart beating quickly.

"Aye, he was there with a dagger in each hand," said Tom.

"Did he – did he return?"

"I saw him helping the Demon Thief back here," said Horace.

A sense of relief washed over her and she released a deep breath. "I will send the monk over to say a blessing over your dead and to give comfort." She picked up her cloak and threw it around her shoulders.

"Thank you, Lady Calliope. Thank you for everything you do." Ida looked up with tears in her eyes as she hugged her scared children to her chest.

Calliope said her farewells, then pulled the hood of her wool cloak over her head and stepped out into the rain. It felt cold against her face, so she pulled her hood lower as she started toward the priory. Part of her felt frightened to be going there, but she needed to see Brother Everad. It wasn't him or even the ruins that she feared. Nor was it the dark, cold, and dreary catacombs that lie beneath the church.

She'd grown up playing in the catacombs and knew them like the back of her hand. The underground passages were like a maze that stretched out in several directions, seeming to go on forever. If one didn't know them well, a person could get lost and never return.

One of the passages led to Scotland, while another led back to the dungeon of Naward Castle. Even her uncle didn't know that the catacombs between the priory and the castle were connected because no one ever had the curiosity to find out where they led. That is, no one but her and possibly the monks.

Hurrying over the wet ground, her soft leather shoes sank into the mud. The falling rain soaked her cloak and made her movements feel slow and weighted. She would go to the priory and talk to Brother Everad, although he had warned her never to come there. She would also take the path through the catacombs back to the castle. Because of the rain, she had no other choice.

None of those things worried her. Even the temper of her uncle, if he found out she was missing, wasn't half as terrifying to her as the thought that she was about to enter the Demon Thief's lair!

Chapter 3

"Brother Everad, I can make it on my own from here," said Rook, making his way down into the catacombs that were deep below Lanercost Priory. He approached his secret room and pulled a hidden lever. The stone slid open, exposing a large wooden door behind it. Rook turned the latch and opened the door that led to his personal space. Once Rook had made Lanercost Priory his permanent home, he'd made sure to fix up a secret room to his liking.

"I will get more water from the creek and be back to tend to your wound," said Everad, holding a lit torch in one hand. Tall shadows danced on the stone walls of the eerie underground chamber.

"Take the horses to the villager's barn first. We don't want to give away our presence here in case the king's guards come looking for us." Rook lit a lantern on a table just inside the room. The soft glow of the flame lit up the area, bringing life to his elegantly furnished room.

"Don't you think Rowen will lead them right here to you?" asked the monk, holding the lit torch higher. The catacombs were dark and musty. The sound of the rain dripping down the antechamber walls in several spots made Rook glad his room was warm and dry.

"If Rowen had wanted to do that, he would have done it by now." Rook grimaced as he limped over to his bed. He reached over and lit a beeswax candle.

"He could have killed you today, my lord," said Everad.

"Aye." Rook removed his weapon belt and dropped it on a nearby chair. His chain mail hauberk followed. "And I could have killed him just as easily."

"Why didn't you?" asked the man. "I know how much you hate your brother for betraying you and Reed."

"That is a good question," said Rook, taking the candle and hobbling over to sit in a chair by the table. A chessboard was set up on the table with the marble pieces atop it already in play. He picked up the knight and turned it over and over in his hand. "Rowen doesn't deserve to be a knight or to have a castle or wealth of any kind." He felt like crushing the knight in his palm but, instead, placed it down gently on the chessboard. "On the other hand, no matter what he did, he is still my brother. He doesn't deserve to die for it, either."

"So you're going to forgive your brother for what he did?" The monk stood just inside the door as he spoke.

Rook's blood boiled at the fact so many lives were wasted today for nothing. The villagers didn't get a shilling from the raid and now they were in a worse situation than before. Plus, the mercenaries were getting restless. Without pay, they wouldn't stick around much longer. His brother, Rowen, could have stopped Rook's men from dying but, instead, he fought for the king.

"Nay!" shouted Rook, taking his arm and swiping it across the chessboard in anger. All the pieces crashed to the ground, hitting the wooden floor with a thunk. "How can I ever forgive him? Things will never be the same between us after what he did."

"Would you have made the same choices as Rowen had you been in his position?" asked the monk. "It was an opportunity that no one could refuse."

Rook didn't know the answer to that. He'd been struggling with the same question in his mind ever since Rowen was dubbed a knight. It confused him and made him feel weary and anxious at the same time. He didn't want to think about this right now, and neither did he want to answer. His leg was bleeding, and he felt like killing someone he was so upset. Still, the monk's question lodged in his brain and he couldn't dismiss it, either. Would he have done the same thing? Damn, the thought of accepting wealth, a title, a castle and being dubbed a knight was very tempting.

"Go tend to the horses." Rook pushed his tall body from the chair and hobbled over to the water basin.

"Aye, my lord. Right away," said the monk, scurrying out the door, leaving it open a crack as he left the room.

Rook blew air from his mouth, then jabbed his hands into the basin and splashed the frigid water against his hot, weary face. Mayhap this would cool down his fiery rage that was burning out of control. He squeezed his eyes closed as he dunked his head in the water, feeling tired, defeated, and irritated as all hell.

The short, quick caws of his raven from the outer crypt caused his spine to become rigid fast. Droplets of water shot across the room from his abrupt action, as well as dripped down his face and neck. Hades, his raven, was alarming him that an intruder had entered his home. He spun on his heel to grab his sword.

Without a candle to light her way, Calliope ran her hand over the rocky walls as she edged her way forward through the dark, foreboding catacombs. Sure she'd heard voices from up ahead, she approached the area silently, aware of every little noise around her. The cry of a bird had echoed through the cavern just moments ago. The catacombs of the dead were no place for a bird. Then again, it was no place for any living thing – including her.

She crept toward the sound and, after a few minutes, she saw the glimmer of light in the distance. Curiosity drew her toward the light like a moth to a flame. She had to know more. Her soaking wet gown and cloak swished over the hard dirt path, dragging behind her as she walked.

She hadn't been in the catacombs for years now. Not since the Demon Thief made this his lair. She'd stayed away for several reasons. One of the reasons being the thought of accidentally running across the bandit in the passages and having her head lopped off by his blade before she could make a plea for her life. But now she had no choice. She needed to get back to Naward Castle before her uncle discovered her missing. In the storm, this was the fastest way to get there. The catacomb passageways wound around, leading right to the dungeon of Naward Castle. If she took the opposite direction, she'd end up in Scotland.

She knew these passageways well, as she'd made a game of exploring them as a child. Growing up, she'd always been much too curious. It had gotten her into trouble more than once.

After the death of her father when she was only ten, she'd been raised by her father's half-brother, Lord Ovid. He never paid her much attention, so she'd been free to explore.

Sometimes she'd get lost in the maze of passageways and be missing for nearly a day. The legends of the catacombs being haunted since the desecration by the Scottish King David two decades ago should have frightened her away. Instead, it drew her closer. Calliope had been surrounded by death her entire life. It took more than just tombs and bones to scare her.

As she got older, she found herself needing to know where every single path inside the catacombs led. And so she'd sneaked down to the dungeon and into the catacombs whenever she had the chance. To her, it was a great adventure.

A raven hopped around atop the sarcophagus of a dead noble, cackling so loudly she was sure it was going to gain the Demon Thief's attention. With the fissure of light coming from one of the stone walls, she could see the bird's slightly curved beak and its beady, little dark eyes. The stone lid of the tomb had the face and body of a noble carved into it. The image of the dead knight had closed eyes and held a stone sword against its chest. Behind it was a large, wooden crucifix rising from the dirt floor.

The raven cackled as if it were laughing at her. Then it hopped atop the cross, using it as a perch. She approached and tried to shoo it away with her hand, but all it did was flap its wings and squawk louder as it vacated the perch and continued to explore the top of several more tombs.

"What is that?" she asked softly to herself, studying the streak of light coming from an opening in the rock up ahead. It looked like it led to a hidden room. This hadn't been here the last time she'd come through the catacombs. She needed to see what it was.

Her curiosity urged her forward without hesitation as she

was drawn toward the light. Without making a sound, her fingers wrapped around the hilt of her dagger hanging from her belt. She gripped it tightly, holding it forward, letting it lead the way as she ventured closer and closer to the hidden room. Her heartbeat quickened. Who or what would she find inside? Hopefully, it was just Brother Everad who lived here with the Demon Thief. Then again, Everad hadn't mentioned a hidden room. He'd only told her to stay away. That made it clear to her that this had to be the Demon Thief's lair. A shiver like icy fingers ran up her spine.

While the catacombs were dark, morbid, and filled with death, this room looked to be light, warm, and full of life. That confused her because when she'd heard from Everad that the Demon Thief lived in the crypts, she pictured him as some monster that thrived on flesh and blood and would shrivel up and die if he ever came into the light.

Ignoring her common sense that warned her to retreat, her desire to know more about this mysterious, dangerous man gave her the courage to move forward.

The raven shrieked from behind her, almost as if it were warning her about walking right toward her imminent death.

Reaching the humongous stone that had been moved aside, she realized there was a wooden door hidden behind it. Opened a little, she could see furnishings inside the chamber. With her dagger clutched in one hand, she leaned forward and pressed one eye up to the crack to get a better look. Oddly enough, it seemed more like the chamber of a noble than the abode of a killer. Silently and cautiously, she reached out her shaking hand, her fingers skimming the gnarled wood of the door. It felt thick and dense and took more than just a slight movement of her wrist to push it open further.

Just one better glimpse of the room and she'd be on her way, she told herself. Her heartbeat pounded in her ears, and her mind scolded her for being so stupid. Still, she did not retreat. Bravely stepping one foot over the threshold, she took shallow breaths as she pushed the door open a little more.

She should have called out and made her presence known since it could be Everad inside. But once she got a better look at the furnishings, she decided to stay silent. Everad may have gone down the wrong path when he teamed up with the Demon Thief but, needless to say, he was still a monk. No monk would be living like this. It would be best to take a quick look and leave without making her presence known.

Three stairs led to a large four-poster bed with ornate designs carved into the wood. It perched atop a small dais in the center of the room. Long, purple velvet curtains hung from black iron rods around it, dressing the bed as if it wore a cloak of protection. Next, her gaze was captivated by a scene painted on a whitewashed wall just beyond the bed. She pushed the door open just a little wider, stopping in mid-motion and holding her breath as the rusty hinges of the door squeaked loud enough to raise the dead. When she was sure no one heard her, she stepped inside the room with both feet to inspect her surroundings. Her eyes scanned the area quickly to make sure no one was there. She released a breath of relief. The room was vacant.

The difference in the warm, dry atmosphere of this chamber compared to the wet and dank passageways of the catacombs was amazing. One lantern and also a candle lit up the spacious area in a warm glow, enabling her to get a better look.

Colorful woven tapestries lined the walls, giving a royal air to the surroundings. Thick wooden beams overhead opened to what looked like vents leading upward in small stone tunnels. She could feel fresh air brushing past her face. A little light from the sky came through the vents as well. The floor was made of wood and felt warm beneath her feet. So unlike the damp earth floors of the village huts.

Candlelight flickered, causing shadows on the walls. When she smelled cinnamon and cloves, she realized it wasn't a tallow candle made of animal fat that was commonly used. Instead, it was of the highest quality, made from scented beeswax. Beeswax candles were expensive and usually only used by nobles or the high clergy.

She glanced back over her shoulder to the darkness of the crypt from which she'd just come. The bird had stopped making noise and she wondered where it went. Holding her dagger in front of her for protection, she padded across the floor toward the whitewashed wall with the mural on it. Calliope marveled at the fact that it looked like the painting was outlined in places by gold leaf.

"It's beautiful," she whispered, reaching out and slowly dragging her fingers across a colorful depiction of two knights jousting at a tournament. In the background of the scene was the castle. In the lists sat a few nobles and some men of the clergy. Oddly enough, she didn't see the king in this painting anywhere. In front of the painting sat a wooden table and two chairs that were carved with intricate patterns and swirls, just like the posts on the bed. Most commoners sat on benches or stools, but these were chairs with backs on them. Her fingers ran over the intricate design, tracing the swirls up and down.

Then she spotted a warrior's chain mail tunic and

weapons on another chair. This had to be the abode of a warrior. The Demon Thief! Calliope's eyes darted back in the opposite direction where she saw a basin of water atop a table near the door. She had been so mesmerized by the beauty of the chamber that she hadn't noticed it when she'd first entered. Even from where she stood, she could see the water was red with blood. A shiver ran up her spine and she realized she'd made a mistake. She should never have entered. A sudden need filled her to get out of the room and back to the castle immediately where she would be safe.

Hurrying back toward the open door, the toe of her mud-soaked shoe kicked something across the floor. Her gaze flashed downward to see the pieces of a chess game scattered across the floor.

Curiosity gnawed at her insides and was the only thing that kept her from running. She hurriedly scooped up a piece with a pointed top, realizing it symbolized a bishop. It was made of a beautiful swirled marble of the finest quality. Her thumb trailed over the top of the jagged, broken stone that had chipped when it hit the floor.

Before she had a chance to inspect it further, a hand clamped over her mouth from behind. She dropped both the chess piece and her dagger as her hands involuntarily rose to try to push the big hand away. She was pulled backward, hitting what felt like a hard chest as the sharp edge of a cold blade pressed up against her throat.

"Make a move and I'll slit you from ear to ear," growled a male voice in her ear.

The Demon Thief! It had to be him. She cursed herself inwardly, now regretting having been so curious. Why hadn't she just ignored this room altogether and gone straight back to the castle instead?

"Who are you?" he demanded to know. Of course, she couldn't answer, because he had his large hand clamped over her mouth. She could barely breathe since he also covered her nose, and had to do something fast before she swooned. The last thing she needed was to be vulnerable in the hands of a killer.

Managing to open her mouth slightly, she bit the man hard. At the same time, she pushed his sword away from her and squirmed out of his arms. Spying her dagger on the floor, she bent over to reach for it.

"Ow!" he spat, sounding surprised. When her hand reached out for her dagger, he kicked it away with his foot, sending it sliding across the room. The raven cried out from the crypt, its wings fluttering as it flew into the room and landed on the floor next to her only weapon.

"You will die for that," bellowed the man, his long fingers closing around her small wrist. She struggled in his grip and, in the process, the hood of her cloak fell away exposing her identity.

"What the hell!" He let go of her wrist immediately as if he were burned and shook his head. "You're a damned girl."

"I am," she admitted, not sure if that made her an easier target in the Demon Thief's eyes or if, perhaps, it was her saving grace. "But you are the one who is damned." Would he kill her now for having such a loose tongue? Would he have his way with her first? Or would he let her go? The way he eyed her up like a wolf that wanted to eat her, she didn't feel like the outcome was going to be a favorable one.

The Demon Thief did not look at all the way she'd expected. She took a moment to survey him now that she'd met him face to face. In her mind, she'd pictured him looking like an ogre with a scarred face, gray skin, broken, rotting teeth and hideous. But this man was handsome! Her gaze swept his body. He was tall and had a wide chest. She saw some huge muscles through the ripped sleeve of his tunic. His hair fell past his shoulders and was darker than the wings of his raven. He had a short beard and mustache that oddly was trim and neat instead of scraggly. But most surprising was his clear, blue eyes. How could a man who lived amongst the dead, raiding, killing and stealing for a living, not have eyes as dark as the devil? Nay, his eyes looked more like the eyes of an angel. Then he said something she wasn't expecting at all.

"You're beautiful."

Rook was not only surprised but also amused to find a woman sneaking into his chamber. He'd hidden behind the open door, meaning to attack the intruder. But now that he saw she was a girl, he couldn't hurt her.

"Why didn't you tell me you were a girl?" he asked, inspecting his bleeding hand and the impression of her bite mark. He could see by the imprint she'd left upon him that she had strong, straight teeth. And lots of them!

The scent of rosewater from her body clung to his skin, reminding him of his childhood days. Living in a hut in Scotland growing up with four females, he'd smelled rosewater on occasion when they'd put it into their bathwater. He shook the thought from his head, needing to concentrate on the matter at hand. This girl had a mean sense of fight in her as well as a lack of fear. He'd never seen another woman like her. Now, thanks to her, his hand was bleeding to match the wound on his thigh.

"Why didn't I tell you?" she asked. "How could I have possibly answered when your paw was covering my mouth as well as my air flow?"

Her voice was like music to his ears and as sweet as the cooing of doves. Just the thought of doves brought up the memories of the birds he and his brothers used to raise with Ross before Edward attacked on the night of Burnt Candlemas. He pushed the thought away, not wanting to think of the man who'd pretended to be his father for the first twelve years of his life. It was too painful.

He felt as if this woman were not just any woman and wanted to find out more. Who was she and why was she here? It wasn't as if he ever had any visitors in the catacombs. Although she had spunk and could act scrappy, he'd had his share of whores and could tell this one was not a strumpet. Neither was she a villager because she looked and sounded too refined.

"Who are you?" he asked again.

"Who are you?" she asked in return.

"Who do you think I am?" He found this little game amusing. It wasn't every day a beautiful woman came into the catacombs to spar with him verbally.

"I think you're the Demon Thief." She raised her chin in the air and matched his stare. "As a matter of fact, I am sure you are the man spawned by the devil who enjoys stealing from our king and killing everyone in your wake."

He chuckled. "You're only partially correct in your assumption." He laid his sword on the bed and moved toward her. In return, she kept backing away from him, heading for the wall.

"My name is Rook the Ruthless. And I am only one-third of the legendary Demon Thief. While it is true that I enjoy stealing from the king, I don't kill unless my life is threatened."

"Stay away! I'm unarmed," she shouted, backing away, keeping her hands in the air where he could see them. Her eyes flashed to the floor where his raven pecked at her dagger and then back to him.

"In case you haven't noticed, I'm unarmed as well." He held his hands up to prove his point. Blood dripped down his wrist from his hand where she'd bit him.

Her eyes opened wide and so did her mouth. "You're . . . bleeding," she said in a gentle, caring voice.

"Aye. What did you think would happen when you sank your teeth into me like you were eating a slab of meat?" He headed toward the basin of water. Slowly, she kept backing away from him, although her eyes didn't leave his face.

Big, round, green eyes like a curious cat studied him coolly. Her long, golden hair was tied back with a burgundy ribbon, but a few strands had come loose and framed her heart-shaped face. Something about her reminded him of the eldest of his three sisters, Summer. Summer had always had her hair coming loose from its binding as well.

He'd gotten a glimpse of his sisters, Summer, Winter and Autumn, at Rowen's wedding. Before that, the last time he'd seen them was the night of Burnt Candlemas when they were naught more than toddlers.

The woman standing before him looked to be no more than twenty years of age. She wore her hair pulled back from her face by a burgundy ribbon. Pink, delicate lips parted slightly, shaped like a bow. Her cheekbones were sculpted and high. The lily-white color of her skin was opposite of someone who spent their days in the hot sun working the land. If he wasn't mistaken, she was a noble. If only he could see her clothes under that dirty, wet cloak, he would know for sure.

He busied himself, rinsing his injured hand in the basin of water, watching her from the sides of his eyes, wondering if she were going to try to escape.

"Will you hold me prisoner here, now that you've found me in your chamber? Or will you let me go?" He noticed she didn't mention the option of being killed. Either she was fearless or daft not to think of that.

"I'm not in the habit of taking a lady prisoner," he said, shaking the water off his hands. "That's more along the lines of my traitorous brother."

"The pirate," she answered with a slight nod as if she understood. She kept her chin raised and her expression emotionless, but he heard a slight tremble in her voice.

"So you've heard. What else do you know?"

"I don't know anything for sure. You see, I am a prisoner in my own home and not privy to anything but idle gossip."

"You are a prisoner?" He eyed her curiously. "I've never heard of prisoners roaming around in the catacombs without being chased by even a single guard."

"That's because no one knows I'm here."

"Really?" He almost laughed when a shadow darkened her face as she realized she'd just given him a perfect opportunity to kill her and get away with it. That is, no one would be looking for her.

"I didn't mean that. Of course, someone knows I'm here. Lots of people." Her eyes left him and she looked to the ground.

"All except your captor I'm assuming?" He chuckled again. It must have unnerved her since she frowned. "Where is your home?"

She didn't answer him and neither did he expect her to

tell him. This one was a mysterious woman, indeed. Slowly, she raised her hands to her head, pulling the ribbon from her hair. Her long, golden locks were released. The waves of curly hair bounced as they hit her shoulders.

Damn, why did she have to do that? He swallowed deeply, feeling his body coming to life by her presence. He'd been wanting to reach out and let her hair down from the moment he realized she was a woman. Now, she was doing it willingly, as if it were an invitation for him to take her. He wasn't sure what she had in mind.

"Here, let me help you." She extended her arm, holding her palm upward as she waited for him to give her his hand. He hesitated, still not sure of her intent. The bow of her lips curled upward as she smiled slightly, hesitant but willing just the same. Finally, he put his hand into hers. "You shouldn't let your wounds go unattended."

"What?" he asked, sure she was offering herself to him, but instead she was only offering her ministrations.

"Your wound needs to be tended to before it gets infected." His heart sank and his visions of taking her to his bed quickly dissipated. Why had he thought she was offering something else altogether? Mayhap it was because he wanted it so desperately right now. She wound the wide ribbon around his hand to stop the blood flow from the bite she'd given him. Her nimble fingers tucked the end of the ribbon under to keep it secure. "That will stop the blood flow for now, but you should also rub an ointment on it." Her eyes fell to his injured leg. "Let me look at that, too," she said, reaching out for him, but he backed away.

"Nay, I'm fine." He didn't want her to touch him again. If she did, he might not be able to control himself. He couldn't take her to his bed without even knowing who she was or why she was there. He used his good hand to rub the back of his neck. "I'd like to call you by name, but you've yet to give it to me."

"It's better if you don't know." She raised her hood over her head again, denying him the visual.

"Nay, don't hide your beauty." He reached out and raised her chin with two fingers. Her body stiffened.

"Don't worry; I'm not going to hurt you." He brought his mouth closer, wanting - needing to taste her sweet lips. He was mesmerized by this woman although he didn't know why. When she didn't fight him, he took the opportunity, lowering his head and gently placing his lips against hers.

Soft, sensual lips melded with his, tasting as sweet as the Black Bun filled with currants and spices that he'd eaten on Hogmanay as a child in Scotland. Longing filled his body to be back in those days, living with the people he loved, feeling safe and happy. But that seemed like a lifetime ago. Now he was a bandit, hiding amongst the dead, living like a creature of the night under the ground. He was alone.

He kissed her deeper, trying to push the thought of family from his mind and let lust fill his head, instead. It was less painful that way.

His kiss became stronger and forceful as he struggled with his inner demons. He slid his mouth down to nibble on her neck. And when that excited him, he sucked her delicate skin in between his lips, letting his teeth graze her flesh much the same way she'd done to him when she bit him. The taste was intoxicating, only making him want more. His fingers curved, gripping her shoulders tightly as he squeezed her flesh beneath his palms. Then he pushed her robe away in one swift motion, needing to see what she wore beneath the rain-soaked wool.

His actions were met by her knee to his groin. He bit back an oath and bent over in pain with his hands between his legs.

"What the hell did you do that for?" he groaned.

"You were trying to undress me."

"I only wanted to see what you wore." Her cloak had opened in the process and he looked up to finally get his answer. She wore a burgundy gown of velvet hidden beneath the cloak. Aye, it was just as he suspected. She wasn't a commoner, but a noble. Now the question was who was she? And from where did she come?

"I don't like being mauled," she snapped. "Now leave me be, you big brute." She gathered her cloak around her, but her hood remained down.

"Brute?" he squeaked out, looking up, but still bent over as he held his hands to his groin. No one had ever called him a brute before. The girl had quite a mouth on her for being in this situation. Bravery was one of her strong suits.

A rat scurried past her feet just then. She jumped and gasped, making him wonder if her previous actions had all been an act of bravado. When she moved, she stepped on one of the chess pieces covering the floor and stumbled. She ended up in his arms with her hands against his chest.

"Make up your mind," he told her. "Do you want me or not?"

"What? Nay!" She pushed away. "There is a rat in here. Or didn't you see it?" Her head nodded toward the floor.

"I saw it." He chuckled and stood up straight, liking the way she clung to him for protection.

"Why are you laughing?"

"I didn't think anything could scare you. Hades, take care of it," he called out. She watched in amazement as his raven squawked and pecked at the rodent, chasing it from the room. "You never know who or what is going to venture inside when the door is left open." She looked up to him and their eyes interlocked. Pools of bright green like the rolling hills of Scotland stared into his eyes, reaching down to his blackened soul. Then her gaze dropped to his mouth. He bent closer, hoping to get another kiss. But to his dismay, the moment was interrupted.

"Rook, are ye in here?" came the voice of his brother, Reed, echoing through the outer caverns.

The girl hurriedly stepped away from him, pulling her hood back up over her head. She shot forward and scooped up her dagger from the floor. Then with one last glance over her shoulder, she hurried out the door and disappeared into the darkness.

"Wait! Come back!" he cried out, but it was too late. His beautiful, mysterious visitor was gone.

Chapter 4

Calliope hurried through the catacombs without a torch, making her way back to Naward Castle. She had been so infatuated with the Demon's Thief's kiss and then so surprised to hear someone calling for him that she'd foolishly ran out of his chamber before she could steal a flame of some sort to guide her way home. However, it didn't matter. She knew these catacombs well and had more than once in the past walked them in the dark when her candle had blown out on accident. It had taken her longer, but still, she had always made it to her destination.

Her heart fluttered in her chest, but it wasn't because she was afraid of the dark or even rats for that matter. She'd learned to push those fears aside when she was younger. She'd only jumped when she'd seen the rat because it startled her. The thing that really frightened her was the fact that she'd liked the kiss of the Demon Thief. If they hadn't been interrupted, she would have let him kiss her again.

"What is the matter with you?" she asked herself, feeling the wall as she walked. Her hand ran over a stone that felt like a star. She slowed, knowing the knee-deep hole as big as her head was coming up. Flattening her body against the wall, she squeezed past it without falling in. She'd managed not to touch the skulls that were embedded into parts of the wall along the way. She also knew where the bodies of dead monks were laid to rest in the crevices in the walls and avoided those as well.

She'd been walking in the catacombs for over an hour now, she guessed. The trip had gone quickly with her thoughts on Rook the entire time. The gate to Naward's dungeon was just up ahead. She only hoped the rusted bars in the gate that had worn through hadn't been fixed or she'd be trapped in the catacombs and would have to call for help. However, since her uncle never even went to the dungeon, she was certain her escape route was still operable.

She'd thought about calling for help while in the lair of the Demon Thief, but something kept her from doing so. While the man frightened her, he excited her at the same time. His ebony hair was as dark as his mysterious pet raven named Hades. Such an odd man. She'd never known anyone who lived amongst the dead before. He didn't even seem to be bothered by the fact there were corpses all around him. She supposed it was because he was used to carnage from so much killing.

She'd been surprised by his secret room. It was warmer and dryer than her chamber in her uncle's castle. He seemed like a man who knew how to make the best of any situation. After all, he'd taken one of the scariest places in all of England and made it his home.

He intrigued her and she was curious to know more about him. She smiled as she thought of his bright blue eyes that seemed clearer than the sky on a summer's day. And his kiss had made her tingle. She'd never been kissed like that by any man before. Of course, she'd only had a few suitors in her life and they'd all been nobles. Their kisses had been stiff and stuffy. The Demon Thief's kiss held power, strength, and most of all – passion.

He'd told her his name was Rook, and she realized it fit him perfectly. Just like the dark bird, he resided over the graves of the dead. She should have been frightened by him just by that fact alone, but she wasn't. Something about being with Rook made her feel special. Perhaps it was the fact he'd called her beautiful. She'd never been called beautiful by anyone before. The mere thought made her smile.

Her hand hit the bars of the dungeon gate, telling her she'd found her way back to the castle. Her body shivered from the cold and her wet cloak felt cumbersome. All she wanted was to get back into her chamber and dry herself in front of the fire in the hearth.

She felt for the hole in the gate and squeezed through.

Seeing the flickering of a torch lighting up the darkness ahead, she made her way forward cautiously. She didn't want to alert the guards that she was there. She also had no idea how she'd sneak out of the dungeon and back into the castle since there was a locked iron gate with a guard sitting on the other side. Of course, if there were no prisoners, the guard wouldn't be posted and neither would the door be locked. Then again, if there were no prisoners then why was there a lit torch in the dungeon at all?

She cautiously made her way past the first barred cell, glancing inside to see that it was vacant. She held her breath and continued forward, not wanting to see inside the holding areas. Even if there weren't prisoners, there might be dead, rotting bodies or bones inside. She remembered once, about ten years ago, she had been playing in the catacombs. When she'd sneaked back in through the dungeon, she saw the bloodied, dead body of an old man in one of the cells with a rat gnawing at his face.

Her stomach lurched at the thought. She stopped for a second to regain her breath. The air stank down here like mold and feces. How could the catacombs smell better than a dungeon of a lord?

She hurried past the next two cells and had almost made it to the iron gate when she heard voices from the guard's room. She stopped next to one of the cells, slinking back into the shadows when she saw a guard approach the outer gate and peer inside. She dared even to breathe, wondering if the man had heard her.

Then she heard the creaking of the wooden door that led to the courtyard and a quick burst of air that smelled like rain filled the chamber.

"There you are," grumbled the guard, leaving the gate to meet the person who had entered. "I was about to come look for you. You're late."

"I was having a drink up on the battlements with the sentries," came the other voice. She recognized the two guards as Ivar and Colbert. They were both shady and couldn't be trusted. She didn't like either of them.

"Keep an eye on things. I'm going to get myself a drink now. What have you got there?"

"It's ale and bread."

"Give me some. I'm hungry."

"Just a little," said the guard. "It's for the prisoner."

"Prisoner?" she whispered just as a hand came through the bars, covering her mouth so she couldn't scream. She bit the prisoner's hand like she'd done to Rook and twirled around to face him.

"Ow!" he cried.

"Wardell?" she whispered in shock, to see her good friend imprisoned.

"What was that noise?" asked one of the guards.

Wardell held his finger to his lips to keep her from speaking.

"I'm hungry," Wardell called out to the guard.

"Keep it down," growled Colbert. "I'm bringing you some bread and ale. Not that you deserve it. I'll be there in a minute."

She heard the guards talking and laughing, and turned back to the boy who was the messenger of the king.

"Why are you in here?" she asked in surprise.

"I could say the same about you."

"That's a long story. Just tell me, why did my uncle imprison you?"

"He accused me of telling secrets. He said someone was giving the Demon Thief information on the king's shipments. Since I'm the king's messenger and there has just been a raid, he accused me of betraying the king. I swear, I didn't do anything of the sort. Now they'll kill me." Wardell's eyes looked sunken, and his body was bruised and bleeding. She felt horrible because the boy had done nothing wrong. If only he knew she was the Demon Thief's informant.

"I'm going to get you out of here," she promised.

"Nay, it's too late. I'm scheduled to hang on the morrow."

"What?" she said, louder than intended.

"That sounded like a girl's voice," said Colbert from the door.

"It's probably that whelp crying again," said Ivar. "You'd better give him a little of this bread and ale since it's his last meal." She heard Ivar leave through the courtyard door. Then came the sound of jingling of keys as Colbert prepared to come to the cells.

"Don't worry. I promise I'll get you out of here before you hang," she said, giving Wardell's hand a squeeze and flashing him a quick smile of comfort.

"Please. Do something," begged Wardell. "I don't want to die. I'm innocent, I tell you."

"I know you are," she said. "Now be strong and don't worry. I'll get you out of here."

She hurried into the shadows across from the cell. When the guard opened the gate and came inside, she quickly slipped out of the dungeon and into the courtyard. It was already night and the torches were lit in the courtyard. The rain had stopped as well.

Making her way past two guards playing dice, she hurried up the stairs of the keep and slipped into the castle.

"There you are, my lady."

She looked up to see Amanda, her handmaid, coming down the stairs.

"Good evening, Amanda." She started up the stairs, keeping her head down and hoping not to see her uncle.

"Your uncle was furious when you missed the main meal in the great hall. He's been combing every room in the castle for the last hour looking for you."

"It's amazing he's even noticed I was gone." Her heavy, wet cloak dragged on the stairs as she climbed, making her feel weak and weighted.

"You are wet with rainwater and covered in mud!" the handmaid exclaimed. Amanda was an older woman with graying hair. She was also the widow of a nobleman, although she was not of noble blood. When Calliope lost her mother at the young age of six, the woman took her to her bosom and treated her like the daughter she'd once had and lost in the plague.

"Amanda, please don't say anything to anyone about this."

"You were outside the castle again, weren't you?"

"You know me too well." Ever since childhood, Calliope had been a handful. She'd disappeared on Amanda more times than she could count. Amanda knew all about Calliope's insatiable curiosity that always seemed to get her into trouble.

"Please don't tell me that you were in the catacombs again," said the woman, almost as if she were able to read Calliope's mind.

"Shhh," said Calliope, looking around as she reached the top stair. When she realized she hadn't been spotted, she bolted toward her chamber. "I don't want anyone to know. Especially not my uncle."

"What don't you want me to know?"

She came to a quick halt and looked up to see her uncle standing in the open doorway of the solar with his young pregnant wife at his side. Ovid had lost his first wife to fever, and all three of his sons followed when they died in battle. Now, in his old age, he tried desperately to have more heirs to take his place and inherit his holdings when he left this earth.

"Uncle," she said in surprise, seeing his eyes settle on her wet cloak.

"You've been outside, that's why I couldn't find you. You better not have been outside the castle walls after I forbade it." His face turned red. Lady Joanna, his wife, laid her hand on his shoulder in a calming gesture. She was four months pregnant but had been looking very pale ever since she found out she was having the baby.

"I'm sure she has a good explanation," said Joanna. The girl was only twenty years of age, just like Calliope. It bothered Calliope that the friendly girl had been forced into a marriage with mean Uncle Ovid.

"Yes. Yes, I do have an explanation," she said, lowering the hood of her cloak. "I was out in the orchard taking a walk when the rain started. I stayed under a tree until the storm passed."

"I don't believe it," said her uncle, slinking forward. His hand snaked out and his fingers closed around her hair. He gave it a hard yank. She shot forward in pain, holding her hand to head. "Why is your hair loose? Have you been visiting the garrison? Or perhaps you're having a tryst with the stable boy, is that it?" He didn't release her hair.

"Nay!" she shouted. "I did nothing of the sort. Now please, Uncle, leave me be."

"My lord," said her uncle's wife. "Please, don't hurt her."

"I'm not hurting her." He released her hair so quickly she almost fell off balance. "If I find out you're lying to me, you'll be locked in your chamber and you won't be let out for a sennight. Do you understand?"

"Of course, my lord," she said, biting the inside of her cheek to keep from saying how she really felt. Calliope didn't fear many people, but her Uncle Ovid had frightened her since the day she was made his ward. She despised him. He was nothing like her father. Had her father known his half-brother was so malicious, he never would have had it set up that upon his death, Ovid would take her into his care. If Ovid hadn't also gained riches in her father's will, she was sure he would never have agreed to take her.

"Go to your chamber without supper," snapped the man, heading down the hall. She turned and bravely asked him what she wanted to know before she lost her nerve to do it.

"Can I at least have bread and ale like I saw the guard taking to the dungeon for the prisoner?"

He stopped and his spine stiffened. He slowly turned around. "Nay. And who told you about my prisoner?"

"No one, my lord," she said, keeping her chin raised. She boldly looked him right in the eye. "I figured it out when I saw the bread and ale being delivered. So who is it you have down there?"

"If you must know, it is your little friend and messenger boy, Wardell. And he's scheduled to die on the morrow."

"You can't do that." She picked up her skirts and started forward, but Amanda held her back.

"Please, my lady, stay quiet," said her handmaid. "You'll anger him."

"I don't care!" she spat, her anger making her forget her fear of her abusive uncle. "Wardell doesn't deserve to die. He's done nothing wrong."

"He's given information to the Demon Thief of the whereabouts and time of each of the king's shipments," said her uncle. "Yes, he does deserve to die."

"Nay." She shook her head furiously. "Wardell would never do a thing like that. You are making a mistake. He is not the informant."

"Really?" Her uncle raised an eyebrow. "Well, then, who do suppose it is?"

"I – I don't know," she said, her gaze falling in the

process. She never could look her uncle in the eye when she lied, and he knew it.

"Unless you can give me evidence that Wardell is not the informant, then he will die on the morrow as scheduled." Ovid turned and headed down the hall, walking at a good clip. She boldly stopped him once again.

"Does the king know you are putting his messenger to death?"

He spun around on his heel, his eyes holding so much darkness that it made her flinch. Then he shot back to her, raised his hand and slapped her face hard.

"Don't worry about something that is none of your business! Now get to your chamber and don't come out until I tell you that you can."

He hurried away with his wife trailing behind him.

Calliope felt tears stinging her eyes, as well as the pain shooting through her jaw from her uncle's hit. Wardell would die and it was all her fault. She rushed to her chamber, ripping off her wet cloak and throwing it on a nearby chair. Her body shivered from anger as well as the cold. After wiping a tear away with the back of her hand, she headed toward the fire burning in the hearth to warm herself. Amanda entered the room after her, closing the door behind her.

"We should get you out of those wet clothes," said the woman.

"I'm too upset to think." She paced back and forth in front of the fire, wondering what to do.

"Come, my lady," said the older woman, bringing a dry sleeping gown and placing it over the chair. "You will catch your death in those wet clothes."

Calliope let the woman help her change. Once she was

changed into her night clothes, Amanda pulled a chair over to the fire.

"Now, sit and warm your bones as I remove those tangles from your hair."

Still in deep thought, Calliope sat on the chair and stared into the flames.

"You really shouldn't rile your uncle so, my lady." She ran a boar-bristle brush though Calliope's hair. "And you really shouldn't be roaming the catacombs alone. It's too dangerous. How many times have I told you that is no place for a lady?"

"I have been doing it since I was eight years old, Amanda. It's no more dangerous now than it was then so why are you so concerned?"

"I heard a rumor that the Demon Thief might live in the catacombs."

Calliope's head snapped upwards making the brush tangle in her hair.

"I'm sorry, my lady," apologized the woman, using her fingers to work the hair from the bristles.

"Who told you that?" asked Calliope, wondering how many knew Rook was hidden in the catacombs. If the king found out, Rook was as good as dead.

"I'm friends with one of the serfs from the village. The woman brings her children to the castle with her when she uses the lord's oven to bake her bread. Her little boy talks a lot. He is the one who told me. Of course, I have no idea if it's true."

"You can't believe all the gossip you hear. Now, please do not repeat that to anyone else."

"What is this?" asked Amanda, pushing Calliope's hair to the side to look at her neck.

Calliope's hand shot upward to cover the spot where Rook had kissed her and raked his teeth against her skin. "I'm sure I just scratched myself in the catacombs since it was dark, that's all."

"It looks like teeth marks or possibly lips," said the woman. "Calliope, I think you'd better tell me the truth. What were you doing in the catacombs?"

Calliope dropped her hand to her side and turned around. She needed someone to talk to. And the only person she knew she could trust was Amanda.

"I was bringing provisions to the villagers and got caught in the storm today," she said, her eyes slowly raising to meet Amanda's.

"Go ahead," said the woman, crossing her arms over her ample bosom.

"I decided to take the catacombs to get back to the castle since it was raining so hard."

"Please don't try to tell me next that you were bitten by a rat because I won't believe it."

"No, I don't suppose you would." Calliope rubbed her neck and smiled. "Would you believe I ran across the Demon Thief and he . . . he kissed me?"

Amanda's eyes sprang open and her jaw dropped. She reached backward for a chair that she pulled up next to Calliope before sinking slowly atop it. "Aye. As crazy as that sounds, I do believe it. Tell me more."

"His name is Rook and he is very handsome." She rubbed her neck and gazed into the fire as she reminisced about their kiss. "I found a secret room in the catacombs. When I went to investigate, he found me."

"You could have been killed," the woman scolded. "Don't you understand how much danger you were in?"

"Nay, you don't understand," she said, leaning back and stretching her legs toward the fire to warm her toes. "He's not like that at all. He could have taken me by force, but he didn't."

"He could have killed you, too!"

"He says he only kills those who threaten his life, so you needn't worry."

"Didn't you do anything to protect yourself?"

"Of course, I did. Since I dropped my dagger, I bit him instead."

"So you attacked him!"

"I did it in self-defense. He had his hand over my mouth and his sword to my throat at the time."

Amanda looked like she was about to swoon. "You are lucky to be alive."

"He kissed me, Amanda. He kissed me and I liked it."

"You are foolish, my lady. Now please promise me you will never return there again."

"On the contrary, I'll need you to cover for me because I plan on going back there on the morrow."

"What?" She sprang to her feet. "Nay, I won't let you."

"You can't stop me." Calliope stood as well. "I'm going to help Wardell escape from the dungeon. I'll bring him through the catacombs and to Rook. I'll convince Rook to protect Wardell since the boy is innocent."

"You don't know that what your uncle said isn't the truth," said Amanda. "The boy could very well be guilty of treason to the king."

"I know for a fact he is innocent," said Calliope, smiling and warming her hands at the fire.

Chapter 5

"Lord Rook, please stop practicing. The meal is ready." Brother Everad made his way out into the courtyard of the priory, calling Rook back toward the small fire he'd made just outside the church entrance. The priory was in ruins since King David of Scotland had ransacked it two decades ago. Before that, it had been used by not only the monks but also visiting barons and even King Edward I for the extended time of six months during his reign as he healed from an illness.

Now, the church was an empty shell, gutted and burned beyond recognition. Other buildings on the premises such as the refectory and the infirmary were in no better shape. Portions of arches and broken pillars towered up into the sky like injured sentries. Only the tall stone cross and the statue of Mary Magdalene in a niche in the wall three stories above the church were untouched. Everything else was broken and crumbling because of the destruction. However, the cloistered walkways that opened to an inner courtyard of dead grass were also in good condition.

The devastation had even extended down into the

catacombs where some of the tombs had been looted and the gravesites desecrated when the Scots looked for booty. Thankfully, the inner depths of the catacombs were still intact, as no one wanted to venture under the earth very far.

Rook's raven sat perched on the dead branches of a tree, watching Rook and Reed practice their sword fight.

Rook had been so upset last night after the battle and so distracted after finding the girl in his chamber that he'd tossed and turned all night. If he hadn't had to stay there to have Brother Everad sew up his leg, he would have gone after the girl himself.

This morning, they'd returned to the road where they'd fought yesterday to collect and bring back their dead. He wasn't one for emotion, but when he saw the wives of the deceased serfs, as well as the children, crying, he wondered if he'd made a mistake in having the villagers fight with them. It had upset him to the point where he couldn't even bring himself to help with burying the dead. The serfs weren't trained in combat like the mercenaries who'd fought at his side. Rook had shown them the basics of fighting and even given them weapons, but it was all for naught he realized. They'd collected nothing from the raid except dead bodies.

The mercenaries that had survived left him last night since Rook could no longer pay them. Even the monks who had inhabited the ruins hoping to rebuild had moved on to another priory for their own safety. Everyone had deserted him.

Was his vendetta against the king so strong that he'd failed to see how it affected the lives of others? He hadn't wanted to think about any of this and that's why he'd decided to burn off some energy by practicing. His brother,

Reed, was still there although the rest of the Scots had left for the coast to catch a ship back to Scotland. Reed only stayed because of Rook's request.

Even the villagers who had survived the battle told Rook they didn't want to fight with him anymore. With so many of them dead now, the others needed to take care of the widows and their children, as well as farm Lord Ovid's land.

Nothing was going right lately and Rook felt like crawling out of his skin.

"Aye, take a break, Brathair," said Reed, sliding his sword back into his scabbard. He'd trained with Rook all morning. "I need to be on my way, Rook. We've managed to secure a ship to take us back to Scotland. If I miss it, I'll be travelin' to the Highlands on foot."

"Then go," said Rook, shoving his sword into his scabbard at his waist. "The legend is over, so it doesn't matter."

Never had Rook felt so defeated. He collapsed atop a rock and buried his face in his hands.

"The legend doesna have to be over," said Reed, sitting down on the rubble across from him. "Mayhap ye can find another army to fight with ye. We still have the Scots."

"Who can I find?" he asked looking up at the sky and shaking his head. "Face it, Reed, it's over. Without Rowen and his men, we can't defeat the king's men. It's only a matter of time before he catches us and throws us in prison."

"Then come back to Scotland with me," suggested Reed. "There's nothin' left here for ye, Brathair. We can make a new life with the MacKeefe Clan."

"Nay." He winced as the stitches in his leg pulled as he stood. Brother Everad had sewed him up right after the girl ran from him last night. "I won't go from one bastard of a father to another."

"Ye and Ross need to make up. It's been too long." Ross had pretended to be the boys' father until the bitter truth was revealed the night of Burnt Candlemas. That's when Rook and his brothers discovered their birth mother was dead and they were bastards of the English king.

"It'll be a cold day in hell before I forgive him. I don't know why you forgave him so quickly for keeping the truth from us for the first twelve years of our lives."

"Scots dinna hold grudges the way ye do, Rook. We let out what's botherin' us and then we move on."

"You still hold a grudge against Edward just as I do, so don't hand me that. And you're not a Scot, dammit. Stop all your tomfoolery of talking and dressing like a Highlander. You're English, so mayhap you should just accept that and move on, just like you say."

"I see." Reed nodded and stood, brushing off his plaid. "Then if ye feel that way, I guess there is nothin' else to talk about. I'll be on my way."

He turned to go, but Rook couldn't just let him walk away. He'd already lost one brother and hell if he'd lose the other.

"Wait, Reed. Come back here."

His brother turned and walked back to him.

"Did ye change yer mind? Ye can bring the monk with ye to Scotland."

"Nay, I didn't change my mind. I'm just wondering if there's a way to get Brody and the crew of the Sea Mirage to change their minds and start working with us again." Rowen had been captain of the Sea Mirage until he'd turned on his brothers.

"Brody is too loyal to Rowen," said Reed, talking about

Rowen's first mate who inherited the Sea Mirage once Rowen decided to give up piracy and stay in England.

"Well, what about the crew? How do they feel?" asked Rook.

"When I visited the ship, I could tell the crew was gettin' anxious. They've been docked for too long and the men are itchin' to raid again."

"Mayhap we can convince them to go against Brody."

"Nay, it'll ne'er work." Reed shook his head. "I couldna even persuade them to talk Brody into givin' us a ride back to Scotland. It was hard enough to convince him to give us a lift here. He doesna want to do anythin' that'll put him at odds with Rowen," he explained.

"Then mayhap the thing we need to do is cause a mutiny on the ship. What if one of the crew was to take over as captain?"

"Who?" asked Reed. "The only one mad enough to try it was Old Man Muck. But now he and Lucky Dog are rottin' in the dungeon of Hermitage Castle thanks to our brathair."

"That's right," said Rook in thought. "Since they're prisoners over the border, there's not much we can do about it either."

"Have something to eat, you two," said the monk, balancing two bowls of steaming pottage in his hands. They sometimes used a small fire in the covered walkways to cook their food, but most of their meals were cold ones. They didn't like to risk the fact that someone would see the smoke and know they were living in the catacombs. Rook hardly even ever had a fire in the winter and learned to live with the cold because he didn't want to be discovered. But now that Rowen was working for the king, it was evident that any day his presence here would be known by all.

Rook took a bowl of pottage and sat back down and started eating. Brother Everad handed the other one to Reed. Even though Reed needed to go, his weakness was food. He gladly accepted the food and gobbled it down while he stood.

"Mayhap yer informant can give us some information and we can catch the king off guard," suggested Reed.

"I think our informant is slipping or possibly no longer on our side," said Rook.

"What do you mean?" asked Everad, being the only one who knew the identity of their informant. The monk was the go-between who brought the messages and information to them.

Rook swallowed down a big spoonful of the pottage and licked his lips. "I'm almost wondering if we need to pay this informant a little visit and rough him up a bit. I think he's led us right into a trap more than once now."

"No, that's not so," said Everad, sounding very upset. "Cal would never do that."

"Cal?" asked Rook, knowing now that something was upsetting the monk. Never once in the past three years had he told Rook and his brothers who the informant was or where to find the man. Everad had told them that it was to protect the identity of the source and that only he would ever know.

"Ye ne'er told us the man's name before," said Reed, taking a moment to look up from his food.

"Nay, he hasn't," said Rook suspiciously. "Something must have Brother Everad so shaken that he was careless enough to slip up and tell us about Cal. So where do we find this Cal?" Rook scooped up another spoonful of food and slid it into his mouth.

"I already said too much," said the monk. "I'm going to go back and clean up the dishes."

"What about the lassie?" asked Reed.

The monk stopped in his tracks. "What lassie?" he asked without turning around.

"I was talkin' to my brathair, no' ye," said Reed. "But now that ye asked, dinna ye remember? Rook told us yesterday that he saw a lassie in the catacombs."

"Mayhap he . . . imagined it," said the monk, not sounding at all like he believed that.

"I didn't imagine a thing." Rook handed his empty bowl to Everad and pushed up to his feet, rubbing his hand that was wrapped in the girl's hair ribbon. "I kissed her."

"Ye did?" asked Reed, handing his empty bowl to the monk as well.

"Nay," said the monk shaking his head. "It was naught but an illusion, I'm sure. You were delirious from being hurt, that's all."

"And what about this hair ribbon wrapped around my hand?" Rook held up his hand to make his point. "She gave it to me right after she bit me so hard she drew blood."

"She did?" Reed chuckled. "Why did ye keep this all a secret until now?"

Why, indeed? Rook wasn't sure. He'd told them he saw a girl in the catacombs, but part of him wanted to keep their kiss a secret. It didn't make any sense, nor did it matter anymore. He'd never see her again. Still, he'd wanted to keep the mysterious woman all to himself and part of him didn't want to share any more information than he needed to share.

"That doesn't matter," said Rook, looking down to his hand and rubbing his fingers over the burgundy ribbon.

"What I want to know is why neither of you even asked me yesterday why I had a ribbon wrapped around my hand?"

"I just thought it was one of yer odd quirks," said Reed.

"Odd quirks? I don't have any." His raven flew up to him, ready to land on his left shoulder. Rook jerked around to make sure the bird landed on his right shoulder instead.

"Like that," said Reed, pointing at his raven. "Ye only let the bird land on yer right shoulder."

"That's because I'm left-handed, like Rowen, unless you've forgotten. I need to make sure my sword arm is free at all times. If you ask me, you're the odd one. Out of the three of us, you're the only right-handed one, and also the only one who looks and acts like a bloody Scot!"

"I've got to leave now," said Reed, looking up at the sky. "Since I'm so late, can I borrow one of yer horses to make it back to the coast before the ship leaves? It's a fishin' ship and the captain is verra impatient. He willna wait a minute past his scheduled time because he thinks the damned fish only bite at certain hours of the day and he doesna want to miss it."

"The horses are in the villagers' barn," Rook told him. "Take Brother Everad's horse and make sure to pay someone dearly to bring it back by tomorrow."

"Do ye perhaps have an extra coin?" asked Reed, shaking the sporran attached to his waist. "My pouch is empty."

"If you didn't give every penny to the Scots, you might have some money for yourself, you fool." Rook dug a shilling out of his pocket and handed it to his brother. Reed just looked at the coin in his palm but didn't leave.

"What's the matter?" asked Rook.

"I was just thinkin'. If ye gave me another shillin' or

two, I might be able to stop at the tavern before I go to get a tankard of ale to wash down that pottage."

Rook grumbled and dug into his pocket and flipped his brother another coin. Reed caught it and smiled.

"Ye ken, another one like this and I'd be able to –"

"Forget it," growled Rook. "If you want more money, then figure out a way for us to continue our raids on the king without losing any more men." Rook knew Reed wanted the extra coin for whisky, not ale. "Besides, you'll have all the Mountain Magic you can drink once you get back to the MacKeefe camp."

Mountain Magic was a very potent whisky brewed only by old Callum MacKeefe, the grandfather of the clan's chieftain, Storm MacKeefe.

"Guidbye, Brathair," said Reed, holding out his hand. Since Rook's right hand was bandaged, he nodded his head. In return, Reed did something Rook hoped he wouldn't do. The fool hugged him and slapped him on his back. Reed had no qualms about hugging anyone, whether they were male or female. Rook, on the other hand, didn't like to show that much emotion. It made him feel vulnerable. He needed to stay strong, so he didn't return the hug.

"What's the matter, Rook?" asked Reed with a chuckle. "I dinna have fleas."

"You know I don't like hugs, so just stop it."

"I'll bet ye hugged that lassie when ye kissed her. What was her name?"

"I don't know," he told his brother. "I couldn't get her to tell me, but I intend to find out."

He noticed someone riding away from the village on a horse. "Damn," he mumbled.

"What's the matter?" asked Reed, looking in the rider's

direction.

"It's Brother Everad. I wonder where he's going."

"I dinna ken. However, it looks like I'll need to use yer horse now, Rook."

"Fine," he said, letting out an exaggerated breath. He didn't like to be without a horse. If trouble arose, he would need to get away quickly. The only other horse was the draft horse that pulled the serfs' plow. That horse couldn't run, let alone gallop, it was so old. "Take it. But if something happens to it or it doesn't make it back into the barn by tomorrow, I'll have your head for it, Reed."

"Dinna worry. I'll try to think of a way to grow yer army again. I'll send a messenger pigeon from the Highlands if I figure it out."

"I'll do the same for you," said Rook. "And don't forget to bring the pigeon back next time. I've only got one left to send you a message if I need it." The pigeons were trained to fly one way only. They'd return to the spot that was their home – with a message attached to the leg. But once they arrived, they needed to be brought back to the other destination so they'd be ready to bring another message if needed.

"I'll remember," said Reed with a wave of his hand behind him as he took off running for the barn. Rook headed back to his chamber. His leg hurt like hell from being on it all day. A short nap while the monk was gone was just what he needed.

He made his way down into the bowels of the church, grabbing a torch and lighting it before heading into the dark with Hades on his shoulder. But not long after he entered the catacombs, the raven became jittery. The bird squawked and shot over and landed atop a large sarcophagus with a carved lid that depicted the noble knight that had been buried within it at one time. The Scots hadn't made their way this far in the tunnels and the grave was untouched when Rook first found it.

Curiosity got the best of him three years ago when he first started raiding. So he'd opened the coffin to find not only bones of the dead man, but a very beautiful sword, a sturdy helm, chain mail, and even a jeweled ring on the man's finger. He'd moved the bones to another part of the catacombs. Then he'd confiscated the buried goods with the help of the monk. They'd done the same to many more of the tombs as well.

He now used the sarcophagus to store weapons he'd collected, as well as shields and other goods he'd taken from the king's dead soldiers over the past three years. Some of the things he'd sold and used the money to pay the mercenaries and serfs for fighting with him. Other things he'd used to complement the stolen goods from the king that furnished his chamber.

Rowen and Reed always wanted to give everything to the Scots, but Rook didn't like that idea. He'd suffered from Edward's hand just as much as the Scots the night the English ransacked and burned Edinburgh and Haddington to the ground. He deserved his share of the booty from the raids and he'd made sure he got it.

He didn't care what anyone thought. He did what he wanted and watched out for himself. He'd always been that way, even as a child. Mayhap, that's the reason he was called Rook the Ruthless.

"What's the matter, Hades?" he asked, holding up the torch to scan the area. The light of the flame cast long shadows on the stone walls. Most of the bones and dead bodies had been moved further into the catacombs but, still, the gravestones and many crosses remained. "Did you hear someone?" He listened carefully and scanned the area again but didn't see or hear a thing. Then, his leg started aching, so he headed to his room to lie down. He thrust the heel of his hand at the secret lever and the stone slid open. Then he pushed the wooden door open with his shoulder.

Hades flew over to him, but he wouldn't let the bird land on his arm. "Nay. You stay out here and let me know if you hear any intruders. What I need is a short nap."

After he closed the wooden door behind him, he yanked at the inside lever and closed himself into his chamber. He'd installed a vent up in the corner of his ceiling that was hidden but allowed him to hear what was happening in the outer chamber even if his door was closed.

Tired and frustrated, he lit a candle and snuffed out the torch. Then he unbuckled his weapon belt and hung it on a hook on the wall.

Rook kicked off his boots and collapsed fully clothed atop his bed. Holding his hand in front of him, he kissed the ribbon wrapping his wound, inhaling the sweet scent of rosewater that smelled just like the girl. The scent was fainter than it was yesterday and he didn't want it to fade away. It was his only reminder that his visitor was not only in his imagination. Pressing his eyelids closed, he tried to imagine the beautiful woman's face, hoping he'd never forget it. Her green eyes were staring at him in his mind. When he looked into them, he saw a spirited woman who had possessed his mind and made his body ache with passion. He wanted nothing more than to kiss her and hold her in his arms once again.

He rolled over and fell asleep, wondering if he was

weakening. He swore he'd never let a woman possess his mind the way Rowen had been changed by his wife, Lady Cordelia.

Ever since Rowen had married the noblewoman and been knighted, Rook felt as if his own world had come crashing down around him. He had thought the three brothers would always be together. They were more than brothers; they were best friends. They'd lived through Burnt Candlemas and also survived being separated for nearly ten years. The fates had brought them back together, but now the power of a woman had torn them apart.

Rook had to find a way to convince the crew of the Sea Mirage to, once again, raid with them. With Rowen's ex-crew behind him, he might be able to convince the mercenaries to return or pay for other hired swords to go up against his father.

Once again, the smell of rosewater drifted through the air and he found himself wanting nothing but his green-eyed beauty. He ripped the ribbon from his hand in frustration and threw it across the room. Dammit, he didn't even know her name.

Tossing and turning on the bed, he finally ended up burying his face in the pillow. Nay, he couldn't get distracted again by a woman, no matter who she might be. And if his visitor ever did wander into the catacombs again, he'd kick her out on her ass. Because if not, he might be tempted to forget everything that was important to him and throw it all away just to hold and kiss her once more.

Chapter 6

The sharp, short cries of Hades woke Rook out of a deep sleep. His eyes popped open, and it took a moment to remember where he was. Not sure how long he'd been sleeping, he'd been dreaming of his female visitor. He'd seen her hurrying through the dark catacombs and she seemed worried.

Sliding off the bed, he donned his weapon belt, feeling the burning in his thigh. He'd been too upset today to care for it properly. If only he could think straight, it would help.

Once again, he heard the sound of his raven calling out. Then he heard what sounded like a female voice through the vents.

Pulling open his door, he hit the lever and the rock that hid his room slid aside. He glimpsed someone run by and decided to follow.

"Who goes there?" he called out, seeing the light of a torch flickering off the stone walls up ahead. Silence. Leading with his sword, he rounded the corner only to come face to face with his mysterious visitor with a travel bag thrown over her shoulder. This time she was with someone - a young man holding a torch.

"Stand back," said the man, blocking the girl's body with his. He looked bruised, as if he'd been beaten. He carried no weapons, but the torch only.

"It's all right, Wardell," she said, stepping around him. "This is Rook. I met him yesterday."

"You again," said Rook sheathing his sword. He felt excited to see her but remained cool and composed since he didn't want her to know. "Why are you in my catacombs? And what are you doing here with him?" He nodded toward the man she'd called Wardell. He looked to be about the same age as the girl.

"We are just . . . passing through."

"Well, get out! These are my catacombs and you don't belong here." Perhaps if he frightened her, she wouldn't use the catacombs as her new road for travel. As much as he wanted her to stay, his head told him she would only bring him trouble. She needed to go.

The girl's eyes opened wide and, by the look on her face, he could tell she wasn't pleased that he'd shouted at her. Her arms crossed in front of her chest. "On the contrary, I've been coming through these catacombs since I was only eight years old. So I'd say you're the one that is trespassing, not me."

"Lady Calliope, don't anger him," said Wardell under his breath. "He could be dangerous."

"Ah, so you have a name after all," said Rook, taking two steps toward them. His raven called out and flew over to settle on his shoulder.

"So now you know," she answered with a sniff, not backing away in the least.

"That name sounds familiar. Where are you from?"

"We're coming from Naward Castle, my lord," said the

boy, getting a stern glance from the girl in return.

"Don't tell him anything more," she warned him.

"Actually, I think you'd better tell me everything and do it fast," remarked Rook. "I don't take kindly to intruders."

"Please, don't harm us, my lord," the boy pleaded. Rook liked the boy using a title to address him, even if he hadn't earned it. "I was imprisoned in the dungeons of Naward Castle just outside of Brampton. I was condemned to death and scheduled to die by hanging today. Lady Calliope helped me escape."

"I see." He stroked his short beard in thought. "So, Lady Calliope, are you some sort of rebel? Helping criminals?"

"He's not guilty and doesn't deserve to die," she spat.

"What was he accused of doing?" asked Rook curiously.

"I am the messenger of the king," said Wardell. "I was accused of being an informant, helping the Demon Thief know where and when to find the king so his goods could be stolen."

That got Rook's attention. "Do you know who I am?" he asked the boy.

"Aye. You are the Demon Thief, my lord. Lady Calliope told me."

"And you're not afraid I'll kill you?"

"If I had stayed in the dungeon, I would have died anyway. So I had no choice but to accept Lady Calliope's help."

"Interesting," he said, looking back down the path they'd taken. "So the catacombs connect to Naward Castle do they?" Although Rook knew damned well they did, he was fishing for information and hoped the boy would spill it.

"Aye, they do," he said. "And in the other direction, they connect to –"

"Hush," said Calliope. "Don't tell him anything else."

Rook wanted to know the answer to that. When he'd first come here to live, he'd explored the catacombs and that's how he knew they led to the nearby castle. However, in the other direction, there were twists and turns, and he'd gotten lost several times and never found out where they ended. Never taking the time to explore further since he'd been busy gathering his raiders and stealing from the king, he'd lost interest after a while and gave up the quest altogether.

"Was it the king who accused you of being an informer?" Rook asked.

"Nay. It was Lord Ovid," said Wardell.

"And where are you escaping to?" he asked, looking around. "Or did you plan on living right here in the catacombs with me?"

"Of course he's not going to do that," said Calliope. "I brought him through here and he's going to . . . to hide out somewhere and then . . . what does it matter what he does?"

"You haven't thought that far ahead, have you?" Rook asked. "Perhaps now that you're a condemned man, you'll want to join me in raiding the king?"

"What?" snapped Calliope. "Of course he would never do that! Wardell is a respectable man and comes from a good family."

Rook chuckled. "People used to say that about me as well."

"Calliope, what am I going to do?" whispered the boy.

"I – we'll think of something," she whispered back.

"Why don't you hide out here for a day or two and think about it," offered Rook. He figured, if this boy was a messenger to the king, he might be able to use that to his advantage. Wardell would know a lot of secrets and be able to help Rook, possibly. That is, if he were willing to betray his king.

"No!" Calliope answered for him.

"Mayhap it wouldn't be a bad idea - for now." Wardell tried to convince Calliope.

"What are you saying?" She turned and stared him in the face. "That would be treason to your king."

"Mayhap I don't have to actually raid," suggested Wardell.

"No raiding?" interrupted Rook. "Then you're no use to me." He turned and headed back toward his chamber.

"Wait!" shouted Wardell. "Mayhap there is something I could do to help you until I decide where I'm going to go."

"Do you know how to fight?" Rook spoke without looking back.

"Aye, I do. I served as a squire for years before becoming the king's messenger. I have assisted my last lord and helped him train for his knighthood."

Rook stopped in his tracks when he heard this. Hades cackled from his shoulder before flying over and settling atop a tomb.

"Are you any good with a sword?" Rook looked back over his shoulder.

"Not only with a sword, but I often jousted against my last lord in practice. I am considering becoming a knight myself someday."

"Not if you team up with the Demon Thief," Calliope told him. "You do that and you can kiss it all goodbye."

"Not necessarily," said Rook, already devising a plan in his head. "I think I'd like to talk with you more, Wardell. I'm happy you stumbled into my dwellings."

"He didn't stumble here. I brought him," said Calliope, setting him straight.

"Tell me, boy. If you aren't the informant, then who is?"

"I – I don't know, my lord," he answered. "I thought you'd know since you were the one being informed."

"The informant speaks through the monk only. I don't know any more than you do about it."

He noticed Calliope looking down at the ground and keeping her mouth shut this time.

Hades cawed from behind him and a voice came out of the darkness.

"Calliope, what are you doing here? And why did you bring him? Do you know how dangerous this is?"

Rook turned around to see Brother Everad standing there, out of breath as if he'd been hurrying.

"Hello, Everad," she said, oddly enough, not using the word "Brother" before his name.

"When I heard a girl was in the catacombs, I hurried to Naward to find you. What I learned from your handmaid is that your uncle is on a rampage because the prisoner he'd planned on hanging had somehow escaped. I knew at once it was you and what you'd done. So I returned here immediately. You need to go back to the castle before your uncle finds you missing."

"I will, as soon as I see to Wardell's safety."

"Brother Everad, you sound as if you're already acquainted with Lady Calliope," said Rook. "Why is that?" Suspicion aroused, he was not going to let anyone leave before he had his answers.

When the monk remained quiet, Calliope took a step forward and put her hand on Everad's arm. "You may as well tell him," she said.

"Tell me what?" asked Rook.

"Brother Everad has been coming to the castle to see me in secret for years now," she said.

"In secret?" asked Rook. "Why?"

"That doesn't matter," said the monk. "What does matter is that Calliope has put herself in much danger by helping a prisoner escape."

"He's innocent," said Calliope, looking over her shoulder toward Wardell. "And he's also my friend. I couldn't let him die when it was all my fault."

"Your fault?" asked Wardell in confusion. "Lady Calliope, what are you saying?"

"You are innocent of any charges because while you might have relayed valuable information that was used against the king, you didn't know that you did it. I'm sorry to have put you in such a position, Wardell. I never meant to hurt you."

"What do you mean?" asked the boy. "I don't understand."

"Lord Rook, I'm sorry I kept it a secret for so long, but I only did it for her own protection," explained the monk.

"Did what?" growled Rook, tired of this conversation.

"The boy is innocent," said the monk. "Because Lady Calliope is the informant."

Chapter 7

Calliope waited for Rook's reaction to what he'd just heard. The man was stoic and didn't show emotion. Perhaps that was part of maintaining his reputation of being ruthless. Why should he even care?

"You?" asked Wardell, breaking the silence, sounding very disappointed. "Lady Calliope, how could you? Why? I almost died because of you."

"The girl just saved your life," grunted Rook. "I'd think that should mean something to you."

"Aye, of course, it does," said Wardell. "But I don't understand why you would use me to get information to pass along to the Demon Thief," answered Wardell. "I thought we were friends, Calliope."

"We are," she answered, reaching out for his hand. Wardell shook his head and backed away.

"I don't want anything to do with you," he spat. "You betrayed me."

"Nay, it's not like that. Let me explain," she begged.

"Brother Everad, perhaps you can take the boy with you

to care for your horse. Check to see if my horse has been returned while you are at the barn," Rook interrupted.

"Of course, my lord," answered Brother Everad, motioning to Wardell. Wardell handed Calliope the torch and stepped around her, scowling at her all the while.

Once they were gone, Calliope looked up to see Rook leaning against a tomb with his arms crossed. The firelight from the torch in her hand cast shadows on his dark face, making her feel uncomfortable. Last time she'd seen Rook, he'd kissed her and she'd liked it. What was the matter with her that she was attracted to such a man?

He chuckled and she moved toward him.

"I don't see that any of this is funny."

"Isn't it?" he asked, reaching out and running a finger over his raven's head. The catacombs were dark and dreary. The man looked like the Greek god Hades, ruling over his underworld with his raven at his side. A shiver ran up her spine.

"Sometimes all the good in the world can't make up for the wrong choices we've made." Now he sounded like the goddess Athena, spouting wisdom.

"Wrong choices?" This angered her to hear him say this when she'd been the one helping him all along. "I helped you and your brothers or haven't you noticed? I'd think you'd be a little more grateful."

"I'm not the grateful type or haven't you noticed?" He stood up and groaned, reaching down to touch his leg. Her eyes followed to his wound.

"You're still bleeding," she said moving the torch closer. "Let me get a better look at that." She reached out to touch him, and his hand shot out and gripped her around the wrist.

"I'm all right."

"I can tend to that wound. Now, stop being so stubborn and let me help."

"Brother Everad will see to it later."

"He's busy with Wardell right now. You could have an infection or the stitches could have broken open."

"Why do you want to help me?"

"Why don't you want me to help?" she countered his question. She adjusted the bag on her shoulder that held healing ointments, sutures, a needle, as well as food and other provisions. She hadn't been sure what shape Wardell would be in when she snuck to the dungeon to help him escape, so she'd brought along what she thought he might need. She also had food and ale since she didn't know how long Wardell would be by himself and didn't want him to go hungry.

"You've helped me enough already by being the informant, although I can't say I understand why you did it. Don't worry about me. You should be concerned with nothing but saving your own skin right now." He limped toward his hidden chamber and she followed. The bird hopped along the tops of the tombs, trailing them.

"Some of us think about the needs of others before the needs of ourselves," she said, causing him to stop in his tracks. She'd been watching the raven and bumped into him, dropping the torch in the process.

"Are you trying to say something?" he asked. "Because if so, spit it out and stop playing games."

She reached for the torch but his boot came down on it and he kicked dirt on it to put out the flame.

"What did you do that for?" she complained, standing up, trying to see him in the dark.

"I don't need it. I can maneuver through the catacombs

in the dark. A flame is only going to gather attention if anyone wanders in here."

"Well, mayhap I need it."

"I doubt it. I saw the way you made your way through the catacombs yesterday without a torch."

"There you go only thinking of yourself again. You are naught but a selfish man!"

"Is that so?" His voice was sultry and much closer to her ear now. "Then why don't I let you tend to my leg after all?"

"All right, I will." She wet her lips with her tongue. "Just light the torch and I'll see what I have in my bag to use on your wound."

"No need for the torch. There is plenty of light in my chamber." She heard him walking away, but stood fastened to her spot. What had she done? Because of her words, now the Demon Thief was taking her to his chamber. Brother Everad and Wardell weren't here, and she wasn't sure when they'd return. The last time she was alone with Rook in his chamber, things had almost gotten out of control. She raised her hand and fingered her neck where he'd left his mark.

"What are you waiting for?" she heard him ask in the dark.

"I – I – it's dark," she said, not sure what to say.

"Come on," he grumbled. She heard him heading back toward her. Before she knew what was happening, he clasped his hand over hers and pulled her along with him.

"Slow down," she complained as he headed through the catacombs at a brisk pace.

"You can handle it," he replied, leading her to his secret lair. She heard the sound of the stone moving to the side. Then he opened the wooden door to the chamber and light spilled out, illuminating him. "Welcome to my humble abode," he said, pulling her inside. His raven flew in behind him. Her eyes fastened to the furnishings of this room again that were far from humble. She turned around when she heard the sound of the stone moving back to cover the door behind her.

"You're closing us in here?" she asked, anxiety coursing through her.

"Unless you want rats wandering in," he said, shutting the heavy wooden door as well. "After seeing your reaction to the rat last time, I thought it better if you weren't frightened again."

"I'm not afraid of rats," she said with a roll of her eyes. She'd been encountering rats in the catacombs for as long as she could remember. "That one just startled me, that's all."

For a moment, she almost thought he cared about her well-being until she heard what else he had to say.

"Well, I'd rather you didn't become startled while sticking a needle through my skin as you tend to my wound."

Once again, it was all about him. She sighed and placed her bag on the table. "Where do you want me to do it?"

"Do it?" His brows raised in response. The soft glow of the beeswax candles made the chamber subdued and enticing.

"I'm talking about tending to your wound," she snapped. "Nothing else!"

"Of course. That's what I was talking about, too. It just sounded as if, mayhap – you had something else on your mind."

Her mouth felt ever so dry and she licked her lips once again. His eyes roamed to her mouth. She felt as if she couldn't breathe.

"How about on the bed?" he asked. His hands went to his weapon belt to remove it.

"All right." She snatched up the bag and darted to the bed. "I'll need water and a cloth to clean your wound if you have it."

"On the table near the door."

She left the bag and headed over to the table. Finding a clean cloth, she dipped it in the basin of water. Last time this water was blood red, but now it was fresh and translucent. "So did you receive your wound during your last raid against the king?" She spoke without turning around.

"Which wound?" he asked. "My hand is still injured as well."

She knew he meant the wound she'd given him when she bit him. She almost felt sorry about that now.

"I'll tend to both your wounds," she said, wringing out the cloth. Then she turned back toward the bed and stopped abruptly, gasping when she saw him lying on the bed wearing naught by his braies.

"What's the matter?" he asked.

"Why have you removed all your clothes?"

"I haven't. I'm still wearing my undergarment. But I can remove it as well if you need me to."

"Nay!" She hurried over to the bed to join him. Shadows danced on his naked, sturdy chest. His arms were large with muscles that looked as hard as rocks in his biceps. Her eyes trailed down his chest to his taut stomach that looked as if she could bounce a coin atop it. His long legs stretched out in front of him and she focused on his wound rather than look anywhere else. "The way you are will be just fine. Now, let me take a look."

She sat down gently on the pallet next to him. Her thigh

touched his. Heat from his body warmed her leg, making her feel as if she couldn't breathe. All she could think of was the kiss they'd shared previously and how it had made her feel.

"How does it look?" he asked, pulling her from her thoughts. She reached out and removed the blood-soaked binding to peruse his wound.

"Everad did a good job with the stitches, but a few of them have broken. You need to stay off your feet for a few days and let this heal."

"That's not an option."

"Your choice. But if I were you, I'd listen to me. I have a lot of experience mending the wounded soldiers of Naward Castle."

"Why do you call him that?" he asked, as Calliope cleaned his wound.

"I'm sure I don't know what you mean."

Rook studied Calliope as she went about her ministrations. He liked having a girl in his chamber. He especially liked the fact she was sitting on his bed next to him and their thighs were touching. He'd never had a woman in his catacomb room and never thought it would ever happen. "I've heard you refer to the monk just as Everad several times now. I find it odd you don't call him Brother."

Her hands stilled on his leg and she answered without turning to look at him.

"I suppose it's because I've known him for a long time and sometimes forget to call him Brother." She dug a needle and thread out of her bag as well as a small bottle.

"He doesn't always call you Lady, either, I noticed. "I've heard him call you just Calliope."

"I told you. We're friends. We've been friends for a long

time."

"And you also told me you are friends with Wardell. How does it feel to have friends?"

Her head turned slowly and her big green eyes peered at him from over her shoulder. "You say that as if you have no friends."

"Now I'm the one sure I don't know what you mean."

"You didn't say how does it feel to have *so many* friends. You just said how does it feel to have friends. Don't you have any?"

Rook didn't like the girl prying into his personal life. So what if he didn't have any friends but the monk. He used to have friends when he was a boy. That is, before he was torn away from his family and driven out of Scotland because of King Edward.

"Just sew up the leg and quit asking so many questions." Her question made him feel like a failure. He didn't have friends. All the villagers feared him. And now the mercenaries had all left him. Hell, besides the monk, he didn't have anyone. Part of him longed for the days when he'd had more friends back in Scotland than he could count. Even being a cursed triplet, the Scots had accepted him and his brothers because Ross was their father. Or so they'd thought he was their father at the time.

She lifted the bottle and uncorked it, then doused the rag with some of the liquid and patted it against his leg.

"Arrrgh," he cried out, feeling the sting against his wound. "What is that?"

"It's just whisky. It helps to cleanse the wound and keep it from getting infected."

"Let me see that," he said, holding out his hand. She gave it to him and he downed the contents, feeling the burn of the whisky traveling down to his gut.

"Why did you do that? I might need more of it."

"I need it more than you ever will. Now sew me up. I'm ready."

She threaded the needle and mumbled something under her breath.

"What did you say?" he asked.

"If you must know, I said you are being selfish again and only thinking about yourself." She stabbed the needle into his flesh and pulled it through. The whisky hadn't helped much. He still felt the pain.

"Aye, I'm the only one thinking about me. With the size of that needle, it feels as if you're sticking a tree trunk through my skin."

"I thought nothing could hurt the big, bad Demon Thief." She finished up with the sutures and continued to bind the wound with a strip of cloth she took from her pouch next. It took all his control not to respond to her last comment. But he didn't want to anger her while she was pushing needles into his flesh. She put down the needle, blotted the wound again, and then rubbed some ointment over his flesh, making small, sensual circles with her fingers. He groaned and closed his eyes as he laid his head back on the pillow. He felt her enchanting touch bringing every part of his body to life.

"What's the matter now?" she asked.

"Nothing. Just finish up, will you?"

"Would it kill you to say a simple thank you?" Her big, green eyes were staring into his soul again. Why did he feel so vulnerable around her? He wasn't used to thanking anyone for anything. He'd given up that notion the night of Burnt Candlemas when he'd found out the first twelve years of his life were nothing but a lie. He hadn't trusted anyone since that night and wasn't about to start trusting or thanking anyone now.

"Take a look at my hand, too, while you're at it." He pushed up to his elbow and shoved his hand in front of her face.

She gave him a disdainful glance and grabbed his hand in hers.

"Careful," he told her. "It's still tender from your bite."

"Is this little thing what you're complaining about?" She gingerly rubbed a finger over the wound that had already started to scab. The feel of her soft skin against his made him groan again. It had been so long since anyone paid him this kind of attention. The last person to do that was Annalyse – the woman who had raised him and pretended to be his mother. She'd always tended to his wounds during his younger years. And he'd always come home bruised and bleeding. Most of the time, it was only from playing rough with his friends. Rook had been a fighter since the day he was born.

"Yes, that is where you sank your teeth into my flesh."

She smiled, showing her beautiful, straight, white teeth. It felt intoxicating, since he was used to only seeing the broken, dirty, and rotten teeth of the mercenaries and villagers. Being in the presence of a noblewoman was something he wasn't used to. But he found himself thinking he could get used to it easily. And that thought unnerved him.

"Your hand is healing nicely and your leg should be fine as long as you keep it covered."

"Are you sure?" he asked, stalling because he liked when she held his hand. "It still hurts. A lot."

"Then, I suppose there is only one more thing I can do to make it feel better."

Before Rook could ask what she meant, she lowered her mouth to his hand and kissed his wound ever so gently.

The feel of her lips against his skin only made the heat in his loins worse. Why did she have to do that?

"All right, my work is done here." She slid off the bed and pushed the rest of her things into the pouch.

"Wait," he said, swinging his feet to the floor. "Where are you going?"

She closed up the pouch slowly, her back to him as she spoke. "If I didn't know better, I'd say you didn't want me to leave."

"Well, what's your hurry?" He walked up behind her and put his hands on her shoulders. "I rather like having a woman in my chamber." He picked up her loose, golden tresses, rubbing her soft silken locks between his fingers.

"So what are you saying?" she asked. "You want me as your friend?"

Friend? That thought almost made him laugh. He didn't want a friend right now. Hell, what he needed was a lover. He lowered his mouth to her neck, pressing kisses against her skin.

She had a sharp intake of breath, tilting her head to the side.

"Why do you gasp?" he asked, kissing her softly. "Do I frighten you?"

"Nay." Her hand shot upward to cover her neck as she turned around. "I should be leaving now."

He noticed an odd expression on her face. It was almost as if she were trying to hide something.

"Give me your hand," he said, reaching out his palm.

"Why?" she asked, her chin rising in the air.

"What is it you're trying to hide from me?"

"Nothing."

He didn't believe her, so he pulled her hand away from her neck. Her eyes closed and she turned her head, acting as if she were dreading his next move. His attention focused on her neck and he saw now why she'd been apprehensive. There in the crook of her neck, he saw bruised skin and the ever so faint impression that looked like scraped skin.

His heart dropped in his chest. Someone had hurt her.

"Who did this?" he demanded to know.

"It doesn't matter." She kept her head down and played with her bag. That's when he noticed something he hadn't before. A red welt on her jawline.

"What's this?" he asked, lifting her chin to inspect it. She hadn't had this mark the last time he'd kissed her. He was sure of it. "Tell me, Callie, who did this to you?"

Calliope felt her heart jump when the Demon Thief used an endearment regarding her name. She liked being called Callie. No one had ever done that before. It was simple, and yet special. It was also very unexpected coming from a hardened warrior.

"I angered my uncle and he hit me," she admitted, rubbing her hand over her jaw. She saw the fire in Rook's eyes when he heard her confession.

"No man will get away with hurting you. I'll kill whoever dares mark your perfect body."

"Then will you kill yourself as well?" she asked. "For you were the one to do this to me the last time I was in your chamber." She held her hair to the side and showed him her neck.

"Nay. I didn't." He shook his head as if he didn't want to believe her.

"Are you saying I'm a liar?"

He hesitated before he answered. "I never meant to hurt you. I'm not used to such a gentle woman with skin as delicate as spun silk."

He hadn't said he was sorry, but neither did she think he would. He was a warlord, a rebel, a bandit and a thief. A man like him was used to taking what he wanted without asking and never saying words like I'm sorry, please, or thank you. She supposed this was the extent of an apology that she'd get from him. After all, he said he would kill anyone who marked her body. He'd even compared her skin to spun silk. She'd never had any man say things like that to her before. It was the last thing she expected to hear coming from the mouth of the Lord of the Underworld.

He dipped his head toward her and she surrendered to his kiss. Her eyes closed as his lips melded with hers and his manly essence engulfed her being. Rook's arms encircled her body and he pulled her closer, his lips parting ever so slightly in the process. Then his tongue slid into her mouth and she tasted the hint of whisky mixed with power.

She should have pulled away and slapped him, but she couldn't bring herself to do it. Something about being in his embrace felt right although it made no sense at all. He was the Demon Thief, one of the most feared and wanted men in all of England who left death and destruction in his wake. This man had no right to touch her or even kiss her for that matter. She was a lady and a noble and should stay clear of men like him. But instead, she welcomed his tongue in her mouth and his body pressing up against hers.

Rook the Ruthless was one of the most handsome men

she'd ever met. Why couldn't he be a knight instead of a bandit?

"My lord, my lord," came the voice of Brother Everad, heard through the venting system. Rook removed his hands from Calliope's shoulders, his face turning upward.

"Something's the matter," he said, running to the door and yanking it open. He activated the lever, and the stone slid open to reveal Brother Everad and Wardell standing there.

"What's wrong?" asked Rook, standing in only his braies. Calliope didn't miss the way Wardell looked first at Rook and then at her. Disapproval was showing in his eyes.

"Lord Ovid's soldiers are headed this way. We saw them coming over the hill on horseback," said Everad. He had a lit torch and stuck it in a holder on the wall outside the door.

"They're looking for me," said Wardell.

"Damn it; I don't need anyone poking around here." Rook dragged a hand through his hair. "Get inside, both of you. Stay here with Lady Calliope while I see what's going on."

"Nay, you can't let them see you," said Everad. "Everyone stay here. I'll go out there. I won't raise any suspicion. I'll tell them I saw the boy riding hard toward the coast an hour ago."

Calliope silently slipped her bag over her shoulder and headed toward the door.

"I'm going to protect all of you," said Rook, standing on one leg as he donned his breeches. "Don't tell me what to do."

Calliope knew she couldn't linger any longer. The guards might be looking for Wardell, but if she didn't get back to the castle soon, they'd be looking for her as well.

Amanda was covering for her, but wouldn't be able to do it much longer. Her uncle would come looking for her eventually. If he didn't find her in her chamber, he might become suspicious that she had something to do with Wardell's escape.

Glancing over her shoulder one last time at Rook, she silently slipped out the door into the dark catacombs, reaching up and sliding the torch out of the holder. Her heart ached to have to leave him, but she had no choice. If she left now, she could be deep into the catacombs before the soldiers decided to search these premises. And with any luck, she'd be back to Naward Castle and in her chamber before her uncle discovered she'd ever left the castle at all.

Chapter 8

"You never should have let her go," Wardell told Rook the next morning, as the two of them sat at the table playing chess. "Lady Calliope could have gotten hurt or even killed. She could be in grave danger."

Rook already regretted telling the boy he could stay there for a few days. After the soldiers had come to the village looking for him, they'd proceeded to search the outer parts of the catacombs last night. Brother Everad had tried to throw them off Wardell's trail, but they were hard to shake. Thankfully, the villagers had played dumb and the soldiers believed them. However, they noticed that several of the village men were missing and they demanded to know where they were.

Brother Everad vouched for the villagers that the men had died from a fever that was spreading quickly. The soldiers, wanting to keep their distance, hadn't pursued their search.

But since they'd come into the catacombs, Rook had to stay in hiding in his chamber with the boy all night long. Wardell was the last person he wanted there with him. He wanted Calliope spending the night with him, but as soon as he'd turned his back, she'd disappeared again. The girl was like a ghost the way she came and left without being seen. He marveled at her ability to maneuver through the catacombs with or without a torch to guide her.

"I am not Lady Calliope's keeper," grumbled Rook, not wanting to hear any more about this. "Now make your move and stop stalling."

The boy's hand wavered above the rook, but then he pulled his hand back and continued talking. "She is an incredible woman, you realize."

"Excuse me, but are you talking about the same woman who tricked you into telling her where and when the king's shipments would be so she could relay the information to the monk who told it to me? You almost died for what she did or have you already forgotten?"

"I haven't forgotten." His hand rose above the rook again, but like before, he lowered it and looked up to Rook and continued talking. "I've been thinking about the situation. Even if she did it, I'm sure she had a good reason. And she saved me from the dungeon like you pointed out, so I can't be sore at her."

"The way I see it, she's ruined your life. Now you're a wanted man just like me. You'll be on the run and have to live in hiding for the rest of your days. Or haven't you considered that fact?"

"Oh. No, I hadn't." Wardell shook his head. "Either way, you should have stopped her from going back to Naward Castle. If her uncle finds out what she's done, there is no telling what he'll do to her."

"I've already seen his handiwork," he said, remembering the bruise on Calliope's chin. It angered him, making his gut twist to think that what the boy said was true. How could Rook know the wretched Lord Ovid wasn't beating the girl right now? He found himself caring about her although he barely knew her. It was an odd sensation since he hadn't cared about anyone for so long. It made him jittery and nervous and he didn't like that. Hell, he didn't like Wardell filling his head with these thoughts! He waited as the boy's hand wavered above the rook again, but his fingers didn't touch it.

"Move the damned rook already before I knock you to kingdom come," he exploded.

Wardell jumped in his chair, pulling his hand away. Then, instead of sliding the rook across the board, he reached for the knight and moved it. "Check," he announced.

"Check? What the hell!" Rook looked down at the board and realized the boy had, indeed, put him in check. Rook had been so distracted with the whelp's infernal talking that he hadn't even seen it coming.

This didn't sit well with him. He and his brothers had learned to play chess as children, as it had been Ross – their father's favorite game. Ross had taught them never to back down until they got the king. In life, Rook and his brothers had played that way as well. When they found out they were King Edward's bastards and that the man wanted to kill them as babies, vengeance boiled in their blood.

They'd worked together for the last three years stealing from the king to make him as miserable as they were. But now his brother, Rowen, had broken the bond between the triplets and betrayed Reed and him. Rowen sided with the king and paid him fealty now. He'd married Lady Cordelia and, because of it, was not only a lord but also a knight.

He stared at the knight on the chessboard, wishing it depicted him. But alas, it represented his brother, Rowen. Rook was represented by the bishop since he lived in the catacombs of the priory. His brother, Reed, was the rook since he lived with the MacKeefes in the Highlands. The MacKeefe Clan also owned Hermitage Castle on the border, having seized it years ago.

"Rowen," he mumbled, knowing now that his brother would be confronting him soon. The pieces of the game never lied. Rowen was coming.

He heard the short, shrill cries of his raven from the antechamber. Heading over to the door, he waited and listened, until he heard the monk's voice coming through the vents.

"Rook. I have information," said Brother Everad.

Rook opened the wooden door and then pulled the lever and the outer stone slid open. Brother Everad entered the chamber with the raven flying in behind him.

"You won't believe this," said Everad, standing in the open doorway.

"Come in and close the damned door before you let in any more rats," said Rook, turning and heading over to the food barrels at the opposite side of the room. He pulled the lid off one of the barrels that contained apples. There were only a few apples left. He knew the other food supplies were very low as well. He needed to do something soon because he was almost out of provisions. His stomach growled and he reluctantly closed the lid. There was no telling how long this food had to last. It would disappear quicker now he had three mouths to feed instead of two. Could things get any worse? "Now, tell me. What won't I believe?"

The monk only closed the door partially and headed across the room to talk to Rook. "I was in the village today talking with the serfs. They thanked me for making up the lie about the fever that killed some of their men." The monk laughed. "You should have seen how fast the soldiers left yesterday, thinking it might be the plague."

Rook sat back down, rubbing his leg and looking at the chessboard. He lifted his hand and moved his king. "There. I'm no longer in check," he told Wardell.

"Yes, you are," said Wardell, moving his queen next. "Check again. You know I'm enjoying playing chess with you as I normally don't have time for such pleasures when I'm always running messages across the land."

"There's more," interrupted the monk. "Actually, it is very disturbing."

"Disturbing?" Rook moved a chess piece once more. Again, Wardell put him in check. The walls were closing in on him and he could feel it. "I'll tell you what's disturbing, is this chess game!" He swiped his hand across the board, messing up the pieces. Normally he won chess when he played against the monk. He had a skill at it and the only one he'd yet to be able to beat was his brother, Reed, who was the master of the game. Wincing in pain, Rook got to his feet. "I can't think straight between the pain in my leg, the boy's constant chatter, and now you rambling on about things that are disturbing." He pointed at the monk. "If you have something to say, spit it out."

"The villagers are contemplating standing up to Lord Ovid."

"What will that prove?" asked Rook. "It'll only get them killed."

"They don't like the way the lord is treating them," the monk told him. "They are starving and have very little wood to make a fire to keep their children warm at night. Some of them have lost their husbands and can't work the land and watch their children at the same time."

"There isn't anything I can do about it," said Rook. "I'm almost out of provisions myself. Not to mention, I've lost my entire army."

"Perhaps we can hunt food for them," suggested Wardell.

"You're already walking on air," said Rook. "Poaching in the king's forest isn't a good idea unless you want to end up with a noose around your neck after all."

"Hello?" came a voice from across the room. Rook looked up to see Calliope peeking around the partially open door.

"Lady Calliope!" Wardell sprang from his chair and hurried across the room. "I'm so glad you've returned."

"I can only stay a little while," she said, putting down a huge burlap sack and pushing closed the door. "If I'm not back in a few hours, my presence will be missed. My uncle is in the practice yard this morning and he will be occupied for the rest of the morning."

"It's so nice to see you again," said Everad.

Calliope looked over to Rook next, as if she were waiting for him to say something as well.

"What's in the bag?" Rook asked. He watched her brows dip and her smile disappear. Perhaps he should have said something else?

"I know how hungry everyone is, so I've brought food." She pulled a loaf of white bread out of her bag – the bread that was reserved for the nobles.

"Good, I'm starved." In two long strides Rook was across the room, his hand grabbing for the bread.

Calliope was taken by surprise when Rook reached out for the food. Did he really think this was for him? And would he even care who she really brought it for? "Nay, not you!" She slapped his hand away and clutched the loaf to her chest. His dark, craggy brows raised in surprise and his bird-like eyes focused on her.

"Did you just . . . hit me?" He rubbed his hand. She hadn't realized it was the same hand that she'd bitten.

"Oh, I'm sorry. Did I hurt you?" She put the bread back in the bag before reaching out and taking his hand in hers. Then she pressed her lips against his palm and kissed it. He swallowed a muffled groan. "Your wound is healing nicely, but you really should keep it covered." Turning back to the bag, she pulled out a bottle of amber liquid next.

"Is that whisky?" asked Rook. There was no mistaking the hope in his voice.

"Nay, it's herb infused ale," she remarked.

"That'll do." He reached out again and when she went to slap him, he caught her hand this time. His striking blue eyes bore into her and his mouth was set in a firm line. "Don't even think of hitting me again."

Then, just when she thought he'd let go of her hand, he surprised her by imitating her action. He pressed his lips to her palm and kissed her ever so gently. The room became silent, except for the pecking noise of the raven as it played with something on the floor.

A heat engulfed her face and she was sure it was becoming red.

"If you aren't going to give us anything from that pouch, then why did you bring it here?" he asked.

"It's for the villagers," she said, letting her hand slip out of his. She bent over and pulled out a rag doll next. "See? My handmaid, Amanda, and I have made some dolls from rags for the children. I also have cheese, sweetmeats, and some dried beef and salted herrings."

"Oh, the villagers will be so happy," said the monk, pressing his hands together. "They have been starving." He looked up to the ceiling and proceeded to bless himself.

"Let's go give them the food," said Wardell, picking up the bag and slinging it over his shoulder.

"Wait," said Rook, stopping them. He perused Calliope. "Do you mean to tell me there is nothing at all for me in that bag?"

"Are you saying you need me to take care of you, too?" she rallied.

She could tell by the expression on his face that he didn't like that question.

"Of course not. I can take care of myself," he answered. "I just thought mayhap you'd bring me something for my pain."

She almost laughed aloud when she saw him rubbing his leg. The big, bad warlord was naught but a simpering child sometimes.

"I suppose there is something you might like in here." She dug into the bag and pulled out a goat's bladder filled with liquid and handed it to him.

"What's this?" He pulled off the cork and took a sniff and smiled. "Whisky. You were holding out on me." He raised it to his mouth.

"I stole it from a guard who was well in his cups last night. He'll never miss it."

"You stole these things?" Rook's hands stilled as he studied her face.

"Of course I did. My uncle wouldn't be generous enough to hand them over had I asked. Besides, you steal all the time, so what does it matter?"

"I just didn't see you as the pilfering type." He raised the goat bladder to his mouth and took a sip and let out a deep sigh. "Aye, that helps the pain."

"Wardell, I'll come with you to pass out the things," offered Calliope. "The villagers might need comforting."

"Nay. You'll stay here with me," Rook ordered. "Brother Everad will go in your place."

"Why?" she asked.

"Yes, why, my lord?" asked Brother Everad. Wardell stared at him, too.

"I – I might need comforting, too." He must have realized how weak that sounded because he quickly added to it. "I need Lady Calliope to check my wound." He stepped around her and reached into the bag on Wardell's shoulder. "You can leave this and this," he said, pulling out the loaf of white bread and some cheese.

"Nay, that is for the children." Calliope yanked the food out of his hands and stuffed it back into the bag.

"We haven't eaten either," Rook told her. "Or is it all right to see your friends go hungry?"

Friends? Did he mean Wardell and Everad or did he consider himself a friend to her as well? Curious, she found herself wanting to stay now. "We'll share this," she said, pulling a small bun that was made of coarse grain out of the bag. "And mayhap just a little of this." She pulled the bottle of mead from the bag next and looked around the room. "Do you have a goblet? Oh, there's one." She found a golden cup on a shelf by the cold hearth and put a splash in the vessel and corked the bottle back up and handed it to Wardell. "Take something for yourself, too, as well as you, Brother Everad."

"Are you certain?" asked the monk. "We wouldn't want

to take food out of the mouths of babes." He glanced over at Rook when he said it. Rook was about to shove the whole bun into his mouth but stopped in mid-motion. His eyes glanced from the monk over to Wardell and then over to her, his mouth wide open in the process. Then he brought the bun away from his mouth and licked his lips.

"I'll bring more food tomorrow as well as anything else that is needed," said Calliope. "Please, go to the villagers now and let me know if any of them need me."

"We will," said Wardell, carrying the sack and heading out of the room with Everad. They closed the door behind them.

The raven cackled, causing her to turn around. Her mouth fell open when she saw Rook sitting at the table, giving his bird a hunk of bread.

"That's not for dirty crows!" Her hands went to her hips. "I didn't risk my neck to bring food for a silly bird."

"Hades is not a crow, even if he is dirty. I wouldn't insult him like that if I were you. He's got a temperamental side." The bird opened its beak and cawed loudly as it if agreed. Then Rook hand fed it a piece of bread. "Come, sit with me," he told her, nodding to the chair at the opposite side of the small table.

After she removed her cloak, she slowly made her way across the room and sat in the chair. There was an awkward silence between them. She watched him eating the bread, still not happy with his actions.

"What's the matter?" he asked, chewing.

"You disgust me."

He stopped chewing, then swished at the bird, sending it flying across the room.

"There, the bird's gone," he said. "Is that better?"

"I'm not talking about the bird. I am talking about you."

He looked down to the bun that was half gone and swallowed. "Oh. Did you want some?" He held it out to her. "I thought you had already eaten. That is, coming from the castle and all."

"You have no manners whatsoever. I can't believe how ruthless you really are. You have earned your reputation."

He put the rest of the bun on the table, uncorked the goat bladder, and took a swig of whisky. His eyes watched her intently over the rim. That dangerous look was back in his eyes and she wished she'd kept her mouth shut now.

"I see." He got up and walked over to the other side of the room and picked up the goblet she'd filled partially with mead. He stalked her as he fastened his gaze upon her, slinking across the floor. Why did she feel like his prey? Then he placed the goblet down on the table with a clunk, right in front of her and settled himself back on his chair. His hand shot out and he slid the rest of the half-eaten bun in her direction. "It's all yours. Eat up!"

She sighed and pushed the bun back toward him. "One act of kindness, just because you had a finger pointed at you, doesn't make up for all the other ruthless things you do."

Rook gulped down another swig of whisky, corked up the goat bladder, and laid it gently on the table. He didn't like anyone making him sound like an ogre. He especially didn't like to hear it coming from such a beautiful woman.

He reached out and started arranging the chess pieces on the board, preparing for a new game.

"I can't help it if you don't approve of me. But I am who I am and I do what I do."

"You could change if you really wanted to."

"Mayhap I like being the way I am and don't want to change." Rook picked up the bishop that had the tip on top chipped off, running his finger over the jagged edge.

"Do you really like who you are?" she questioned. This seemed to upset him. He gripped the marble bishop tightly in his hand.

"Why does it matter?" he asked, his demeanor becoming perturbed. "I've had a hard life and I've learned to survive. I may be a cutthroat and a thief and a lot of other things, but at least I am loyal and would never betray one of my own blood."

"This has something to do with your brother, Rowen, doesn't it?"

He sprang up out of his chair and paced the floor. "I don't like you asking so many questions about me. Talk about something else."

"Like what?" she asked, taking a sip of the mead from the golden chalice. She was sure Rook had stolen this from the king. Her finger trailed around the smooth rim as she wondered how it would feel to be as wealthy as King Edward.

"Let's talk about you," he said, causing her eyes to snap upward.

"What about me?"

He returned to the table and sat down on the chair with a thump. She noticed the way he bit the inside of his cheeks. He was still in pain from his wound.

"Tell me about your childhood. Do you have brothers and sisters? Are your parents still alive?"

That was one subject she didn't care to speak of. "Here, have some whisky. It'll help the pain in your leg." She handed him the goat bladder again. His hand reached out and covered hers.

"You are avoiding my questions and that makes me think you have something to hide."

She let out a breath and nodded slightly. "You're not the only one who has had a hard childhood."

"Tell me about it." He took her hand in both his hands now and rubbed a finger in gentle circles atop her skin, staring at her with those dazzling blue eyes that drew her into his world. She felt tense, but enjoyed his touch. "Perhaps some whisky would help you relax." He tried to give her the whisky, but she pulled out of his hold and took a sip of mead instead. Putting the goblet down next to the chessboard, she figured he wasn't going to let her out of here before he got some answers.

"I am . . . an only child," she said, not able to look him in the eye. "My father was a knight and my mother was a wonderful woman. She died in childbirth along with my baby sister when I was six years old. My father was so heartbroken that he never remarried."

"So when did you come to live at Naward Castle with your uncle?"

"I've always lived at Naward. It used to be my father's castle."

"It was?" That seemed to take his interest.

"Yes. My Uncle Ovid is my father's half-brother. He lived with us along with his wife and three sons. But his wife died of a fever years ago."

"What happened to your father?" he asked.

"I'm getting to that. You see, my father was good friends with another lord who had a son named Alexander that was a good eight years older than me. So he betrothed me when I was just a child."

"Then why aren't you married?"

"I would be, but Alexander died in battle."

"Fighting for the king," he said, nodding his head.

"Nay. Fighting my uncle."

"What?"

"My uncle never liked Alexander or his family, even though my father was good friends with them. So when my betrothed came with his father and some of their soldiers to meet me, my uncle started a fight. It turned into a horrible battle. Alexander ended up killing one of my cousins – but it was only to protect himself since they were fighting against him with my uncle."

"So what did your father do?"

"My father knew my uncle started the fight. Although he mourned the loss of his nephew, he still wanted the alliance. But my uncle started killing them off, crazy that he'd lost his son. By the time it was over, all three of his sons had died, and so had Alexander and his father."

"So what did your father do to your uncle?"

"He was so distraught that he did nothing to my uncle. He arranged for the bodies of his good friends to be returned and was busy making sure Alexander's family wouldn't turn into his enemy after this."

"So he succeeded?"

"Yes and no. He managed to convince Alexander's family he did nothing against them and the whole thing was a horrible misunderstanding."

"I can't believe they didn't come for revenge," said Rook, shaking his head.

"Not everyone settles things with revenge," she told him. "My father pointed out that he'd also lost three of his nephews in the fight, so they called a truce."

"Your father should have killed your uncle. What was the matter with him?"

"My father was a good and just man. Ovid was his half-brother. He knew that blood was thicker than water."

"Hah!" Rook blew a puff of air from his mouth. "That was his first mistake."

"It was his last mistake," she corrected him. "He was found dead with a dagger sticking out of his back the next morning."

Calliope's eyes filled with tears as she remembered the horrible day. She'd had nightmares for years wondering what really happened and didn't like to talk about it.

"Are you all right?" his hand was back atop hers.

She bit the inside of her cheek so she wouldn't cry and continued. "I'll never forget seeing my father's dead, bloodied, mangled body lying there on the ground with a dagger sticking out of his back. He never had the chance to defend himself. Who would be such a coward?"

"Sounds to me like it was your uncle." He nonchalantly took another swig of whisky.

"I thought so, too, at first. However, my uncle said he saw the whole thing from the battlements. He said one of Alexander's soldiers snuck back into the castle and killed my father. My uncle tried to stop him, but by the time he descended the battlements, the attacker had disappeared and my father was dead."

"And you believed that?" asked Rook.

"I had no choice. I was just a child and my uncle swore this was the truth. There were a few guards who vouched for his story." She shook her head and bit her lip. "Uncle Ovid took over my father's castle that day and has raised me for the last ten years." The tears flowed faster and her body trembled. "I'm sorry but this is too upsetting to me. I can't speak of this anymore."

He reached out and brushed away her tears with his thumb. Then he stood up and pulled her into his arms.

"Shhh," he said, hugging her close to his chest. His hand smoothed over the top of her hair. "It's all right now." He guided her to the bed where they sat down together.

Feeling foolish, she wiped away another tear and faked a smile. She had to change the subject. "So, let me see how your wound is healing."

"Now?" His eyes darted toward the door and then back again. "All right." He stood and released his breeches, dropping them to his knees. She reached out and gently touched his stitches. He winced in pain.

"The stitches seem to be pulling, but the wound has closed up nicely," she said. "Lie down and I'll remove the sutures so that they won't pinch you anymore."

He removed his breeches all the way and lay down on his back on the bed. Calliope used the tip of her dagger to cut away the thread, and then cleaned and rewrapped his leg.

"I'm sure you'll be fine now. You are a very fast healer. You will feel pain for a while, but there doesn't seem to be an infection. The wound is healing nicely, although you will have a nasty scar."

"It won't be the first scar," he said. She was about to get up off the edge of the bed when his hand shot out and stopped her from going.

"Oh, did you want me to check your hand as well?" She inspected it.

"Nay, I want you to examine something else for me."

"Another wound?" she asked, hoping that was what he meant.

"What does this look like to you?" He pointed to his cheek.

She narrowed her eyes and turned her head, studying his handsome face. "I don't see anything."

"Look closer."

When she leaned in to take a better look, he wrapped his arms around her and kissed her. He'd tricked her, but she no longer cared. Calliope needed some love and attention after reliving the death of her father. She was getting used to kissing him and had lain awake last night wondering if she'd ever have the chance to do it again.

Her hands rose to his shoulders. Her eyes closed and she leaned her body over him for another kiss. Her breasts pressed up against his chest and she liked the way it felt being so close to him.

"That is a horrible story you told me," he said.

"Do you feel pity for me?" she asked, kissing him again.

"Nay. I pity no one," he answered, caressing her shoulders and kissing her on the neck. Her head went to one side and she let him do it.

"Why don't you pity anyone? Why are you so ruthless?"

"I don't know. I just feel nothing anymore. Ever since the night of Burnt Candlemas."

"Tell me about it."

"Not now." His hand slid down her body, his fingers closing around her breast. She moaned from the intimate gesture as she kissed him again. Then his mouth was on her neck and trailing lower. His fingers kneaded her breasts right through her gown. She felt the flicking of his thumbs across her nipples, making them go erect under the cloth. She moaned again in pleasure.

"Do you like that, Callie?" he asked, his kisses trailing

down to her cleavage.

"I – I do," she said, throwing back her head. Then he mouthed her nipple right through her clothes and, this time, she felt fire between her legs. What was it with Rook that he could excite her so easily? He had the means to make her squirm with desire. Curiosity made her want to know how it felt to make love to a man.

"My lord, we've returned."

Her eyes flew open and she jumped off the bed. Everad was there, standing in the open doorway with his mouth hanging open.

She noticed the laces on her bodice had opened during their foreplay, so she quickly ran for her cloak and threw it over her shoulders.

"I've brought back your sack," said Wardell entering the room. He stopped in his tracks when he saw Rook lying on the bed in only his tunic and braies. "What's going on here?"

"I tended to Rook's wound." She snatched the bag out of Wardell's hand. "It is late and I must return to the castle now. Goodbye."

She ran out the door, not even looking back over her shoulder at Rook. If she did, she would feel so wanton. What had she done? She was a lady but hadn't behaved like one today.

"Wait, Calliope," came Wardell's voice from behind her. "Will you return on the morrow again?"

"I don't know," she called back, collecting the torch she'd left burning in the wall holder and heading into the darkened catacombs. "I don't think so."

Her words said one thing, but her heart said another. Who was she fooling? There was no doubt in her head she wouldn't sleep tonight, thinking about the time she'd spent with the Demon Thief. There was also no doubt that she'd return on the morrow to continue where she'd left off with the dark and handsome man, Rook the Ruthless.

Chapter 9

Calliope made her way to the great hall with Amanda at her side the next morning, having dreamed of kissing Rook all night long. She'd sneaked back into the castle last night by way of the dungeon. It was empty and there'd been no guard posted at the door. She'd barely made it back to her room without being seen. Amanda had told her uncle she hadn't been feeling well and was taking a bath and going straight to bed last night. Thankfully, Lord Ovid hadn't questioned it.

Now, Calliope would have to face her uncle. She hoped she could look him in the eye when she lied or he might figure out she had something to do with Wardell's escape. Her cloak with the deep pockets covered her gown today. It would be needed during the meal.

"How are you feeling this morning, my dear?" Her uncle walked up with his wife, Joanna, holding on to his arm. She looked pale and sickly.

"I am well, Uncle, thank you. How are you, Lady

Joanna? You look pale today."

"There is nothing wrong with my wife," said Ovid. "She is pregnant with my heir."

"I am feeling a little ill today, but perhaps if I eat something I will feel better," said Joanna.

"Where have you been, Calliope?" scoffed Ovid.

"What do you mean? I'm right here, Uncle." Calliope faked a laugh and her eyes darted from one person to the other. Her body tensed and her tongue felt too big for her mouth. Her uncle was about to ask her about last night. She would have to lie and try to stay calm as she did it.

"You were missing last night."

"I was taking a bath." Trying to look straight at her uncle when she spoke didn't work. Her gaze dropped down to his chest. "And then I went to bed early." Now she was staring at her feet.

"So your handmaid told me. Of course, if I find out that either of you is lying to me –"

"My lord, I feel ill. Can you escort me to the dais table?" asked Joanna, taking Ovid's attention away from Calliope.

"You really are ill, my dear?" asked Ovid, turning his attention to Joanna. "I hope nothing is wrong with the baby."

"I'm sure after some food I'll feel better." Joanna looked over her shoulder and smiled slightly at Calliope. Calliope smiled back and nodded her thanks for the distraction.

Seated at the dais, Calliope kept her cloak on. When her uncle wasn't looking, she snuck some bread off the trencher that she shared with Lady Joanna and stuck it in her pocket. When she looked back up Joanna was staring at her with big, brown eyes.

"Saving a little for later in case you get hungry?" she whispered.

"Yes. That's what I'm doing."

Calliope nibbled at the food. When Joanna turned her head, she took a small Cornish hen and slipped that into the other pocket. Joanna turned back to the plate and giggled. "My, you are hungry today to have eaten that so quickly."

"Yes, I am." Calliope licked her lips and nodded.

"Bones and all."

"Oh." Calliope's heart dropped. Joanna was wise to her ways.

"Server, please bring more food," called out Joanna raising her hand in the air.

"Where did the food on your trencher go?" asked Ovid, stretching his neck, not able to believe it was all gone.

Joanna rubbed her stomach. "Little Ovid is hungry today."

"Oh, then, by all means, bring lots more food. I won't have my baby hungry." Ovid picked up a thick slab of beef, slapping it onto the trencher. The juices from the meat were bloody and dripped down into the trencher – an old, stale crust of bread. "Have some carrots and a little cheese as well." Ovid started stacking food up onto the trencher. "Here is some chicken and root vegetables and don't forget about the tarts." He topped off the heaping pile of food with several cherry tarts about the size of her hand.

Then, once Ovid was busy in a conversation with one of his knights, Lady Joanna took the beef and put it on a cloth used to wipe their hands. After wrapping it up, she slipped it onto Calliope's lap. "Here. In case you have guests," she whispered. Then she handed her two tarts which Calliope quickly slipped into her pockets. A hound came to her side, pushing his nose against the package on her lap.

"Nay, get away." Calliope shoved the hound away, but

the animal smelled the meat wrapped up on her lap and wouldn't leave. Its tongue curled and lapped at the cloth covering the beef. "Shooo, go. Get away from me."

"What's going on?" growled her uncle.

Calliope's eyes met with Joanna's. Then Joanna nudged the trencher with her elbow and it landed on the floor between them. Not only the hound, but several other dogs ran up and gobbled up the food. "Oh, how clumsy of me," said Joanna.

Her uncle didn't look happy. Calliope figured this would be a good time to slip away with her booty. She stood up, but when she did, she realized the blood from the beef covered the front of her gown.

"Calliope, what's that on your gown?" asked her uncle.

Joanna saw it too and hurriedly got to her feet. "My lord, I'll be going back to my chamber to lie down now."

"I'll escort you." He started to rise, but she stopped him.

"I'll be walking with Lady Calliope. We'll need to stop by the garderobe on the way there."

"Then I'll wait."

"She has her courses and will be embarrassed if you escort us," said Joanna under her breath. "Or cannot you see the evidence on her kirtle?"

"Ah, yes, I can." Lord Ovid cleared his throat and sat back down, looking the other way.

Once they left the great hall and were out in the corridor, Calliope spoke to Joanna. "Why did you help me?"

"I helped you because I want to be your friend, Calliope. I know you've never liked me, but we are the same age. I don't have many friends and hope you'll be mine."

"Why would you think I didn't like you, Lady Joanna? I've never said that." They continued to walk.

"You didn't need to." Joanna rubbed her belly. "Ever since I married your uncle, you have avoided me."

"Please forgive me. It wasn't you I was trying to avoid, but my uncle."

"I know Ovid isn't easy to warm up to and has done many awful things. But still, no matter how dark a man is, there is always some light in his soul. Always remember that."

She thought about Rook and the darkness surrounding him. He was a ruthless bandit who cared about no one but himself. He didn't pity anyone. And the poor man had no friends. He lived like a hermit, hidden away in the underworld amongst the dead. There wasn't much that should make her like him – but she did.

"Do you really believe that, Lady Joanna?"

"I do." Lady Joanna headed out to the courtyard with Calliope at her side. "Sometimes we forget that the men we love are warlords. All they know is fighting and killing, and we need to show them that there is so much more to life."

"But how?" she asked. "If a man is set in his ways, I don't believe a woman could easily change his mind."

Lady Joanna giggled. "No one said it was easy, Calliope. But what is life without a challenge?"

"I think you're right." Calliope walked into the stable with Joanna. "Do you love my uncle?"

"I was forced to marry a man twice my age," she said. "I don't love him, but I do care for him. I am eager to give him an heir."

"Ever since the death of his sons, an heir is all that seems to matter to him."

"Isn't that so for every man?" she asked.

"Only men who have something to leave their son. If a

man has nothing, I don't believe children are important to him."

"You sound as if you are speaking of someone you know. Are you?"

They stopped in front of a stall. Lady Joanna motioned for the stable boy to saddle a horse.

"I – I'm not sure," Calliope answered.

"Is he the one you are bringing the food to, my dear? You've been sneaking out of the castle for a while now, haven't you?"

She thought about telling Joanna the truth. She wanted and needed to talk to another woman of her status about her predicament. But in order to do so, she would have to divulge that she'd been dishonest. If her uncle discovered she'd helped Wardell escape and was meeting in secret with the king's enemy, she would be in terrible trouble. Nay. She needed to keep silent.

"I've been taking food to the serfs in the village, my lady, but I beg you not to tell my uncle."

"The serfs?" she seemed surprised.

"My uncle treats them terribly and they are ready for an uprising against him."

"Oh, no."

"Their children are starving and their hovels are cold with no wood for a fire. If they all died tomorrow, my uncle's only regret would be that he has no one to tend to his crops."

"I didn't know this," said Joanna. "I will talk with your uncle."

"Nay!" She said it a little too loudly and the stable boy looked up. "Please, say nothing," she whispered.

"You don't need to worry about Morton," she said,

nodding to the stable boy. "He is a friend and won't say a word to Lord Ovid about anything he hears."

"Are you sure?" She eyed the boy who just smiled at her. He was new at the castle and she'd never taken the time to talk to him yet.

"He can hear, but he cannot speak," she said. "He came from my father's castle. I have learned to understand what he wants to say by reading the motions of his hands and face." The boy waved his hands in the air and touched his face and heart.

"Why can't he talk?" she asked.

"He was an orphan that was brought to us by his nursemaid when he was a baby. There was a fierce battle and he was on the wrong end. His tongue has been cut out."

"Oh, how horrible," Calliope cried, her hand going to her throat.

"Morton says he likes you and wants to be your friend."

"Tell him, I'd like that," she said.

Joanna smiled and held her hand out toward the boy. "He heard you, Calliope. He is mute but not deaf. I've had him saddle a horse for you to take to the village. That way you won't be gone so long and, hopefully, my husband will not notice."

"But I can't go outside the castle walls. My uncle has forbidden it."

"He won't have to know. Morton, take the horse outside the castle and bring it around to the postern gate for Lady Calliope."

"The postern gate?" she asked.

"That is what you use to leave the castle, isn't it?" asked Joanna. "That is the only other way out and I know you haven't been leaving by the front gate."

"Yes. That's right," she said since she did use the postern gate on occasion. She didn't want to tell Joanna about using the catacombs from the dungeon because she wasn't exactly sure she could trust her. Even if the woman was sincere, there was always the chance she'd slip up and tell her husband. If Calliope's uncle knew his wife was helping her, he might take the back of his hand to her as well. Calliope didn't want her or anyone else to get hurt.

"When you return the horse, tie it up outside the postern gate in the brush," said Joanna. "Then come tell Morton and he will retrieve it."

"Thank you," said Calliope, turning to go.

"Wait." Joanna stopped her. "Do the villagers have horses to feed as well?"

She thought about Rook's horse, as well as the monk's. The villagers only had an old plow horse, but the horses were apt to be hungry since it was already autumn. Come winter, there would be little grass for the animals to eat.

"Yes, a few."

"Then I'll have Morton tie a bag of oats to the horse as well. You can tell the villagers it is compliments of the lady of the castle."

"I will," she said with a smile, happy to have someone on her side. "Thank you, my lady."

Joanna rubbed her belly again and held on to the gate of the stable. She looked even paler than before.

"Will you be all right?"

"Don't worry about me, Calliope. Now go to him and take all the time you need. Your uncle is leaving to see the king in the morning. He'll be occupied with preparations tonight. And then you'll have a sennight to do as you please."

"Thank you, my lady," she said, not missing the fact that Lady Joanna had said go to *him*.

"Do you love him?" she asked, as Calliope turned to go.

She stopped in her tracks, pondering the thought. "He is dark, my lady. Very dark. I have never met anyone as dangerous as him, but yet I've seen a spark of light within him that draws me to him like a moth to a flame."

"That is how it starts," she told her.

"How will I know if I'm in love?" she asked, looking over her shoulder.

"I cannot answer that, but my guess would be that if that spark turns into a flame, it's probably going to keep growing. That, I'd say is love."

Calliope hurried across the courtyard, keeping her cloak pulled close so she wouldn't lose the food. Would that spark that started between her and Rook turn into a flame? Curious, she needed to find out. Now, her thoughts were focused on nothing else except the notion of what it would feel like to make love to a man.

Chapter 10

Rook raised his bow and nocked an arrow, aiming for the buck he spied through the trees. He sat atop his horse while Wardell sat mounted on Brother Everad's horse next to him. He'd only taken the boy with him to hunt because Everad looked weary from Wardell's constant chatter as well.

Wardell had been eager to come along. But the deal was he needed to remain quiet. He'd accepted the challenge and had done little talking since they entered the woods.

Letting his arrow fly, it embedded itself into the hind end of the buck. The deer went running through the woods. Rook's jaw clenched and he shook his head.

"We've got to bring it down before it gets away." Rook urged his horse forward with Wardell right behind him.

"There it is," said the boy, pointing in the direction of the deer. The animal, being wounded, had slowed down. Rook lifted his bow again and took the deer down with one last shot.

"There is a pheasant," said Wardell, pointing toward the brush.

"Leave it. It's small and too far away. You'll never hit it from here. We need a hound for that," said Rook.

"I've got it," said Wardell, preparing his arrow and pulling back the bowstring. The pheasant took off into the sky.

Rook shook his head. "I said to just –" He stopped his words in midsentence when Wardell's arrow made a clean shot and brought down the bird.

"Are you sure you're only a messenger?" asked Rook, impressed by the accuracy of the boy's aim.

"I have a skill for weapons and hunting. I told you, I served as squire for a long time."

"I see. All right, let's collect our kills and take them back. Everad will have the cook fire ready. I'm so hungry I could eat this whole buck by myself."

* * *

Calliope stopped her horse at the ruins of the priory as Everad came out to greet her.

"Everad," she said, getting off the horse and hugging the monk.

"Calliope! You've taken a horse and traveled outside the castle in the daylight? What if Lord Ovid finds out?"

"He's busy preparing for his trip tomorrow," she told him. "Besides, Lady Joanna is helping me."

"Is that so?" The monk released her and looked her in the eye. "Where is Ovid off to now?"

"Joanna says he's going to see the king."

"What could he possibly be doing? Why would he want to see Edward?"

"I couldn't say." She looked around the crumbling ruins, but didn't see Rook anywhere. She wondered if he was in his underground chamber.

"He's not here," he told her.

"Who?" she asked.

"Rook. Don't pretend you're not looking for him. I know you better than that."

"I was looking for Wardell." Her eyes dropped down to his chest as she said it.

"Then why can't you look me in the eye?"

She let out a sigh. "Oh, all right, you caught me. I make a horrible liar."

"That you do." He reached out and ran a loving hand over her hair. "But that's what I love about you, Calliope. You have a good heart and won't end up like me."

"You had no choice, Brother," she said. "You weren't destined to be a monk and we both know it."

"All that matters is that you stay on the right path. I'm not sure sneaking around the catacombs, smuggling out prisoners, and kissing bandits is a good start."

"Perhaps it's not my calling to be a lady."

He reached out and squeezed her shoulder affectionately. "I don't want to ever hear that again. Do you understand?"

"When will you stop trying to look out for me?"

"Never. Now, tell me why you're here."

"I've brought food," she said, pointing to the travel bag on the horse. "And Lady Joanna sent oats for the horses, although the serfs might eat the oats instead."

The monk stared at Calliope's gown. "By the Rood, did Lord Ovid strike you again?"

She was perplexed at first until she realized he saw the bloodstain from the meat.

"No. That's from the beef I smuggled onto my lap during the meal. I've got it in the travel bag. Would you like some?"

Brother Everad's eyes traveled to the bag tied to the horse. His tongue shot out to lick his lips. She knew he was hungry. "Nay. Take it to the villagers. I'll wait for Rook and Wardell to come back from the hunt."

"What if they don't catch anything?" she asked. "At least take a little."

"They'll bring food back, I'm sure," said Everad. "Rook never misses when he aims to catch . . . something."

"Or someone?" she asked with a smile. "After all, that is what you were thinking, weren't you?"

The monk's face darkened. "He's not right for you, Calliope. He'll only bring you trouble."

"I'll decide that, not you. I'm going to take the food to the village." She mounted her horse, ignoring the words of wisdom. Everad was right. Rook was trouble. But part of her was attracted to anything that was off limits. Rook the Ruthless was the last person she should have her eye on and, somehow, that made her want him even more.

Calliope dismounted in front of Ida's cottage. The door opened and two of the older children, a girl, and a boy, ran out to meet her.

"Lady Calliope, you're here," said the boy.

"Yes, Stanley, I am." She reached out and ruffled the boy's hair. He was approaching the age of about ten. Soon, he'd grow and be stronger and more help in the field.

"Did you bring us anything?" asked Martha, who was eight.

"I did," she answered.

Ida hurried out of the house next with her younger

children, Matthew and Mary, clinging to her skirts. Mary was clutching one of the rag dolls she'd made.

"Lady Calliope, I'm so glad to see you." Ida looked worried and her eyes were sunken on her face.

"I've brought food," she told Ida, showing her the travel bag. "I've got more food in my pockets, as well as a flagon of wine and sweetmeats, too."

"We could use food," said the woman, not smiling at all.

"Ida, is something the matter?" She knew it must be a strain for the woman since she lost her husband, but something else seemed to be troubling her.

"Children, take the things from Lady Calliope and carry them into the house," instructed Ida.

Calliope untied the goods from the horse and handed everything to the children. "One of you go and get the neighbors, too," said Calliope. "We will share the food."

"I'll go," said little Matthew, running to the next hovel. Once the children were gone, Calliope spoke to Ida. "Tell me what's troubling you."

"It's the baby," she said. Calliope first realized the woman wasn't holding the youngest girl, Etta.

"Is she sick?"

"She's had a fever for the last two days. I've been up day and night trying to take care of her as well as the other children. Between that and working the fields to bring in the crop for Lord Ovid, I feel as if I'm going to collapse."

"Let me see Etta. I've brought my bag of herbs along and, mayhap, I can make up a healing poultice or some tea to help."

She entered the hovel and went straight to the baby, picking her up and cradling the child in her lap. The little girl cried. Calliope could see the baby's hand in her mouth.

When she put her finger in the baby's mouth, she felt the sharp edges of two teeth poking through her gums.

"Ida, she's teething. That's why she's got a fever. You have been through this before with your other children, why didn't you notice?"

Ida's face turned red and then she started crying. "I'm so tired I didn't even think of it. And I miss Hank so much. I could just die."

"What's the matter, Mommy?" asked little Mary, tugging on her mother's skirts.

"Nothing, darling," she said, pulling her child toward her. Calliope's heart went out to the woman and her family, as well as all the people of the village.

"I brought along some spices in a pouch and I think the cloves will help little Etta's pain." She dug the things out and called Mary over. Stanley and Martha walked into the house carrying the bags of food. "Will you children help me prepare a meal while your mother rests for a while?"

They all nodded. Then Matthew ran into the house being followed by Tom, Horace, and their families.

"The boy says you brought food," said Horace.

"Our families are hungry," added Tom. "Where is it?"

"It's not much, but I'll bring more tomorrow." She pointed toward her offering.

Tom looked into the bag and shook his head. "This isn't the way it's supposed to be," he said. "We're all so overworked, hungry and tired that to die would be a blessing."

"Nay, don't say that." Calliope rocked the crying baby. "We'll get through this together. But you all need to be strong."

"It's all that Demon Thief's fault," cried Tom's wife.

"It's because of him we're starving and our loved ones have died. We should never have joined with him to go against the king."

"We're doomed," cried out another woman. "When Lord Ovid finds we haven't harvested the crops, he'll beat us."

"The king is bound to find out we helped that bastard and we'll all be beheaded for it," wailed another.

"Let's get him!" shouted one of the men, causing an uproar amongst the villagers.

"Get who?" came a deep voice from the door, causing everyone to go silent. Calliope looked up to see Rook standing in the doorway. Outside was his horse with a dead deer tied to it. With him was Wardell with a pheasant dangling from a rope at the side of his horse.

"Rook!" She handed the baby to Ida and started across the room to him. Everyone remained silent. "Why are you here?"

"We don't want you here," came a voice from the crowd.

"Leave us alone," said someone else.

Rook glared at the serfs. His hand wavered over the hilt of his sword. "I was out hunting and only stopped because I saw a horse here and wondered who had come to visit."

"That's my horse," said Calliope. "I took it instead of walking today. I brought food for the villagers and I've got feed for the horses as well."

"Well, don't let me stop you." He turned to go. "I won't stay where I know I'm not wanted."

Calliope had to act quickly to remedy this tense situation.

"Rook has brought you venison from the hunt," Calliope called out to the villagers, causing Rook to stop in his tracks and slowly turn his head.

"What are you doing, Calliope?" he mumbled.

She pushed through the crowd of people, making her way to his side. "Trust me. It's for the best," she said in a soft voice. Then she turned around and surveyed the hut filled with people. "It looks like they've bagged a buck and a wild pheasant as well," she said, stretching her neck to see outside. "That'll be plenty of food for everyone. The extra can be smoked or dried, so you'll have food during the winter."

"He didn't bring it for us," said Tom with a snort. "Hell, he'll probably keep it all for himself. He always does."

"Nay, you're wrong, Tom." Calliope hoped to smooth things over between them.

"He doesn't care if we live or die," spat Ester. "He didn't even tell us he was sorry for the deaths of our loved ones."

"Neither did he help bury their bodies," said someone else. "He made the monk help us instead.

"Tell them, Rook," she said, looking up into his bright blue eyes. "Tell them that you've hunted for them and will do so again whenever they need more food."

"That's poaching," said a woman. "It's from the king's forest. We can't eat it. The king will have us killed."

Rook's chin rose at the mention of the king. He looked over the heads of the crowd. "I can do whatever I want. And the more I take from the king, the better. If you don't want the food, then starve – I don't care. But if any of you want to take the risk, then get the buck off the horse and take it to the back of the hovel where we can gut it and prepare it for cooking."

Calliope looked to the villagers eagerly. They were glaring at Rook and she knew they didn't want to trust him again after they'd followed him into battle and lost so many of their men.

"What is taking so long?" asked Wardell, pushing his way into the room. "Is there something going on here?"

"Rook has offered the venison to the villagers since they are starving," Calliope announced.

"He did?" Wardell looked up at Rook and nodded his head in approval. "We've also got a pheasant and two hares that I caught." He looked up at Rook who was scowling at him now. "That is, if the Demon Thief decides to share."

"The Demon Thief is dead," mumbled someone from the crowd.

"What was that?" Rook looked up sharply, his jaw twitching and his eyes narrowing in the process.

"I think you should take the offer," Calliope told the villagers, stepping in front of Rook in a feeble attempt to put space between him and the serfs who were angering him at the moment. "Rook has nothing but your well-being in mind. I'm sure he'd like to share the pheasant and two hares as well. Wouldn't you?" She played a dangerous game with the Lord of the Underworld and wasn't at all sure he'd play along. Her heart thumped so loudly as she waited for his answer, that she swore everyone could hear it.

Finally, Rook nodded his head. "Let's get moving," he said. "We have animals to gut and clean before nightfall."

The villagers hurried out the door, led by Wardell, to get the food. Calliope released a breath of relief and smiled. Perhaps Rook did have a spark of light inside him just like she and Lady Joanna had discussed. And hopefully, that spark of light would continue to grow brighter and bring the man out of his dark ways before it was too late.

Chapter 11

Hours later, Rook watched as Calliope engulfed herself in the lives of the villagers. They'd ended up bringing the meat to the fire that Brother Everad had set up in the courtyard of the priory.

Everyone had eaten their fill and tempers were relaxed now that people weren't hungry.

Rook sat next to Calliope on a log, finishing off his portion of venison, giving pieces of it to Hades. The bird sat perched on his knee.

"Thank you for trusting me," she whispered, leaning over and bringing her mouth to his ear. Her body touched his and he wanted to put his arm around her, but he didn't. Not in front of all the villagers.

"Umph," he mumbled, taking a drink of the wine. He'd brought a barrel of wine up from the catacombs that he'd stolen on one of his raids. She'd even convinced him to share that with the villagers, although he didn't like the idea. Was it because he trusted her that he'd agreed to feed the people? He wasn't so sure. But when he heard the villagers talking about not wanting to hunt in the king's forest, he knew he wanted to help them. Helping someone didn't feel natural to him. Neither did he pity the fact they didn't have enough food. That's just the way he was.

"You have a good heart, Rook," Calliope said, gazing up at him with those innocent, trusting eyes. Didn't she know he was a black-hearted devil? He'd learned to be that way ever since the horrible night of Burnt Candlemas when his life changed forever.

"I have no heart. I did it to spite the king," he admitted, admiring the golden goblet he'd confiscated on a raid before bringing it to his lips.

"That goblet is made of gold, isn't it?" she asked.

"What's your point?"

"I was just thinking how much money that would bring in if you sold it."

"Now, why would I want to do that? I like having a few nice things in my life."

"I just thought you could do it to help the villagers." She splayed out her hand, pointing to the men, women, and children. "They have very little at all."

"Haven't I helped them enough for one day?" Everything she said always came back to the serfs and it was making him ornery. Their welfare didn't rest on his shoulders. They were vassals of Lord Ovid, not him.

"I was just thinking – they need help bringing in the crops as well. If we all –"

"Stop it, Calliope," he said, no longer wanting this problem placed on his lap.

"It would be a kind gesture," she continued, not listening to his warning. "They need the help since so many of their men died."

"And that's my fault?" He took another drink of wine, looking at the cup rather than at her. His raven squawked and hopped from one of his knees to the other.

"You were the one to bring them into battle although you knew you didn't have enough men to win without Rowen and his crew."

"That's enough!" he spat, throwing down the goblet and getting to his feet. His raven shrieked and took off to the sky. Rook stormed off to the catacombs to be alone. At least it would be quiet there without someone constantly pointing out his flaws. He made it through the church and down the steps to the bowels of the priory. He walked in pitch darkness to his chamber without a torch to guide him. He had just entered the room and lit a candle when he heard her voice from behind him.

"Here, take it." Calliope followed him with the golden goblet in her hand. He'd been moving quickly in the dark and she'd managed to keep up with him. That impressed him. He was especially impressed by the fact he'd never heard her following him. "I'm sure you don't want to lose this."

She walked over and set down the goblet on the table. As soon as she did, he pulled the hidden lever and closed them inside together, proceeding to close the wooden door as well.

"What are you doing?" Her cockiness diminished quickly. She wasn't so brave when they were all alone. It was just the two of them now and she didn't have her precious villagers to rely on.

"I close the door so rats don't come in. I thought you knew that by now." He unclasped his weapon belt and removed it. Then he proceeded to sit on the chair at the table that held the chessboard.

"You didn't need to close the inside wooden door, too."

"Yes, I did," he said, pulling off a boot and looking up at

her with a sardonic grin. "That way, when this black-hearted bastard kills you, no one will be able to hear your screams for help."

Her eyes almost bulged from her head and he had to hold back from laughing. Her fingers gripped her cloak tightly as she held it closed around her neck. "Pardon me?" she asked, standing frozen to the same spot.

"That's what you think of me, isn't it? That I'm ruthless, I care for no one but myself, and would slit the throat of someone I care about without even batting an eyelash – just for fun."

"I – I don't think that about you at all." Her gaze fell.

"Then why are you staring at the ground? It's because you can't look me in the eye when you lie." He pulled off his other boot and threw it to the floor. "What does it matter? It's all true." He turned and studied the chessboard. He and Brother Everad had started a game this morning before he went out on the hunt but they hadn't had time yet to finish.

"So you really would slit my throat although you care about me?" She swallowed deeply when she said it.

"Now your presumptions are clouding your judgment, my dear." With one finger he slid his bishop across the board. "Who said I was talking about you?"

"Oh. Well, you did make a comment about no one hearing me scream when you killed me. However, I would like to think that was only an ill jest and naught more."

"It was." He studied the board. "And like I mentioned, the rest of what I said had nothing to do with you."

"So you're saying you don't care for me? Not even a little?" She sounded so disappointed. Gradually, she released the tight grip on her cloak and strolled over and slid her body atop the chair opposite him.

"Did you want me to care for you?" he rallied, still staring at the board.

She paused before she answered. "Nay. Not at all. Why should I care?" She pushed the opposing queen across the board, scooping up the bishop in return – the one that was chipped at the top.

"Damn! Why'd you do that?"

"This piece represents you, doesn't it?" she asked, holding the piece and turning it around in her palm.

"You know it does. I told you that the other day."

"It's chipped at the top and damaged," she pointed out.

"It fell off the table. So, what of it?" He nudged a pawn forward.

"You're damaged, too. But like this broken chess piece, you can also be mended."

"That piece is made of marble. It's ruined and there's no way to fix it. It's broken and that's the way it'll stay. Now, stop lecturing me about things of which you know nothing. It's too late for me, Calliope. No one can help me, so just accept it. I can't change!" He got out of the chair and plodded over to the washstand. Leaning over, he glimpsed his weary reflection in the water, not sure he liked what he saw. He closed his eyes so he wouldn't have to look at himself. Using both hands, he splashed water on his face and let out a frustrated breath.

"I don't believe that for a minute," came Calliope's reply, followed by the sound of the padding of her feet across the wooden floor as she made her way over to him. "I've already seen you change – a little. If you were beyond help, would you have taken in Wardell in his time of need? And you fed the villagers today with the meat from the hunt, as well as shared your cask of wine. Those were good things, not something a black-hearted man beyond hope would do."

"I was tricked into doing every one of those things by you."

"Are you saying I'm capable of controlling you?"

He gripped the sides of the washstand and opened his eyes. Not liking the way she spoke to him, he wasn't about to let her leave here thinking she could control him. No one could and he needed to make that clear.

"No woman is ever going to control me. So get that idea out of your head right now." He stared at the wall and gritted his teeth.

"You're just afraid that you'll end up like your brother, Rowen, aren't you?"

Calliope knew she'd pushed Rook too far when he spun around and she saw the fires of hell in his eyes. It was either that or the reflection of the lit candle on the table.

"Don't ever mention his name to me again. I only have one brother and his name is Reed. Do you understand?"

"So now you deny your own blood? Just like you deny being a bastard of the king? That is selfish, Rook." She couldn't help it and had to say that to him. It probably wasn't a smart move, but he needed to hear it.

"What do you want from me?" he ground out. "I have done everything you wanted just to please you, but still you are not happy."

"That's why you did those things?" she asked in surprise. "For me?" She wasn't quite sure how she felt about it. It rather touched her but, at the same time, she didn't like the idea that his heart hadn't been in the decisions.

"Does that surprise you?"

"Well, if you're not letting a woman control your

actions, then I'd say yes. I'm very surprised."

"I think you talk too much," he said. "Mayhap you should leave now."

"Leave? Is that what you want?"

"There's the door," he said, nodding toward the other side of the room. He said the words but, if he wanted her to leave, why didn't he open it for her?

"I'm sorry if I upset you." She took one step closer, testing the waters. "I only meant that I see a spark of light in you that I'm sure can grow into a flame."

"Oh, there is a spark there," he said. "That I won't deny. But I'm not sure it's the same kind of spark you're thinking of right now." He reached out and pulled her into his arms forcefully. Her chest smashed against his. "It's already grown into a fire that's threatening to consume me." He dipped down and kissed her, and she didn't fight him. But tonight was different. His kiss didn't hold the care and gentleness in it that it had previously held. This time, it seemed forceful as if he were trying to prove something to her.

"Rook, don't," she said, putting her palms against his chest.

"Why not?" he asked. "I know you want it, too." He lifted her in his arms, bringing her over to the bed. Panic filled her body. She wanted to make love to a man, but not like this.

He dumped her atop the bed and then straddled one large leg over her. His long hair hung down around them as he kissed her mercilessly.

"Nay!" she said, pushing against him. Then he changed his actions as fast as he'd started. Reaching down, he brushed his lips against hers and kissed her gently. Then he caressed her shoulder with one hand in a very caring way. The tip of his finger on his other hand brushed across her cheek in a whisper of a promise. This was the way it should be.

Her hands settled against his chest as their kisses became more and more fulfilling. A tingling sensation ran across her skin as every part of her body came to life with his magical touch. She relaxed instantly. All fear of the man left her and she daringly trailed her fingers down his chest and to his waist.

"What are you doing?" he asked in a sultry voice. Their mouths were almost touching.

"I've been wondering what it would feel like to make love with you, Rook. Now, I'll finally know the answer."

She figured that would propel him forward. Instead, he rolled off her body in haste and bounded off the bed.

"Well, you're going to have to keep wondering, aren't you?"

"What?" She sat up, confused as to what just happened. "Are you saying you – don't want to do it?"

"Look at you," he said, nodding to her soiled gown. "You've got blood on your gown and your body is almost as dirty as mine. Now, do you think I'd want to bed someone under those conditions?"

She felt the stab to her heart from his words. Was he purposely trying to be so calloused and ruthless? "You're just doing this to spite me, aren't you?" She swung her legs off the bed.

"I told you – no woman controls me. Not even in the area of coupling."

"You had this planned all along, didn't you? You wanted this to happen."

"You're right, Callie, I did."

Why did he have to call her Callie? It only made her want him more. She felt as confused as he looked right now. His hardened words couldn't keep her from seeing the disappointment in his eyes that they'd stopped. He'd gone from being generous to being black-hearted and downright scary, to gentle followed by ruthless, all in a matter of minutes.

"I don't want to play games with you, Rook. I care about you and I'm only trying to help you."

"Don't care about me," he told her, shaking his head and holding up a palm to her. "And I don't need your help. I've survived on my own since childhood and I'll continue to do it. Also, before you say another word, I don't want your pity. I was cursed the day I was born a triplet bastard of the king on the Feast Day of the Holy Innocents and I've learned to live with it."

"Tell me what happened." Curiosity made her want to know more about this dark man.

"There is nothing that matters anymore."

"Nothing but your vengeance for the king," she corrected him. "That seems to be the driving force behind everything you do. Mayhap no woman will ever control you, but it's obvious that King Edward already does."

"That's not true!" His face became hardened and she knew she'd struck a nerve. "The king doesn't have any control over me."

"Prove it," she daringly challenged him. "Do something of your own choosing that is not done in hatred against your father."

"Don't call him my father." A muscle twitched in his clenched jaw.

"Why not? Everyone now knows it's the truth. You need to accept it."

The cry of his raven sounded through the vent and Rook's attention snapped upward. "Someone's here."

"There are a lot of people out there, most of them villagers," she reminded him.

"Nay. My raven tells me it is a stranger."

The outside stone door was heard sliding away. Rook grabbed his weapon belt and headed over to collect his boots.

"My lord?" came Brother Everad's voice as the wooden door opened. He held a lit torch in his hand. "There is a stranger who has approached the village and now has shown up here." He stuck his head inside the room, looking first at Calliope and then at Rook as if he didn't approve of them being together behind closed doors.

"Who is it?" Rook asked, having already donned his boots. He fastened his weapon belt around him.

"I don't know. It's a young man and he doesn't seem to be able to speak."

"Morton," said Calliope, hurrying out the door. Making it through the catacombs and out into the courtyard, she discovered the sun had already set and it was getting dark. Calliope hadn't meant to spend so much time here. She saw the boy on his horse, waving his hands wildly in the air trying to relay a message to Wardell.

"What does he want?" asked Wardell, making a face and looking at Morton as if he thought the boy was daft. The serfs had all gone back to the village and the fire that had cooked their meal was smoking as the embers glowed red.

The boy handed her a missive. She took it and opened it to read it in the moonlight.

"What is it?" asked Everad, walking up behind her with the torch. Rook was with him.

"This is the stable boy from Naward Castle," she explained. "His name is Morton and he is mute."

"Who sent the missive?" Wardell was curious and peeked over her shoulder as she read it.

"It's from my uncle's wife, Lady Joanna," she told him. "She's telling me to hurry back to the castle because my uncle is asking for me."

She stuck the missive in her pocket.

"I'll escort you back to the castle," said Rook, surprising her.

"I've got Morton with me. I don't need you. But thank you just the same." She mounted her horse, preparing to leave.

"It's not safe, Calliope." Rook mounted his horse as well. "I'll protect you."

"My lord, is it wise for you to be seen out in the open and so near a fortified castle?" asked the monk.

"I am going along to protect Lady Calliope and I'll not hear another word about it," Rook told him.

"She'll need my protection as well," said Wardell, throwing his bow over his shoulder and mounting the monk's horse.

"Nay, you'll stay here," ordered Rook. "Help Everad clean up and douse the fire. If Ovid comes looking for her, the villagers will need protecting."

"I don't need either of you, now just stay here," protested Calliope.

Rook rode his horse to her side, the moonlight casting a purple sheen on his ebony hair. He looked dark and dangerous in the night. It suited him. He was the lord of darkness, so why shouldn't he feel at ease traveling under the cover of darkness?

"I told you, Callie, I don't let any woman tell me what to do and neither will I ever. I've decided to escort you back to the castle, so there is nothing you can say to change my mind. Now shall we?"

He led the way. Calliope and Morton followed. Then his raven shrieked and she ducked as it flew right over her head, landing on Rook's shoulder as he rode.

She smiled to herself because, mayhap, she'd reached a part of Rook today after all. Perhaps that small spark of light had grown. And even though he denied it, she had a feeling that he did care about her.

Chapter 12

They approached the postern gate of the castle and Calliope glanced over at Rook. "Thank you for the escort, but you should leave now."

"How will you get in?" he asked.

"I'll sneak through the postern gate while Morton takes the horses around the front and to the stable."

"I'll meet you here on the morrow at midday. Watch for my raven and you'll know when I've arrived."

"Why?" she asked, sliding off the horse.

"You are planning on returning on the morrow, aren't you? For the sake of the villagers," he added quickly. "I don't like you traveling alone. It's not safe and I will escort you."

"Of course." She flashed a smile. "For the villagers," she added, and headed toward the postern gate as Morton continued toward the front gate with the horses. She looked back over her shoulder before she stepped through the opening and saw that Rook was waiting and watching to make sure she got inside safely. With his raven on his shoulder and all dressed in black, he looked devilishly handsome in the moonlight. Her heart soared. He wanted her to return and was even coming to get her. He did care for her after all.

She'd just made it through the postern gate and was in the garden when a male voice stopped her in her tracks.

"Where have you been, Niece?" asked her uncle.

Her body stiffened. She turned around to see the man sitting on a stone bench polishing his sword in the moonlight.

"Uncle," she gasped.

"Don't think I don't know you've been sneaking outside the castle walls. What do you take me for – a fool?"

"I – I felt like going for a walk."

"It's no use, Calliope. I saw my wife sending the missive with the mute. Now, why don't you try the truth?"

Her heartbeat sped up as she considered lying to him. She had to tell him something and didn't want him to find out about Rook. Then she thought of the poor serfs. The way her uncle treated them only made her angry.

"If you must know, I was in the village."

"Ah." He stood up and slid his sword back into his scabbard. "And why would you be going there?"

"I bring the serfs food from the castle," she blurted out. "You treat them unfairly and they are sick, starving, and even dying."

"How dare you go against my word!" His hand shot out and though she moved her head, she wasn't fast enough. Her uncle clipped her on the jaw. "My soldiers tell me that when they went to the village to look for the missing prisoner, they discovered that several of my serfs had died from a fever. Is this right?"

"Yes, they are dead," she said, doing her best to continue

staring at the top of his head in the dark. If her eyes dropped just once, she was sure he'd hit her again.

"I can always tell when you're lying, Calliope."

"I'm not lying. They died, just like I said." She stared at his forehead, hoping he wouldn't mention the fever again.

"You haven't dropped your gaze, so I suppose you tell the truth. But I don't want you going anywhere near the village if there is a fever spreading through there. You will stay inside the castle walls. Do you understand? You are not to go anywhere without my permission."

"Of course, my lord," she said, looking downward.

"I will see that you are controlled, as soon as I return from my visit with the king in a sennight."

"What do you mean?" Her eyes lifted.

"I am going to hold a tournament as soon as I return. The winner will receive your hand in marriage."

"Marriage?" Her mouth opened in surprise. This was the last thing she expected.

"If you are married, I know your husband will keep you under control. And if you're pregnant and bearing his heirs, you'll not have time to be worried about peasants. That will keep you where you belong." He stormed off toward the keep with Calliope on his heels.

"Nay, please Uncle. I don't want to be married to a man I don't even know."

"Perhaps you will know him. After all, some of my knights will be competing as well."

She didn't want to marry any of his knights. The ones that didn't have wives were either undesirable or elderly. She wanted to marry a man she loved and not be traded off like a side of beef at the market.

"I don't want to marry any of your knights," she said.

"It doesn't matter what you want. I've already instructed my guards to post the details of the competition in the morning. I'll also send missives to the neighboring castles, as far as the coast. This contest should be quite large."

"Please, don't make me get married."

He stopped in his tracks and turned to face her. "You have no say in the matter, Calliope. You are already well past marrying age at twenty years of age. If you don't marry now, no one will ever want you. As it is, I'm going to have to offer one hell of a dowry to entice any man to marry a woman of your age who cannot seem to follow orders." It was legal and also common for girls to marry as early as the age of twelve and boys at fourteen. By twenty, most girls had already had three or four children.

"But, Uncle –"

"I'll not hear another word about it."

Calliope ran through the courtyard and up to her chamber where she cried herself to sleep.

* * *

"You surprise me with your skill in wielding a sword," said Rook the next morning as he sparred in the ruins of the priory's courtyard with Wardell.

"I not only handle a sword with grace, but you should see me joust," answered the boy.

"Hold up," said Rook, with his hand in the air. Over Wardell's shoulder, he saw Brother Everad cleaning fish that he and Wardell had caught in a nearby stream early this morning. Rook wanted to have a special meal when he brought Calliope here today.

"What is it, my lord?" asked Wardell, taking on the habit

of calling him lord since the monk did it. Rook could get used to this title.

"I've always wanted to learn the joust," he admitted. "Can you teach me?"

"I suppose so," said Wardell, looking around the grounds. "But we'd have to make a quintain to use for practice.

"Brother Everad, could you devise such a thing?" asked Rook.

"Yes, I'm sure there are enough bits and pieces of rubble that I could put together to make a mock quintain," said the monk.

"Then do so. I know where we can get some young trees to whittle into jousting lances," said Rook. He looked up to the sky. The sun was getting higher. He'd have to make this fast so he could still get to the castle by midday to get Lady Calliope.

"I am looking forward to this," said Wardell. "I've often wondered why the king made me his messenger when I had been his best knight's squire for years."

"You were squire to the king's best knight?"

"Aye," he answered proudly. "Sir Benton is one of the best in the land at jousting. He was also the king's champion."

"What did Sir Benton say when the king made you a mere messenger?" asked Rook suspiciously. Something didn't sit right with him and he smelled foul play in this story.

"He didn't say anything. I was replaced by another squire."

"Didn't you ask the king why he was making you a messenger?"

"I've learned never to question King Edward," said the boy. "I know the king must have a good reason to do what he did."

"Yes. I'll bet he does." Rook would have to think about this later because he didn't like what he was hearing. He also didn't like the fact Calliope was able to spring Wardell from the dungeon so easily and the fact that the guards gave up so fast while looking for an escaped prisoner. He'd have to find out more about this from Calliope. But right now, he was going to learn a skill he'd always wanted to know. He was going to learn to joust. That is, he would learn the skill of a knight. No matter how good Sir Benton was at jousting, Rook's goal was to become even better. And with the boy's help, he'd get what he longed for after all.

Chapter 13

Calliope stood atop the battlements the next morning, watching her uncle and his entourage heading away from the castle because of a summons from the king. He'd be gone for a sennight and that was exactly the amount of time she had to figure out a way to stop his silly notion of holding a tournament to marry her off.

Her heart belonged to Rook now and she only wanted him. But Rook wasn't eligible to compete in the competition since he was a bastard. Even if he could, she didn't think he would. While she knew his longing to be a knight, she also saw the turmoil in him that stemmed from the vengeance he held toward the king.

"Lady Calliope, why are you up here?"

Lady Joanna climbed the battlements to meet her.

"I thought you went with your husband," she said in surprise to see her.

"Nay. I wasn't feeling well and preferred to stay here rather than to travel." She held her hand to her stomach and looked very gaunt.

"What is the matter, Lady Joanna?" she asked. "Is it

something with the baby?"

"I – I don't know," she told her. "I haven't felt the baby move for days now. I also retch constantly and have started bleeding."

"Have you told my uncle?"

"Nay." She shook her head. "He is counting on this baby to be his heir and I didn't want to worry him. I'm afraid, Lady Calliope. If I lose this baby, Ovid will not want me. He wants a strong woman who can birth him many heirs to inherit his lands and castle."

"I see," she said, reaching out for Joanna's hand. "But you need to tell him. Let me call the midwife to take a look at you."

"Nay." She shook her head. "I will tell Ovid when he returns. I'll not have rumors about this floating around the castle in his absence."

"Lady Joanna, you haven't been married long to my uncle, but I need to tell you that he is an evil man, no matter if you think so or not."

"Don't say that."

"It's true. He killed a good man to whom I was betrothed because he didn't want my father, his half-brother, to make the alliance."

"I'm so sorry. I didn't know."

"He inherited the castle and lands from my father, but he shouldn't have."

"Oh, you feel as if you should have inherited everything?" asked Joanna.

It was so much more than that, but she couldn't tell her. Neither did she want to worry the woman anymore. She'd already said too much.

"I am a female and couldn't inherit anything, anyway,"

she said. "And even if I marry, it won't make a difference."

"You're thinking about the tournament he's planned for you to marry you off, aren't you?"

"I am," she admitted with a slight smile. "I know any woman of my age should be thrilled to be getting married to a noble. But I don't feel that way."

"You've fallen in love with another man, haven't you?"

"Nay. I haven't." She focused her gaze over the edge of the wall. Joanna laid her hand on Calliope's shoulder.

"It's who you've been sneaking away to see, isn't it?"

She didn't want to lie anymore. What she needed was a woman – a noblewoman with whom she could share her secrets.

She looked back out to the rolling hills in the distance as she answered. "I am in love with the Demon Thief," she admitted before she could change her mind. When Joanna did not answer, she slowly turned her head to peek at her.

The woman was smiling. "I know," she said.

"You know? How could you?"

"I saw him bring you back to the castle last night when I came up here looking for my husband. I thought it could be the Demon Thief. When I asked Morton about it, he nodded to confirm my suspicions."

"Oh, please don't tell anyone, Lady Joanna. If so, Rook would be in grave danger."

"Your secret is safe with me," Joanna assured her.

Calliope stuffed her hands in the pockets of her cloak, trying to get warm. And when she did, her fingers closed around the marble chess piece she'd stolen from Rook. She held it up to look at it, running her finger over the chipped top. "I saw that spark in Rook of which you spoke. And I think he is changing, though it's ever so slowly. In time, I'm sure I could get him to change his ways."

"Be careful, Calliope," said Joanna. "No man wants a woman controlling his thoughts and actions. That will turn him away faster than the plague. Just love him and, hopefully, he will want to return that love all on his own."

"Such words of wisdom. Thank you." Her heart went out to Joanna. She was such a kind and loving girl. Calliope knew she'd never find love with Ovid. The woman deserved someone so much better than him. Still, there was nothing she could do to change things.

"What have you got there?" asked Joanna, rubbing her stomach again. She reached up and tucked an auburn curl of hair behind her ear.

"This is a piece from the chessboard that symbolizes Rook," she explained, holding it up so Joanna could see it. "It's chipped and I want to fix it."

"Just like you want to fix him?"

"I suppose so." She studied the piece. "Do you think Morton could use something from the stable to help me smooth down the chipped top?"

"I believe so. And if you visit the blacksmith, I'd bet he could smooth it down as well. Just tell him you're doing it for me."

"Thank you," said Calliope, reaching over and giving Joanna a hug.

"Why are you thanking me? I haven't done anything."

"You've given me hope. Hope for Rook. And even if it's not meant for us ever to be together, I'm going to do all I can to help the spark of light within him grow. That's the least I can do before I'm married off to a man I don't love and am taken away from him forever."

* * *

Rook hid in the brush by the postern gate at midday, waiting for Calliope to join him. He'd sent his raven over the wall nearly a quarter of an hour ago to let her know he'd arrived. The bird had returned, but Calliope hadn't shown up yet. He had the feeling he was being watched. Slowly, he slid his sword out of the scabbard, ready to attack if needed. It wasn't until he saw the sea hawk high in the sky above the trees that he knew who it was.

"Rowen." His brother's name sprang from his lips like an oath. Rook tasted the bitter betrayal of his brother on his tongue. He was about to go find him when he heard another sound and turned around to see Calliope heading through the brush, looking for him.

His raven squawked and headed up into the sky. Calliope saw it and headed in his direction.

"Rook?" she called out softly.

Rook sheathed his sword and pulled himself up onto his horse and headed toward her.

"I thought you weren't going to show." He scanned the area for possible guards. When he didn't see any, he reached down for her. "Give me your hand," he said, scooting off the saddle to the back of the horse to make room for her.

"A guard was patrolling the back of the castle and I had to wait for him to leave," she told him. She handed him a bag of food first. He tied it over the pommel and then proceeded to lift her up in front of him. As they rode off, her golden tresses brushed past his cheek in the breeze. Her hair felt like silk against his rough skin. She also smelled like rosewater.

His raven led the way. When he saw the raven and the hawk making circles in the sky, he knew his brother was close.

"Hold on tight," he said into her ear as he wrapped an arm protectively around her. "I'm going to pick up speed."

"What's the hurry?" she asked as Rook brought the horse to a full run.

"I've got a lot to do today." He looked back over his shoulder to see his raven flying toward the priory. The hawk was gone.

When they finally rode up to the ruins, Rook's ears were almost shattered by the sound of a screaming baby.

"What the hell?" he grumbled, when he saw Brother Everad pacing the courtyard with a baby in his arms. He dismounted, then reached up and helped Calliope from the horse. Her small waist felt nice under his fingers. So did her hands on his shoulders as her body slid down his to the ground. He wanted more than anything to kiss her right now, but the piercing cry of the baby rattled his brain as well as his nerves.

"Brother Everad, can't you silence that thing?" he asked. "The baby is going to alert others that we're here."

"I'm sorry, my lord," said the monk, looking as flustered at Rook felt right now. "I can't get it to stop crying."

"What is it doing here in the first place? And where is Wardell?"

"I'm here," said Wardell, rounding the corner with a child on his back, one in each arm, and another two clinging to his legs so he could barely walk. "The village women brought their children by for us to watch so they could work in the fields."

"We're not playing nursemaid, now get rid of the

children and get back to work on our project," snapped Rook. "What gave them the idea they could do this in the first place?"

"I might have mentioned that I'd help watch their children," said Calliope.

"You?" asked Rook. "Then why didn't they bring their children to the castle instead?"

"Because I told them to bring them here. It's much closer. Besides, they are too frightened of Lord Ovid to leave their children anywhere near him."

"And they're not frightened of leaving them near me?" asked Rook in astonishment. What was happening here? The Demon Thief was the most feared legend of the land. The villagers, even though some of them had fought with him, had always feared him. Until now.

"I told them not to fear you," said Calliope, causing his gut to twist into a knot. "Besides, I think you've redeemed yourself and your horrid reputation when you gave them the meat from the hunt yesterday."

Rook knew that action would come back to haunt him. And while it had felt good to help the serfs, he didn't want to make a habit out of it. He had other things on his mind. Such as how he and Reed were going to plan their next raid against the king when Rook no longer had anyone to fight with him.

"How far did you get on the quintain?" Rook asked the monk.

"I haven't been able to do much since I've had a baby in my hands since you left," Everad told him.

"The little one is teething and needs some more clove oil on her gums." Calliope took the baby from the monk. Wardell headed away with the children still clinging to him while Everad followed.

"Can you bring me the clove oil from the bag?" asked Calliope, rocking the baby in her arms. Rook liked the way she always cared for everyone. She also looked good with a baby in her arms. She was a natural mother and would make some lucky man a good wife someday.

He dug around in the bag, but it was so filled with food, drinks, herbs, and even clothing, that he couldn't find what she asked for. "I don't see it in here anywhere," he said, his head down as he searched through the bag. The baby continued to cry.

"Here, I'll find it." She pushed the baby into his arms and, involuntarily, he took the child. He held the baby out from his body with both hands as she wailed.

"I'm not comfortable with this," he admitted. It had been a long time since he'd held a baby. He'd held his sisters in his arms when they were babies, but that was so long ago that he forgot how to do it.

"You look like you're afraid of the poor thing." Calliope giggled, digging her hand deeper into the travel bag. "Haven't you ever cared for a baby before? The baby will pick up on your fear."

"I have, and I'm not afraid. Not of a baby." He held the little girl closer against his chest just to prove it. When he did, the baby started sucking on his finger. Magically, she stopped crying.

"You have the golden touch," said Calliope, finally finding the bottle and pulling it out of the bag. "I think little Etta likes you."

"Mmph," he mumbled, almost liking the fact the baby took to him so easily. It made him feel special.

"Here, I'll take her," said Calliope with outstretched

arms. He almost hated to give the child up. She gathered the baby in her arms and proceeded to rub clove oil on Etta's gums. The baby fell asleep snuggled to her chest. "What is that tree doing on the ground?" she asked, looking over toward Wardell who was now running around like an idiot with the children laughing as they tried to catch him.

"That is supposed to be a jousting lance that Wardell should be whittling."

"A jousting lance?" She shifted the baby in her arms. "What for?"

"Brother Everad is making a quintain and Wardell is helping me make lances because he is going to teach me to joust."

"Really? Whatever for? I hardly think you'll ever use the skill. After all, jousting is only for knights. I don't see that you'll ever have the opportunity to use it."

When he didn't answer, she looked up and could see it all clearly now. Her mouth opened in surprise. "You want to be a knight, don't you?"

"Nay. I never said that." He headed away and she followed.

"Why else would you want to learn to joust?"

"I want to learn any skill I can that will help me in my raids against the king."

"I thought you weren't going to raid anymore now that you have no army."

"Who said that?"

Now it was her turn to be quiet. "I suppose I just presumed that."

"That is always your problem. You presume too much." He picked up a knife and started to pull the bark off the tree.

"That is going to take a long time. Perhaps you should

have help."

"I had help," he growled, whittling faster. "That is, until the priory was turned into a nursery."

"Lady Calliope, I'm so glad you're here." Ida walked up to greet her, taking the baby from her. "Was little Etta any trouble?"

"Not at all. Rook was able to calm her down just by holding her. He's good with babies."

"He held my baby?" asked the woman with concern in her voice.

"Aye, and she's still in one piece. Surprised that I didn't swallow her whole?" Rook looked up and sneered on purpose as he used his knife like a madman on the tree.

"Oh!" Ida jerked backward and held her baby close.

"Rook, stop it," Calliope scolded. "Ida, don't be frightened. Rook is just jesting with you."

"Are you sure?" he asked, waggling his brows, moving the blade even faster.

"Ignore him. Now, tell me what is going on in the village," said Calliope. "I brought food and supplies for everyone."

"Thank you, milady, but it'll be a long time before any of us can sit down and eat. We're so far behind in harvesting the crops that it'll never get done."

"Just do your best, Ida. Lord Ovid is away for a sennight, so you have some time before he shows up to collect the harvest."

"Thank you, my lady." She looked down to what Rook was doing and whispered. "What is he doing?"

"He's making a lance. Brother Everad is constructing a quintain so Rook can learn the joust."

Rook groaned inwardly, wishing she hadn't told that to

Ida. Next thing, he knew, she was going to say he wanted to be a knight as well.

"I'm working on learning new skills for the next raid against the king," he told her.

"I see," said Ida. "You know, my Hank was a woodcutter and taught almost everyone in the village how to whittle. Even the elderly who can't tend the fields can whittle faster than anyone I've seen."

"Perhaps they could help you, Rook," suggested Calliope.

"Nay, they couldn't," said Ida.

Rook figured the villagers were still angry with him and hated him.

"Why not?" asked Calliope.

"Because we've had to send the elderly out to the fields to tend to the crops since we are so short on help. I cannot thank you enough for telling me to bring the children here," said Ida. "It has freed up many of our women so they could work in the fields as well."

Rook almost asked why they didn't have the elderly watch the children or just put the children to work. But before he could, Wardell walked up to join them. The children were now bothering Brother Everad instead.

"Do you need help bringing in the harvest?" asked Wardell. "I'd be happy to assist you."

"No, you wouldn't," said Rook. "You've got work to do for me."

"I'm sure the elderly would be happy to whittle your lances while Wardell helps them in the fields," suggested Calliope. "They could use the assistance of an able-bodied man."

"I'm certain Brother Everad would want to help, too,"

added Wardell.

"Nay, you're not going to help them in the fields." Rook looked up to see Calliope scowling at him. Wardell and Ida were staring at him as well and he didn't like the way it felt. It felt so much better yesterday when the serfs smiled at him and thanked him for the food. He wanted to feel like that again. Plus, he wanted to please Calliope. He cleared his throat and continued to whittle. "That is, you're not going without me." Shoving his dagger back into his weapon belt, he got to his feet and wiped the dust from his hands on his tunic.

"Oh, thank you, Rook," said Calliope, rushing over and giving him a hug. She kissed him on the lips right there in front of everyone. Rook was so shocked he didn't know what to say.

"I'll get Brother Everad," said Wardell with disappointment in his voice. Rook was sure Wardell liked Lady Calliope. It did Rook's heart good to see that Calliope liked him, instead.

Once again, he found himself letting a woman control him. While it irked him, it also oddly felt good to help others. He shook his head, wondering what was happening to him lately. It was so unlike him. He was softening and wasn't sure it was a good thing. After all, he had a reputation to uphold. If he wasn't careful, he was going to end up like his brother, Rowen, before too long.

Chapter 14

For two days now, Rook had helped the serfs tend the fields, which kept him away from what he really wanted to do. But the kisses from Calliope in thanks were worth it. He had the villagers thanking him for helping, as well as for hunting for them. It felt good to work with the land and reminded him of his days as a child in Scotland.

He and his family had farmed the land, as well as learned to fight and be part of the clan. His father, Ross, even raised birds. Rook and his brothers had loved the birds. That was the reason he and his brothers all had birds today.

"Rook, look what the villagers have finished for you," said Calliope, heading across the field toward him with a few of the children helping her to carry the jousting lances.

Rook wiped the sweat from his brow with the back of his hand and threw down his shovel. He'd dug up more beets in the past two days than anyone could eat in a lifetime.

"Let me see," he said, taking one of the poles in his hands. The villagers had done a good job. The wood was smooth and there was even a pommel to grip on the end.

Wardell made his way through the fields to see it as well.

"That's pretty good," said Wardell, taking the other pole and testing its weight. "However, real jousting lances have a guard over the hand and it needs to be a little longer," he said as he inspect it.

"We'll work on it," said one of the teenage boys. "I'll tell the elders right away."

"I'll come with you to instruct them." Wardell took one pole while the children took the other and headed back to the huts.

"They do excellent work, don't they?" Calliope reached up and put her arms around Rook's neck. "And so do you." She kissed him right there out in the open, and he let her do it.

His hands slipped around her waist and he pulled her closer. He hadn't had any intimate time in private with her lately since he'd been so busy helping the villagers. Every morning, he snuck to the castle to bring Calliope back with him. Then every night, he escorted her home again. He didn't like having to stay hidden with her. But he did like the fact the villagers didn't judge him for kissing a noblewoman when he was naught more than a bastard. Even if he was of noble blood.

"I'll have Morton bring the cart tomorrow to collect the harvest," announce Calliope. "The crops will be back at the castle before my uncle returns. Hopefully, that will satisfy him and keep him from sending his reeve to the village or from coming here himself. The serfs are happier when he stays away."

"I'll be glad to finally start training to joust tomorrow," Rook told her. His raven landed atop a fence and cackled. "Someone's here." He peered across the field to see a man sitting atop a horse watching them. Rook's hand instinctively covered the hilt of his sword. Pushing Calliope behind him, he said, "Stay back."

"Who is it?" She peeked out from behind him. A cry of a hawk from the sky made him realize who watched him. Rowen.

"It's no one," he said, turning and guiding her back toward the hovels. "Calliope, tonight I'd like to spend time in my chamber – just the two of us."

"Don't you want to share a meal with the villagers?"

"On the contrary, I'd like you to ask Brother Everad and Wardell to leave us alone."

"How will I explain that?"

"Tell them someone has been watching me and I'd like them to stay in the village tonight in case there is trouble."

"All right. I will."

"Meet me back in my chamber within the hour. I have a special surprise for you."

"I can't wait," she said with a smile. "Is this surprise something that will please me?"

"If it doesn't, then I've lost my touch satisfying a woman."

She kissed him again. This time, it was so passionate that he wanted to take her right there in the field. She'd said she wanted to make love with him and tonight was the night he was going to grant her that wish. Matter of fact, it was his wish, too.

* * *

Calliope felt her stomach fluttering as she made her way to Rook's chamber in the catacombs nearly an hour later.

She'd given the message to Wardell and Brother Everad. They promised they'd stay in the village to watch over the serfs tonight. She might have also given them the idea it was so Rook could take her back to the castle and get away from crying babies.

However, she had to make it sound that way, because Wardell fancied her. Plus, Brother Everad thought she should be with a noble knight and not a bandit. This way, they wouldn't suspect that she might stay the night with Rook. If he had a romantic evening planned, then she would be the one to suggest she stay instead of going back to the castle.

Her uncle wouldn't return for days yet, so that wasn't a problem. Lady Joanna knew Calliope's secrets and her handmaid, Amanda, was good at covering for her absence.

She entered the catacombs and the darkness surrounded her. She'd been spending so much time in the outdoors and the sun with Rook that it felt awkward coming back to the dark. However, this time she felt as if it wasn't Rook who would be tempted by the darkness. This time, it would be her.

Was she selfish by wanting to make love with Rook when she knew in less than a week she'd be married to someone else? She hadn't told Rook of her uncle's plans. She also wanted to spend every last minute with him before she got married. If she told him of the competition, he would probably not even kiss her anymore. Nay, she couldn't live with that idea.

The door to his chamber was open slightly. A pleasant aroma drifted through the catacombs as she made her way past the ancient, dusty tombs. Keeping her eyes focused on the crack of light coming from his chamber, she ignored the evidence of death all around her and walked forward toward the light.

"Rook? Are you in here?" She pushed the door open slowly, shocked to see a wooden tub filled with water in front of the hearth. She'd never seen a fire in here before, but now there was not only a glowing fire but also a spit with a wild pheasant roasting over the flames. A heavy iron pot was filled with vegetables up to the rim, bubbling in what smelled like a wine broth. One of the loaves of bread she'd brought from the castle, as well as two apple tarts, kept warm on the bricks next to the fire.

"Come in and close the door." Rook stood at the table, staring down at the chessboard. He wore only a pair of braies and nothing else. His raven hopped around pecking at the chess pieces.

She turned around to close the door and he stopped her.

"Wait," he said, shooing his raven off the table. "Hades, you stay out of here tonight. Calliope thinks you're a dirty bird."

The raven cawed its disapproval, flew across the room and then out the door.

"I don't think Hades is too happy," she said, shutting the wooden door.

"He wasn't happy keeping the rats at bay either while we waited for you. The rodents smelled the food and kept trying to get in."

"This is unbelievable," she said, walking in a daze over to the tub. She reached down to feel the soft flower petals floating atop the water. She heard him closing the stone door behind her. "The water is hot," she said in excitement.

"Yes. I kept warming water over the hearth. I also had hot stones on the bottom of the tub to keep the water from getting cold."

Next, she heard the sound of a key being turned in a lock. She spun around to see Rook locking the door. "I didn't know that door had a lock," she said, thinking of all the times that someone had walked right in when they were kissing.

"I've never needed a lock before tonight."

"Really? Why is that?"

His body glistened in the amber light of the candles as he made his way across the room. His eyes were dangerous, and lust dripped from his words when he next spoke.

"Because tonight I'm going to give you what you've asked for, Callie."

"Do you mean –"

"That's exactly what I mean." He reached out and slipped her cloak from her shoulders. It fell to the floor and pooled around her feet. "I haven't been able to think of anything but making love to you lately." He lifted her chin with two fingers and grazed his thumb across her lips. "You are so beautiful and kind. And I am so undeserving of someone like you."

"Nay, don't say that." She kissed him gently, staring into his mesmerizing blue orbs. She saw her reflection in his eyes and also the fire burning in the hearth. "You deserve so much more than you think. You are a good man, Rook. Never forget that."

"I don't want to talk about being good or bad tonight. Because what I have planned is going to be very good, but also bad at the same time."

"I – I'm ready," she said, licking her lips, scared but excited at the same time. Tonight, she'd know what it felt like to make love to a man. Not just any man, but Rook – the man with whom she'd fallen in love.

"Not quite yet," he said, removing her gown next, leaving her standing there in nothing but her thin shift. "First, we will bathe together and cleanse our bodies and our souls."

"I'm not quite sure a mere bath can cleanse one's soul." She was thinking about the fact she hadn't told him she was to be married soon.

"My soul will never be clean with all the darkness within it." He removed her shift and let his eyes trail down her naked body. "But your soul is beautiful and will always be." With the gentlest of touches, he skimmed his fingers down the front of her, making her shiver with desire. Once they were both naked, he lifted her in his strong arms and carried her to the tub.

Her skin was on fire touching his bare body. She could even feel the crisp curls of hair on his chest. She hadn't allowed herself to look below his waist yet. Instead, she kept her focus on his face.

"Your lips are like sweet, ripe berries ready to pluck from the vine." He kissed her gently. "I feel as if with just a taste I am heady." He stepped into the water and hunkered down, bringing her with him. She settled into a sitting position, the water just covering her chest.

"This feels good," she said, leaning back against the edge of the tub and closing her eyes. "Where did you get a tub?"

"It's left over from when the priory was intact. Not everything was stolen or demolished when King David and the Scots destroyed it decades ago."

"I know," she mumbled with her eyes closed. "I'm glad they didn't demolish the large stone cross or the statue of

Mary Magdalene in the alcove above the church door."

She felt his hands on her shoulders as he scrubbed her arms with soft soap. It wasn't the coarse, harsh, lye soap used by peasants, but rather soap that was scented with the essence of roses and cinnamon. That, mixed with the tantalizing aroma of their meal and the smell of the scented beeswax candles, made it hard to remember she was in a chamber in the crypts rather than the solar at her castle.

"Let me wash you and then you can do the same to me." His fingers traveled in sensual circles, trailing from her shoulders down to her breasts. His thumbs rolled her nipples and she felt herself go taut. Her back arched of its own accord. He splashed water over her chest and then lowered his head to gently take one nipple between his lips.

His mouth was warm and his tongue talented. He suckled at her breast like a babe. A fire of desire grew in her belly. Then she heard herself gasp at the feeling of pleasure.

"Do you like that?" he asked in a low and sultry voice.

"I do," she admitted.

"We need to make sure we don't miss a spot." His hand slipped between her thighs as he covered her mouth with his. He spread her legs with his hand and, before she knew it, she felt him playing with her folds and entering her with one finger.

"Ooooh," she moaned, closing her eyes and leaning her head back again.

"I want you to feel pure pleasure tonight," he told her. "And I want to be the one to give you that pleasure in any way possible."

"You're off to a good start," she admitted, wondering what else he would do.

"Now it's your turn to wash me." He guided her hands

into the bowl of soft soap.

"I – I'm not sure I can do this."

"Why not? Are you frightened of me?" His eyes were hooded and lust emanated from him. Yet, he was gentle and kind at the same time.

"Nay. That's not it. It's just that I've – never done something like this before."

"All the more reason to take your time to enjoy it," he told her, taking her hand and rubbing it against his chest. "You said you wanted to feel the experience and I am going to grant you your wish. Unless you've changed your mind for some reason."

This would be the perfect time to tell him about her wedding. But curiosity ate away at her and she had to know what came next. Nay, it was too hard to turn away now and neither did she want to. She'd dreamed of this and wanted it more than anything. Tonight would be the night she made love for the very first time.

"I haven't changed my mind, nor will I," she whispered, using both hands now as she rubbed them against his chest.

"Good," he said, capturing her hands in his. "Now, lower." He guided her hands below his waist under the water. She rubbed him and then felt something growing. It surprised and frightened her, and she tried to pull away. But he took her wrists in his and stopped her. "Try it again, but this time, slower. And this time, don't pull away."

She did as he instructed, taking his male form into both of her hands. Before long, she felt him growing longer and harder in her embrace. As she ran her fingers up and down his shaft, he laid his head back on the rim of the tub and moaned in pleasure. His eyes were closed and this gave her the courage to explore further. Her fingers roamed lower and she felt more of him. Then his swollen member pulsed against her hand and it scared her and she pulled away.

"I think it's time we get out of the tub," he told her, standing up. Water dripped from his glorious body, making him look like a god of the sea. She couldn't bring herself to look below his waist and kept her eyes on his face instead.

"Don't you want to see how I look when I'm aroused?" he asked.

"Nay," she said and her eyes lowered with the lie. Now she stared at his chest.

"You're lying, Callie," he said with a chuckle.

"Nay, I'm not." Her eyes dropped lower. This time, she found herself staring at his manly beauty. So big, so long, so hard.

"Let's go over to the bed, shall we?"

"Yes," she said, stepping from the tub with his guidance. He reached over and patted her body dry with a towel.

"Callie, I'm finding myself very attracted to you." He kissed her once again.

"And I, you."

"I know this is your first time, so I'm not sure we should continue. If you ever get married, your husband is going to want a virgin."

"Then I'll lie and tell him I'm a virgin."

"With your maidenhead gone?"

"My maidenhead was gone when I fell from a tree and hurt myself as a young girl. It is no secret."

"Then I see no reason not to continue. Do you?"

"Nay." She closed her eyes and shook her head. "I want you, Rook. Please. Don't tease me when I'm ready to shatter."

She must have said the magic words because he stopped

asking questions. He scooped her up in his arms and laid her on his bed. This time, when he covered her with his body, it wasn't harsh or forceful. This time, he was gentle and caring, taking the time to please her before he pleased himself.

After he'd kissed every part of her and used his magic to make her feel euphoric, she felt as if she were about to burst with desire. He slid his length into her a little at a time until she felt as if she wanted him in his entirety.

His hands cupped her buttocks and he tilted her pelvis upward as his glorious length entered her fully. He slid in and out, slowly at first and when she felt comfortable, his thrusts became faster. Before long, she picked up the rhythm and they were doing the dance of love. Her body tingled and heated up until she felt as if she were going to burn up. Then she felt the pulsing deep down to her core. She closed her eyes and opened her mouth and released a squeal of delight.

"Let loose, Callie. You don't need to hold back."

She did let loose and found her peak as her body melded with Rook's and they became one. It felt as if nothing else mattered in life. She was with the man she loved and she wanted him to know it.

He spilled his seed within her, making her climax once again. "I love you, Rook," she cried, causing him to still. Then he removed himself from atop her and got off the bed.

"Let's get cleaned up and have something to eat," he said.

"All right," she answered, feeling confused why he hadn't returned her profession of love. Mayhap it was too much to expect from such a hardened man. She hoped her words hadn't scared him away.

After a while, they sat at the table finishing their meal.

"This pheasant was the best I've ever eaten," she told

him, putting a bone down on the silver platter she ate from and wiping her hands on a cloth napkin. It was obvious the fine things they used had been stolen from the king. She picked up the gold goblet and took a sip of mulled wine. Rook had gone to so much trouble to make things special for her that it made her feel honored and like a queen.

"You deserve only the best, Callie. But I could never give you the things I really want to give." He reached out and cupped her cheek with his large hand. She closed her eyes and leaned into the touch. It felt good and she never wanted it to end.

"I wish I could give you what you deserve as well," she told him. "After all, you are the son of a king. You shouldn't be living in a tomb, hidden away from the rest of the world. You should be living in a castle, honored and respected, and as an icon for the people. You are an excellent warrior. You should fight for the king instead of against him."

"Never." He dropped his hand to the table and the mood was ruined.

"Tell me what happened to you as a child, Rook."

"I don't want to talk about it." He started to get up from the chair, but she reached out and took his hand.

"Please." She smiled gently. "I'd like to know."

He hesitated for a moment, then sighed and ran his hands over his face. "All right," he said. "You were honest and told me all about your childhood; I suppose I owe you the same."

She hadn't told him everything. But she would – in time. "I'd like that," she answered.

"I grew up in Scotland. My mother was English and my father was from the Douglas Clan. Or so I thought. My brothers and I are triplets, as you know."

"Yes. I understand that twins and triplets are feared and thought to spawned by the devil."

"That's right. We *were* spawned by the devil." He shoved the platters aside and dragged the chessboard in front of them. Then he plucked the marble piece that depicted the king from the board. "We didn't know he sired us until my father – Ross, spilled the secret one night. It was the night of Burnt Candlemas. Edward and his troops were ransacking the coast, killing all who crossed his path, and burning everything." His fist squeezed the marble piece and Calliope thought for sure it would turn to dust.

She reached over and pried his fingers from it, placing the piece back on the board. "So what did you do when you found out?"

"We were only twelve at the time. But my brothers and I were so angry that we wanted to kill the king. I went out to the barn to get our swords and the horses with Reed. Rowen stayed in the house for another minute. I think that's when my mother told him he was the first-born triplet. That's why Rowen betrayed us. He figured he was entitled to land, wealth, and riches, being the first-born. Or at least that's what he thought. Edward has many sons and we were nothing but the babies of his mistress. I think Edward feared us since we were triplets. He ordered us all killed as babies."

"Oh, that's terrible!"

"My mother – or the woman I thought was my mother, Annalyse, also had three daughters with Ross."

"So you have sisters?"

"They are really cousins since Annalyse was my mother's twin sister. Their names are Summer, Autumn, and Winter."

"Where are they now?" she asked.

"Annalyse was so angry with Ross for betraying her late sister's last wish of never telling us who sired us that she took the girls and the handmaiden and left for England the night of Burnt Candlemas. They live with Rowen and his new wife, Cordelia, in Whitehaven now."

"Have you gone to see them?"

"Nay. Why would I? They are all dead to me." He continued to put more pieces on the board.

"Surely your sisters didn't do anything wrong. Why do you hold anger toward them?"

"I don't." His hand slowed as he arranged the pieces. "I just can't see them. I'm a bandit. Besides, Rowen is there."

"Mayhap it's time you make up with him."

"Never!" His fist came down on the table, making the chess pieces jump. "He betrayed us. He turned his back on us and now pays allegiance to the king instead."

"I heard he's been knighted as well. Aren't you happy for him?"

"Why should I be?" he snarled. "Rowen doesn't deserve it."

"Don't you ever wish you were a knight, too?"

His eyes flashed over to the painting on the wall, fixating on the knight in the scene. She saw the hunger and desire in his eyes. It didn't matter how he answered because she knew the truth now.

"Are we done with this conversation?" he asked in a low voice.

"Nay." She picked up a few pieces and started to set up her side of the board. "So what happened after you and your brothers left that night?"

"We tried to take refuge in a church, but Edward's men didn't regard it as a place of sanctuary. They invaded and, at the same time, so did a band of pirates."

"Ah. So that is why Rowen was once a pirate."

"Yes. They abducted him that night and raised him as one of them. Reed escaped and went to the Highlands to live with Ross, who was injured. My family was friends of the MacKeefe Clan who took them in. I, on the other hand, was shuffled off into the catacombs by an old monk. He took me to safety. But after too long he said I needed to leave the area. He brought me to the border and handed me over to another group of monks. Before we could get into hiding, we were attacked by ruffians. I knew how to fight and was able to save Brother Everad from being killed, but I was only a boy. One sword wasn't going to ward off all the bandits. So I escaped with Brother Everad and he brought me here to Lanercost Priory. The ruffians followed, but we were able to hide in the catacombs."

"So why didn't you go back to the monastery with Brother Everad?"

"I thought you were friends with him. Didn't he ever tell you?"

"Nay. She ran her finger over one of the pieces and looked downward. "He said it was best I didn't know."

"One of the monks that died said with his last breath that I was a curse. He said it was because of me that they all went to their deaths. Everad probably would have left me as well if I hadn't saved his life. He was a very young monk and is only a few years older than me."

"Yes, I know."

"Instead of leaving me alone in the catacombs, he vowed to stay and help protect me."

"How did he think he was going to do that?" she asked.

"I taught him how to fight and kill," he said, biting his

bottom lip. "I took a man of the cloth and turned him into a murderer. He couldn't go back to the monastery then. So instead, he joined me on my quest. Years later, I eventually formed a small army to go up against the king."

"So you found your brothers then."

"Not right away. It was nearly ten years before we were reunited. I was on the docks one day and saw Rowen in the crowd. He was there pirating. We formed an alliance with my army and his crew and made our way to Scotland to find Reed. From there, we decided we'd make Edward miserable for ruining our lives. We vowed to raid him instead of killing him because we wanted him to suffer for not only wanting us dead but also for the all the needless deaths on Burnt Candlemas."

Rook stared off in deep thought. "The day the three of us reunited was when the legend of the Demon Thief was born. But now Rowen has betrayed us. We can't continue raiding without him and his crew. Because of him, the Demon Thief has been laid to rest. Now, I will forever be just a black-hearted bastard living like a rat in the dark, my only hope being to survive another day."

"Then leave here," she told him. "Come out of the dark and into the light."

"I can't. This is all I know." He clenched his jaw. "I live for revenge, Callie. You don't understand. I am not one of your noble knights, nor will I ever be. I was cursed the day I was born and I will die cursed as well because of the things I've done."

"Rook, you are a good man," she murmured. "I've seen a spark of light within you that has grown to a flame in just the past few days."

"You don't know me so don't pretend you do." He

finished setting up the pieces and found one missing. He looked under the table and then scanned the floor.

"I believe anyone can change. No matter how much they are damaged."

"I can't change and I won't! Now, I don't want to talk about this anymore. I'd like to play chess, but a piece seems to be missing."

"So it is." She made her way to her cloak still on the floor and slipped her hand into the pocket. "Which one is missing?"

He took a look again at his board and shook his head. "It's my bishop. This is a bad omen. That piece represents me."

"That piece is the one that was broken, wasn't it?"

"You know it was, Callie. It's got to be here somewhere." He leaned over and looked under the table again.

Her fingers closed around the polished piece that the stable boy and blacksmith helped to fix. Taking her seat again, she held out her hand and slowly opened her fingers. "Is this what you're looking for?"

He looked at her hand and then his eyes met hers in confusion. "You had it?"

"I did."

"You stole it from me? Why?"

"I borrowed it," she replied. "I fixed it, Rook. Look." She lifted her hand higher.

He plucked it from her palm and held it up to his face. Then he ran a finger over the smooth surface.

"It's not broken and jagged anymore," he said in astonishment.

"Nay, it's not. I fixed it, Rook. So you see, you can be

fixed as well. You don't need to remain the Demon Thief, living in hiding and amongst the dead your entire life."

He didn't say anything, just put the piece down on the board.

"I'll bet if you reconcile with Edward, he would even make you a knight like your brother, Rowen."

His attention flashed over to the painting on the wall. She saw the longing in his eyes when he looked at the scene with the knight and the joust.

"I don't want to be a knight and I don't want to be like my brother."

"Of course you do. Isn't that why you want to learn the joust? You can change, Rook. I can help you do it."

He stood up so fast that the table moved, shaking all the chess pieces.

"You can't fix everything, Callie, so why don't you just stop trying?"

"But Rook. Wouldn't you rather live in a castle instead of in the morbid crypts amongst the dead?"

"I think it's time for you to leave now. Get your cloak; I'm taking you back to the castle."

"You're taking me back?" She stood up, confused. "I thought I was going to spend the night."

"I've reconsidered. It's too risky. If your uncle finds out you were gone all night, he might hit you the way he has before."

"Oh," she said, rubbing her face just thinking about it. "You're not angry with me, are you?"

His eyes took on a tired look and the life drained from his face. "Nay, not at all, Sweetheart." He leaned over and kissed her atop the head. "I'm only thinking of what's best for you."

"You're right," she said, not really believing him. But still, she didn't want to end their special night together on a bad note. "Thank you, Rook. For the best night of my life."

He didn't say anything, but just nodded slightly and headed for the door.

Chapter 15

Rook tucked the wooden lance under his arm and kicked his heels into his horse, urging it toward the homemade quintain. A canvas bag filled with sand hung from one side of a swinging wooden arm that fastened into the ground. On the other side was a wooden shield he'd collected from one of the battles with the king's men.

He was also dressed in his chain mail, wearing a helm and holding another shield, all part of the booty from one of the Demon Thief's raids.

"Faster. You need to go faster," called out Wardell from the sidelines.

"Be careful, my lord," came Brother Everad's warning.

The tip of the pole hit the center of the shield, but Rook wasn't fast enough. The quintain spun around and hit him in the back, sending him falling from his horse. He landed face down on the ground with the lance and shield atop him.

"Almost," said Wardell. "Did you want me to show you again how it's done?"

"Nay," he growled getting to his feet and throwing his helm to the ground. He'd been so distracted this morning that he couldn't concentrate. After Calliope had told him she loved him last night, he had wondered if he'd done the wrong thing by making love with her.

The part that really bothered him was that she fixed his broken chess piece. She'd also said she could help to fix him. That made him feel so pathetic! He wasn't one who pitied anyone, but lately, he'd been pitying himself. He didn't want any woman trying to fix him. She'd already influenced him so much that he no longer knew who he was. If he didn't watch it, he'd end up like his brother, Rowen.

Just the thought of Rowen seemed to materialize his brother. Hades cackled from atop the ruined wall to tell him they had a visitor. When he heard Rowen's osprey in the sky, he knew at once who was coming to see him.

"Someone approaches on horseback," said Wardell, picking up his sword.

"Who is it, my lord?" Brother Everad collected a dagger in each hand.

"Put away your weapons," he told them as his brother rode up alone on horseback. "It's just my traitorous brother."

"Rook," said Rowen, stopping his horse opposite Rook. His hawk swooped down from the sky. Rowen held out his arm to make a perch for the bird. "I need to speak with you."

"So talk," he said, brushing the dust off his clothes.

"Alone." Rowen nodded toward Wardell and Everad.

"Leave us," ordered Rook, heading toward his brother.

"Are you sure, my lord?" asked Everad. "Perhaps we should stay close by, just in case."

"If my brother is here to kill me, then it is I who will fight him by myself," said Rook. "Go to the village and see that the serfs stay away from here. Just in case." His hand wavered over the top of his sheathed sword.

Wardell and Everad reluctantly headed away.

"What do you want?" asked Rook, curious as to why his brother was there. "If you're going to try to explain to me why you betrayed us again, I don't want to hear it."

Rowen lifted his arm and sent Mya, his hawk, back into the sky as he dismounted. The hawk landed close to the raven atop the ruins. "Rook, I've seen you with the girl from Naward Castle lately."

"I know you have. I've seen you spying on me."

"I wasn't spying. I was looking out for you."

"Me?" Rook asked in surprise. "Don't you mean you were looking out for Calliope? After all, I'm sure you probably think I have no right being with a noblewoman."

"I never said that. You are a wanted man, Rook. All it would take is one eager archer from the battlements and you could be dead," he said from atop his horse.

"Why do you care?" Rook stormed back over to his horse, tying it to a tree. "All you care about is your newfound wealth, your castle, and your knighthood."

"You neglected to mention my wife. Cordelia is pregnant with my child."

"What do you want me to say? Congratulations? Are you forgetting that since we're not legitimized, your child, as well as mine, is still going to be a bastard?"

"Are you having a child?" he asked, looking from the corner of his eye. "You've been bedding Calliope, haven't you?"

His heart almost stopped. He had bedded her and, in reality, there was a chance she could be pregnant. He'd never given it a thought at the time. Had he for one minute thought she'd end up pregnant and he'd have a bastard child, he would never have done it.

"You have bedded her. I can feel it in here," Rowen said, thumping his leather-clad fist against his chest. Being triplets, they'd often shared each other's feelings.

"All right, so I did. What difference does it make?" Rook headed over to pick up the shield from the ground.

"Do you love her?"

Rook's hand stilled above the shield. Then he released a breath, picked it up in two hands and stood up. "Did you really come all the way here from Whitehaven to ask about my love life?"

"Nay. I came here to show you this." He dismounted his horse and took a rolled up parchment from inside his surcoat and handed it to Rook.

"What is it?"

"Something I think you need to see."

Rook stuck the wooden shield under his arm and unrolled the parchment, reading the words on it. The shield fell and hit his foot when he saw the announcement that Lord Ovid was offering Calliope's hand in marriage to whichever nobleman could win a tournament. It would be held within the week.

"Ow," he said, moving his foot, almost dropping the parchment. "Where did you get this?" he asked. "It can't be real."

"Oh, it is. And there are at least a dozen more notices posted all over the land. If you left your mole-hole once in a while, you'd know that."

"How long has it been posted?" asked Rook, staring down at the notice.

"For the last three days."

"Three days?" His head snapped upward. "Then Callie knew about this before we made love."

"Callie?" Rowen chuckled. "Oh, my brother, I can see you have gone and fallen in love with someone you cannot have. Just like me."

"I'm nothing like you! I wouldn't betray those I care about." He slapped the parchment against Rowen's chest.

"I didn't know you actually cared about anyone but yourself. And I wouldn't be so eager to point a finger at me when your lover more or less betrayed you as well."

"Get out of here, Rowen, before I make you leave. And don't think I won't."

"I'm not done talking to you yet."

"We're done. Now leave." In anger, Rook drew his sword. Rowen's eyes fell to Rook's weapon, but he did nothing to meet him in challenge.

"I won't fight you, Rook. God's eyes, you're my brother. Now put away your sword."

"You should have thought of that before you made an alliance with Edward. By right, you should kill me now. Isn't that what Edward wants?"

"Nay. He wants to make an alliance with both you and Reed. He wants to stop fighting against you and be on the same side."

"How could you think I'd even consider it?" asked Rook. "After everything Edward has done to us? I would never align with our king."

"Never?" Rowen's eyes traveled over to the jousting pole and quintain. "Then why are you training to be a knight? You've always wanted to be a knight, so don't deny it. You are the son of the king! You should have a castle, wealth, and a title of your own. Edward can give that to you if you just pledge your allegiance to him and stop fighting against him."

"You have no idea what I want!" spat Rook. "Now I'm not going to tell you again – get out!" He brought the tip of the sword to Rowen's throat. Rowen's eyes interlocked with his, showing disappointment.

"I don't think you have the guts to kill me," he ground out.

"Do you really want to make that presumption?" Fire burned in Rook's veins.

"I did what I had to, in order to keep you and Reed safe, and at the same time not lose the woman I love and our child. You would have done the same if you were in my place."

"I wouldn't."

The sound of a horse and cart coming over the roughened ground caught Rook's attention. He hadn't gone to pick up Calliope at the castle today because he wasn't sure what he should do with her after last night. Now she was with the mute boy and they traveled with a wagon of supplies. "Callie," he said under his breath. The tip of his sword lowered from Rowen's throat. Rowen's gloved hand shot out and hit his blade away.

"Wouldn't you?" asked Rowen, looking first at Rook and then at Calliope approaching in the wagon. "We are triplets, Brother. We share the same blood, the same thoughts, and the same feelings. I know we were filled with hatred for a long time, but it's time to let that go now."

"I can't," he spat.

"You need to change."

Rowen was starting to sound like Calliope and that bothered Rook immensely.

"What are you going to do about this?" asked Rowen, holding out the missive. "Are you really going to let her marry someone else?"

"I don't have a choice, do I?"

"Don't you? If you loved her, you'd find a way."

Rook ripped the missive from his brother's hand, wanting to punch him right now.

"Get the hell out of here, Rowen. I'm not going to tell you again. I'm the legendary Demon Thief, not one of the king's lackeys like you."

Rowen mounted his horse and held out his arm. Mya landed with stealth and grace upon it. He gently ran a finger over the bird's head. "The legend is dead, Rook, face it."

"It's not dead. Reed and I will make sure the Demon Thief lives on and Edward gets what he deserves."

"We both know that can't happen without my crew and me."

"You're not a pirate anymore, Rowen. You have lost the Sea Mirage as well as your crew. So mayhap your crew will be loyal to us now, instead."

"Brody is the captain of the Sea Mirage now. He will always be loyal to me no matter what. There is no way he'd ever let the crew side against me."

"Leave!"

"I will." He turned to go, with his hawk rising up into the air to lead the way. Then he looked over at Calliope approaching and turned back once more. "It's never too late to make a new legend, Rook. Think about that. It's all I ask."

With that, he took off over the land, riding away, looking like the nobleman that he now was.

* * *

When Morton stopped the cart by the ruins of the priory,

the villagers, as well as Wardell and Everad came running to greet them. Calliope had seen Rook talking to a man on a horse. Because the man had a hawk with him, she guessed it was his brother, Rowen.

"Lady Calliope, what have you brought us?" asked Ida, rushing toward the cart carrying her baby. Her other children followed.

"Morton, show them what we've brought them," said Calliope, getting out of the cart and heading over to Rook. He was standing by the homemade quintain, looking at something in his hand.

"Rook!" She shouted and waved her hand in the air. "Wait until you see what I have for you. Wardell, Morton, can you bring the surprise over here for Rook?"

She headed across the rubble with Wardell and Morton following, carrying two jousting lances each. They were followed by Ida's son, Stanley, who carried jousting helms. She didn't understand why Rook hadn't come to meet her at the castle today and wondered if it had something to do with last night. While she thought it was the best night of her life, she wasn't so sure Rook had felt the same way.

Everything she said seemed to upset him. And when she gave him the chess piece, she thought he'd be happy but, instead, it seemed to make him very mad.

"I've brought jousting lances from the castle, as well as equipment," she said, making her way over to him. "I thought it would be better if you got to experience the actual thing."

"Look at this, my lord," said Wardell with a whistle. "These are some of the finest jousting lances I've ever seen. They are weighted perfectly."

"And these helms have visors that move up and down,"

said Stanley, examining the helms.

"They are nice," said Everad, putting the lances down at Rook's feet. "Did you want to give it a go with the real thing?"

"Once you're better at it, we'll joust against each other," said Wardell.

"Put everything back in the cart. I don't want it," growled Rook.

"What?" asked Calliope. "Why not?"

"Because I don't need your help," he snapped. "I'm not even sure I want to learn the joust anymore. Brother Everad, throw the quintain into the fire."

"Into the fire?" asked the monk with wide eyes. "I just spent backbreaking hours making that for you. Are you sure, my lord?"

"I'm not going to tell you all again. Get those things out of here."

Rook stormed off to the catacombs, causing Calliope to stand there with her mouth gaping wide.

"What is the matter with Rook today?" she asked

"He had a visit from his brother," said Everad. "Perhaps they had a spat."

"Did you want us to put these back in the cart, Lady Calliope?" asked Wardell, balancing a jousting lance over his shoulder.

"Nay, not at all. Leave them here. Rook will want to try them once he's snapped out of his foul mood. Have Morton take the cart to the village and load up the harvested crops. Make sure the serfs keep enough food to feed themselves for a while."

"But Lord Ovid won't like that," said Wardell.

"My uncle doesn't need to know. I'll tell him the crops

just weren't as plentiful this year."

She hurried after Rook, finding him entering his chamber. She snuck in right behind him.

"What are you doing here?" he asked, spying her over his shoulder.

"What's wrong, Rook? You seem out of sorts today."

"You tell me!" He slapped a parchment into her hands. As soon as she looked down, she knew what it was.

"Oh, this. I meant to tell you."

"When? You knew about this and yet you didn't say a word when I took you to my bed."

"Would that have made a difference?" she asked. "I thought you bedded women for pleasure only. Why would you even care?"

"Because I do. I care about you, dammit!"

"You . . . do?" It was the last thing she expected him to say right now.

"How could you let me think I had a chance with you when you were already scheduled to be married to another man in less than a week?"

"I – I'm sorry. I suppose I was afraid you wouldn't make love with me if you knew."

"You're damned right I wouldn't have."

"Why not?"

"Callie, you are a noblewoman and you must marry someone of the same status."

"But you are noble, too."

"I'm a bastard. That's different."

"I don't see how. The king is your father, so that should count for something."

"For what?" he yelled. "If you even think for one minute I am eligible to compete for your hand in marriage then you are delusional. Even if I did, as soon as I entered the castle, I'd be apprehended and hauled away to the dungeon to be executed."

"I didn't know you were interested in marrying me, Rook," she answered softly. Her heart soared. Just thinking of possibly being Rook's wife was very exciting.

"I'm not interested," he said, sinking down atop his chair and staring at the chessboard. "I'm just angry with you because you betrayed me. Just like my brother."

"How did I betray you? I've given information to the Demon Thief where to find the king for your silly raids because Brother Everad asked me to do it. I've never told anyone you were hiding in the catacombs. I've even brought you food and drink and now jousting equipment as well. In my eyes that is the furthest thing from betrayal."

"I think you'd better leave, Calliope. I don't want to talk to you right now."

She knew he was upset with her since he hadn't called her Callie, but she couldn't leave before they made amends. If she did, she might never see him again. Next time, she'd be married to a nobleman that she didn't love. Both she and Rook would live the rest of their lives feeling miserable.

"I'm not leaving until I feel like it." She crossed her arms over her chest.

"My lord?" Everad stuck his head around the partially open door.

"Get her out of here!" He stood up and overturned the table this time. Now, all the chess pieces were on the floor.

"You'd better go, Calliope," said Everad, placing his hand on her back to guide her to the door.

"I don't want to leave like this."

"It's for the best," the monk told her.

"Please, talk to him," she begged. "Let him know I'm sorry and that I love him."

"Love him?" Everad shook his head. "Nay, Calliope, you can't love him. He's a wanted man and no good for you."

"I believe he is good for me. He's just a little confused right now. If I could just talk to him once more, I'm sure I could fix things between us."

"Stop trying to fix me," Rook growled from across the room. "Stop coming here and bringing things! And for the love of God, stop telling me what a good man I am, because I'm not! Do you hear me? I'm the Demon Thief and I will live the rest of my days trying to bring down the king. So stop trying to change that."

"I didn't mean –"

"Go!" He picked up the golden goblet and threw it across the room. It hit the painting of the knight on the wall, chipping his painted armor.

The tears welled in Calliope's eyes. She didn't know what she'd done wrong. Turning, she ran to the cart to get back to the castle, not sure she ever wanted to see Rook again.

Chapter 16

Rook emerged from the catacombs the next morning, having thought things over last night. He knew he could never compete for Calliope's hand in marriage, but why should that keep him from learning the joust? He had the equipment and he also had Wardell to instruct him. He would hone his fighting skills and, hopefully, he could rebuild his army soon.

"Brother Everad," he called, looking around the shambles of a courtyard. The jousting lances Calliope had brought were still lying in the rubble. He knew she wouldn't listen to his orders. The monk was at the far side of the courtyard poking at the ashes of a glowing fire.

"Aye, my lord." Everad put down the stick, brushed off his hands, and ran over to greet Rook. It was a blustery day and the sky darkened. Rook could tell a storm was brewing on the horizon.

"I've decided I will learn the joust after all. Set up the quintain and fetch me my horse."

Everad made a face. "I'm sorry, I can't do that."

"Why the hell not?" Rook pulled on a leather gauntlet as he spoke.

"Because I don't have the quintain."

"Well, where is it?"

"Right there." He pointed his finger at the fire.

"God's teeth, you burned it?"

"That was your order yesterday, so I followed your instructions."

"Since when do you ever listen to anything I say? I was angry at the time. I didn't mean for you to actually burn it."

"Would you like me to start working on a new one?" asked the monk sheepishly.

Rook looked at the sky and then at the poles. Then his eyes fastened on something blowing around the grounds. He walked over and stomped his foot on it. Bending down and picking up the parchment, he realized it was the bann announcing the competition that offered Calliope's hand in marriage to the winner.

He found himself longing to go to the competition. He couldn't stand the thought of Calliope being married off to someone else. All he wanted was to feel her in his arms again and kiss her sweet lips. While she aggravated him to no end at times, he still liked being in her company. It felt good to have a woman around, even if she did have him doing things he would never have done on his own.

Pain shot through his heart and he threw the missive to the ground. If only he weren't a bastard and a bandit, then mayhap he'd have a chance of being Calliope's husband. If only he were a nobleman and a knight.

"No, don't bother with a new quintain," he said. "It'll be raining soon. Find Wardell and tell him we're going to joust against each other."

"But you're not ready yet, are you?" asked the monk.

Rook gritted his teeth. The passion to learn the joust was so strong within him that nothing else mattered.

"I'm as ready as I'll ever be, and there is no time like the present."

"Here comes the boy now," said Everad, pointing to Wardell riding toward them on Rook's horse.

"Good morning," said the boy with a smile.

"It's going to be a hell of a morning if you don't remove your body from my horse anon," snarled Rook.

"I hope you don't mind I borrowed your horse this morning, but it was too far of a walk, and I wanted to return before it rained."

"I do mind. Don't do it again," warned Rook.

"Where were you?" asked the monk. "I saw you ride out early this morning."

"I saw how upset Lady Calliope was when she left here yesterday. I snuck to the castle to try to find her and make sure she was all right."

"You did what?" asked Rook, not liking what he heard.

"I didn't think you'd be going there today," said Wardell. "Or will you?"

"Nay, I'm not going to the castle. And do you know how stupid that was of you to do that? If they had found you, they would have thrown you back in the dungeon."

"I was careful, my lord. Just like you."

"Rook wants to joust with you today," Everad told Wardell.

"Ah, yes. I can't wait." Wardell hopped off the horse and headed over to the jousting lances.

"I've already burned the quintain as he ordered, so you'll be jousting with him one on one," explained the monk.

"We'll need the jousting helms and also armor to protect ourselves," said Wardell, inspecting one of the lances. "Even though the tips of the poles are blunted, it is very dangerous. We'll need shields, too."

"The helms Calliope left are still here," said Rook. "And I have everything else we need. Just follow me." Rook led the way back into the catacombs. Wardell followed as Everad tended to the horse.

Once inside, Rook lit a torch and stuck it into an iron holder on the wall. Then he headed toward the biggest sarcophagus that had an ornate image of a knight carved into the stone lid. "We'll have everything we need in here." Putting his hands on the heavy stone, he pushed it aside. The scraping of the stone as the lid moved echoed through the dark, dank, cavern.

"I never really noticed how eerie it is down here." Wardell picked up the torch and held it up to see the walls better. "Why are there so many holes or shelves in the walls?" he asked.

"Those are where the dead bodies are stored." Rook went about what he was doing.

"I don't see any bodies," Wardell said with a shaky voice.

"That's because I've moved most the bodies over the years when I made this my home."

"I hope there's not a body in there," said the boy, taking a step back as Rook slid the heavy lid of the sarcophagus open.

"Not anymore. I moved it. Now I use this spot to store things."

"Store things? Like what?" Rook's raven flew into the catacombs and landed on a crucifix atop another burial spot.

"Like this." He took the torch from Wardell and held it up to the coffin so the boy could see inside. "The spoils of war."

Inside, he'd been keeping things he'd absconded for the last three years every time they came back from a raid on the king. Most people would think it was morbid or immoral to take the chain mail, armor, weapons, and shields off of the dead soldiers, but he didn't. They were dead and didn't need them, so what did it matter? Then again, his actions could be part of the reason people called him Rook the Ruthless.

"You have some nice things here," said Wardell with wide eyes, running his hand over the hilt of a sword. Next, he picked up a chain mail tunic and proceeded to put it on.

"They should be nice. They came from the dead soldiers of the king."

Wardell's hands stopped as his head poked out of the chain mail. "So I'm wearing something that was taken from a dead man?"

"That's right." Rook put down the torch and dug into the coffin. His raven cawed and hopped around the rim. "Does that bother you?"

"Not unless I'll be cursed by putting it on. I won't die from it, will I?"

Rook grabbed a greave, the metal plate that covered the shin, and scooped up more plate armor to cover their arms and legs. He would have to wear chain mail over his chest. "I haven't died yet. And I've been cursed since the day I was born. I wouldn't worry about it if I were you. We have other concerns," he said hearing the thunder rumble through the cavern walls. "It's going to rain soon and I'd like to get in some practice before it does."

"All right, let's go."

"Wait," said Rook, stopping the boy. "Tell me. How was Lady Calliope when you saw her this morning?"

"You care for her, don't you?" asked Wardell.

"Just answer the question and keep your comments to yourself."

"I wasn't able to get into the castle. There were extra guards posted, even at the postern gate."

"Has Lord Ovid returned?" asked Rook.

"I don't believe so. I didn't see his banner of residency flying from the battlements."

"Then Calliope posted the guards," he said, feeling a stab to his heart when he said it.

"Why would she do that?" asked Wardell.

"Because she no longer wants me coming to the castle. It's her message to me to keep away."

"I don't think she'd do that, would she?"

Thunder rumbled again from outside and, with it, grew Rook's anger. "I don't care what she does and I don't care who she marries. I need to learn the joust in order to fight the king. Now, are you going to teach me or not?"

"Of course," said Wardell. "I'm ready when you are."

Ten minutes later, Wardell and Rook were seated atop their horses dressed in chain mail, metal platelets covering their arms and legs, helms, and leather gauntlets. It started to rain slightly, but they were still able to practice. Brother Everad ran back and forth between them, helping them to lift their lances and get them into position. Rook used the good lances that Calliope had brought from the castle. They were quite a bit heavier than he'd anticipated, but of far better quality than the lances made by the villagers.

"Now, to start out, you need to know there are two types of jousting," said Wardell. "The first is the joust a plaisance which is a series of elimination jousts over a few days. The second is the pas d'armes or passage of arms where a knight sends out his proclamation and takes on all challengers of a joust that is scheduled for a certain place and time. Did you know that jousting replaced the Gladiatorial games in the arena? Actually, tournaments and jousting are credited to a Frenchman named Godfrey de Preuilly back from 1066."

"I don't care nor do I need to know about the history of jousting," said Rook, looking up to the threatening sky. "Now just tell me how to hold the lance and where to hit you."

"It's not that simple, my lord. There is a process to it. And then there are points awarded to how many lances are split, where you hit your opponent, and if you fall off the horse."

"Just the basics." He looked up to the sky again. The rain started falling faster.

After a few minutes of instructions, Rook was in position for his first joust against Wardell.

"My lord, you are holding the lance in your left hand," said Wardell.

"That's right. I fight left-handed."

"The joust will only work if both the opponents are using the same hand with the lances angled toward each other."

"Then fight with your left hand."

"I can't. And if you want me to teach you, you need to learn to hold the lance in the other hand."

"Fine. I can fight either way, so let's just do it."

"I will take it easy on you since you aren't experienced at this," said Wardell, lowering his visor.

"Nay! Just fight how you normally would. I don't need

any special pampering. If I'm going to learn to do this, I want to do it right."

"All right, then, if you say so," Wardell answered.

Everad gave the signal and they charged their horses toward each other. Rook missed Wardell altogether, but the boy hit him so hard, the lance shattered and Rook fell from his horse. Everad rushed over to help him. Rook pushed up to standing position, madder than hell.

"What did you do that for?"

"You told me to fight like I normally would," came Wardell's reply. "Are you hurt?"

"Nay, I'm not hurt, you fool. But you broke one of the lances. We only have a few. Now, try not to break them or we'll have nothing to use for practice."

"But the idea of the joust is to break the lance," explained Wardell.

"Not today it isn't." Rook pulled himself atop his horse. "Now, do it again and try to refrain yourself from breaking any more lances."

"Yes, my lord."

After several more passes, Rook felt as if he were starting to get the feel for jousting. Rain soaked them, but Rook didn't want to stop. He felt now as if he'd be able to knock Wardell on his ass. He hadn't liked the fact that the boy had done it to him. This time, he was going to hit hard with the lance to prove that he knew what he was doing.

"My lord, can we retreat until after the rain has stopped?" asked Wardell.

"One more pass and then we'll take a break for something to eat," said Rook.

He held the lance vertical and started forward. The horse whickered from beneath him as it splashed through the puddles of the courtyard. As he approached Wardell, he moved his lance to a horizontal position, holding tightly, and securing it under his arm. He aimed the blunted tip of the lance straight for the center of Wardell's shield.

With a powerful hit, the tip of his lance connected with Wardell's shield. The lance shattered and the sound of the splitting wood filled the air. Pieces of wood flew in all directions as Wardell's body twisted and became unstable. He fell backward on his horse but didn't fall off. However, the impact of Wardell's lance hitting Rook, caused him to become unbalanced. And when his horse slipped in the mud, Rook found himself falling to the wet ground for the second time that day.

Thoughts filled his head of rebuilding his army and teaching each of his men to fight like this against the king. Then he'd teach Reed and his Scots as well. All they'd need were more horses. The villagers could make the lances. With each battle, Rook would collect more and more armor and weapons. With a skill like this, they'd be able to grind Edward's soldiers into the earth easily. Eventually, Rook's army would become unbeatable.

He hit the ground hard, landing in a puddle. The water splashed up on him, but he didn't care. He felt powerful and like a knight. No one was going to stop him now. He got to his knees, removed his helm and threw it into the air as he let out a whoop of excitement.

Just then a jagged bolt of lightning from the sky struck his helm. Instantly, thunder crashed louder than he'd ever heard it, rumbling the earth beneath him. His body tingled and he swore the hairs on his arms stood on end.

"My lord!" Brother Everad grabbed the reins of the horse. "Your helm has been struck by the hand of God!"

Rook struggled to stand in his plate armor. His eyes opened wide when he saw his helm split in half and smoking. He moved forward slowly, eyeing the helm curiously. Carefully reaching out to touch it, he jerked his hand away when he realized the helm was hotter than the fires of Hell.

Hades cried out from atop the church, and flew down and landed on Rook's shoulder.

"I think that's enough practice for now," said Rook, still staring at the helm. That could have been him if he hadn't taken it off. Was God punishing him for his thoughts? Was this some kind of warning? He no longer knew.

"Aye, that will be all for today."

Chapter 17

It had been days now since Calliope had seen Rook and she missed him with all her heart.

She stood atop the battlements this morning, looking out over the vast, rolling meadows and open land at the pavilions dotting the surface. Competitors were already arriving for the tournament and setting up their tents outside the castle walls. Extra guards had been posted around the castle and also at the postern wall according to her uncle's wishes before he left. This made it impossible for anyone to come or go without being seen. Calliope hadn't wanted Rook to come for her at first since she felt angry and hurt, but now she'd changed her mind. Still, as far as she knew he hadn't even tried to see her.

She'd told the guards not to hurt anyone if they appeared at the postern of the castle, but to alert her instead. Wardell had approached the castle but returned to the catacombs when he saw the guards. The guards recognized him as the escaped prisoner and wanted to go after him. If it weren't for Lady Joanna telling them to leave the boy alone, Wardell would be back in the dungeon right now.

"Calliope, come down from here. It is cold and windy."

Lady Joanna appeared at the top of the battlements looking at her. Her cloak blew open and she tried to hold it closed. The pregnant woman's face was even paler than it had been days ago.

"I just wanted to come up here to clear my head," said Calliope, still looking for Rook. It was hard to accept the fact he wasn't coming for her.

"Your uncle will be home in a few days," said Joanna. "You should be preparing to meet the competitors who will try to win your hand in marriage."

"I don't want to marry any of them." She looked over the wall of the battlements at the knights. Their banners boasting their crests fluttered from tall poles and were also draped across their tents, announcing their arrival.

"I know you don't, but you don't have a choice."

"I'll run away where my uncle can't find me. I won't attend the tournament and be traded away like meat at the market."

"You have fallen in love with someone you can't have." Joanna's brown eyes met hers. The woman reached out and took Calliope's hands in her own. "I understand, but I can't say that your uncle will."

"Aye, I suppose you are right," she admitted, feeling sorry that she hadn't tried harder to make amends with Rook. "But I can't just give up and never tell him how I feel. I need to go to him."

"I don't think it is wise at this point," said Joanna. "The guards will see you leave and follow. Do you want your secret being revealed? That would put your lover in jeopardy as well."

"Nay, I don't want that to happen. He's already accused me of betraying him. If I lead the guards right to him, I'll never forgive myself."

"Then stay here," said Joanna, flinching and holding her hand against her stomach. "If he loves you, he'll come for you."

Calliope shook her head, feeling the tears stinging her eyes. "I don't know if he will," she said. "It's too risky."

"Love is worth the risk," said Joanna. Then her eyes rolled back in her head and her knees buckled beneath her. Calliope lunged forward and caught her as she fell.

"Someone, help her," Calliope shouted. Several guards atop the battlements ran over to collect Lady Joanna.

"Take her to the solar, quickly," she ordered. "And someone send for the healer as well."

"Aye, my lady," answered one of the guards as they took her away.

Calliope glanced over her shoulder once more, hoping to see Rook. Instead, she saw more knights approaching for the competition. Her uncle would be home any day now. And when he returned, Calliope's life as she knew it would be over. She would be married off to a man she neither knew nor loved while Rook disappeared into the night forever. She'd never see him again.

That was one thought that scared her more than anything else. Life without Rook at her side was going to be very sad and lonely.

* * *

Rook was pleased with his progress concerning the joust, and also obsessed with it. He spent all of his time practicing, even though Wardell and Everad told him they needed to rest.

He hopped off his horse, heading for a trough of water that the monk had filled from a nearby stream. After removing his helm and gauntlets, he splashed water on his face. Looking down, he stared at his reflection. His long, dark hair touched the shoulders of his chain mail tunic. The metal platelets he wore for the joust glittered in the sun. He hadn't shaved in days now and the stubble on his face was getting thicker, turning into a full-blown beard. He had been trying not to think of Calliope, but he stayed awake nights wondering if he'd ever forget her.

He looked like a knight now and was getting experienced at the joust. Part of him wanted to march into the tournament with his head held high, competing with the rest of the nobles for Calliope's hand in marriage.

"What takes your thoughts, my lord?" asked Everad coming to his side. "Is it Lady Calliope?"

"Aye," he admitted, splashing more water on his face. "I suppose it is. I only wish I could see her once more before she's married."

"I tried to go to the castle to get her, but I couldn't get in," said Wardell, walking up behind them. "There are extra guards posted. Probably because of all the knights making camp outside the castle, waiting for the tournament."

"Were there many of them?" Rook asked.

"Aye. And I'm sure more every day."

"I need to get a message to her." Rook ran a hand through his hair and paced back and forth. "Everad, you go to the castle for me."

"Me?" asked Everad, shaking his head. "Nay. I won't be able to get inside either."

"Why can't you just enter through the front gate?" asked Wardell. "You're a monk. No one will suspect you."

"I'm not welcome there," he said.

"Why not?" asked Rook. "After all this time, you've never told me what happened that you are afraid to go to Naward Castle."

"It's not that I'm afraid," said the monk. "I've been banned from there by Lord Ovid himself. If I go back, it won't be pretty."

"What could you have done that upset the man so much?" asked Rook with a chuckle. "After all, you were banned from there when I first met you ten years ago. And you're not much older than me, so how could you have angered anyone?"

"Lord Ovid sees me as a threat," answered the monk.

"A threat?" Rook laughed harder. "Don't lie to me, because I'll never believe that."

"What is the message you want to give to Lady Calliope?" asked Wardell.

Rook sighed, no longer wanting to fight the feelings inside. "I should have told her how I felt about her when she said she loved me. I need to think of some way to stop that tournament from happening. I want Calliope to stay with me. I don't want her to marry another man."

"What do you mean?" asked Wardell. "Are you saying you want to marry her?"

"Nay, you can't," said the monk.

"I wasn't saying that," said Rook, glaring at the monk. "But tell me, why are you so against Calliope and me being together?"

"Because you are a bandit, a warlord and a thief," answered Everad.

"Well, thank you for reminding me of my downfalls," said Rook. "But if Calliope loves me and I love her, then why should she marry one of those knights? She can stay right here with me."

"In the catacombs?" asked Wardell. "That's hardly a place for a lady."

"Eventually, we can find a new place to live."

"I don't think she'd want to stay with you," said Everad. "It's not right. She's a noble and belongs in a castle."

"I know that," said Rook. "And if I must remind you, I'm a bastard. I couldn't marry her if I wanted to, nor would I want our children growing up as bastards."

"Then what is it you're saying?" asked Wardell. "You don't want another man to marry her, but you won't marry her either?"

"Aye. Nay." Rook felt flustered, not at all sure what he was saying. "I don't know," he growled. "I haven't thought it all through yet. All I know is that I want her here with me."

"You can't give her a thing!" shouted the monk. "She deserves better than you. She is worthy of a noble who can protect her and give her wealth and respect. She will never have that with a bastard."

Rook shook his head, not sure where this hostility was coming from. He'd never known Everad to speak out against him and this was very out of line. "What is it that's causing your concern?" asked Rook. "Something has been troubling you ever since I met Lady Calliope. Now, why don't you just come out and say whatever it is that's making you act this way."

"You can't marry her, Rook, I'm sorry. She needs to marry a noble and have many children. That way, if the day ever comes that Ovid dies, and if for some reason he doesn't have an heir, she'll be able to inherit her father's castle."

"She lives there already so that's just as good as owning it," answered Rook.

"Nay, that's not sufficient. We need it for our own, the way it should have been to begin with."

"We?" Rook raised a brow. "Is there something you're not telling me?"

"It's about time you knew, I suppose," said Everad. "I don't want you to marry Calliope because you will ruin everything, being a bastard. Don't you understand? We've waited so long and need to take back from Ovid what he stole from us."

"Us? Bid the devil, Everad, please don't tell me you're secretly Calliope's lover. If so, I'll kill you."

"Nay, you've already seen to filling that position," said the monk, looking first at Wardell and then at Rook. "It's worse than you think. You see, I'm Lady Calliope's brother."

Chapter 18

"Brother?" both Rook and Wardell asked at the same time.

"Egads, Everad. Why have you never told me?" Rook threw his hands in the air.

"I stayed silent to protect her," said Everad. "If our uncle found out I was sneaking in to see her he would have hit her or punished her. Or killed her, as he'd once threatened to do."

"Say it isn't so," spat Rook.

"Do you have any other siblings?" asked Wardell.

"Nay. There is just the two of us. When my father died, I should have inherited the castle. But I was young and Ovid was my father's half-brother. He wanted to inherit the wealth of my father. So he sent me to the monastery to become a monk."

"That's awful," said Wardell.

"So you want the castle back as your own?" asked Rook.

"Nay. I can't. I took the vows of a monk, even if I didn't keep them. The king would never let me inherit a thing now. My only hope is for Calliope to marry someone worthy. Then when my uncle dies, and he hopefully has no living sons to inherit, my sister can claim what is rightfully ours."

"I see," said Rook with a nod of his head. "I suppose you have good reason not to want me to marry your sister."

"You couldn't anyway," said the monk. "You said so yourself."

"But his brother married a noblewoman," Wardell pointed out. "All you would need to do is make an alliance with the king. He could even dub you a knight like he did for Rowen."

Rook knew better than anyone that this would be the simple solution. But to do that and, hopefully, claim Calliope's hand in marriage, he'd have to betray his brother, Reed. He still felt sore at the way Rowen had turned his back on them and he wouldn't do that to Reed no matter how much he loved Calliope. Reed was of his blood and he would never forget it.

"Nay, I'll never align with Edward," said Rook. "I made a vow to stay loyal to my brothers and I won't turn my back on Reed the way Rowen did to us. It's been too long without a raid. I need to talk to Reed. With the knowledge of the joust, I think we can build a strong army and use lances to fight - if we could only get a hold of some horses. Everad, send out the last courier pigeon with a note attached to its leg. Tell Reed to bring his men and come quickly. With the distraction of the tournament at Naward Castle, this might be the perfect opportunity to make our dear old father miserable once again."

* * *

Calliope waited until nightfall. As soon as things were quiet in the courtyard, she sneaked out of her chamber and toward the dungeon. After spending most of the day with Lady Joanna, she'd had a lot of time to talk with her as well as think about Rook. Joanna was still in bed and probably belonged there. But with Lord Ovid returning any day now, Calliope knew this would be her last chance to see Rook before she was married.

Hiding under the hood of her cloak, she hurried across the cobblestones, making her way to the dungeon. If she took a horse, it would be faster, but there was no chance of that happening. The castle gate was already closed for the night, not to mention there were even more knights camping outside the gate in preparation for the joust. She would never be able to pass them unnoticed.

Making it to the door of the dungeon, she opened it slowly and stepped inside. There was no guard posted since they had no prisoners. She held the door open a little, looking back into the courtyard once more. When she was sure no one was looking, she reached out her hand and grabbed the burning torch from the iron mount on the wall. Then she brought it back into the dungeon and closed the door.

After opening the old gate, she slipped past the empty cells. She hurried to the broken gate at the other end, stepped through and made her way into the tunnels of the catacombs.

Rook lit a candle, removed his chain mail, armor platelets, and tunic, and collapsed on a chair in his room feeling exhausted from practicing the joust all day long. He leaned forward and rubbed his hands over his weary face. Then he gingerly reached out and poked at the wound on his leg. It had been hurting lately. Without Calliope there to tend to it, he wasn't even sure if it was infected or not. The monk could have looked at it, but Rook hadn't taken the time to ask him.

Rook's ability to ride while carrying the lance was strong now and his aim was getting better every day. Even using his right hand, he was fearless. He prided himself on the fact he was picking up the skill so quickly. With Wardell's help in guiding him and the help from the serfs in continually supplying new lances to replace the broken ones, things were running smoothly. Even the monk was useful, acting as both his and Wardell's squire.

He pushed up from the chair and waded through the chess pieces spewed about the floor, never having picked them up after losing his temper with Calliope. The truth was, as much as he loved the game, he couldn't concentrate enough to play it anyway.

Calliope weighed heavy on his mind. He missed her so much his heart ached. Was this love, he wondered? He craved her body, but it was so much more than lust. He'd never felt this way about a woman before. Calliope said she saw a spark in him that was growing to a flame. That there was light inside him, although all he could see was darkness. Without her there to fan the flame, that spark would go out quickly.

He got off the chair and picked up the golden goblet, turning it over and rubbing his fingers across the smooth surface. Calliope had told him to sell it. To use the money for those who needed it, like the villagers. The serfs were supposed to be taken care of by Lord Ovid, not him. Ovid had more than enough wealth to make them happy. Rook only had what he stole from the king. His father.

He sauntered over to the wine cask at the opposite side of the room, thinking about how good he felt helping the villagers by hunting for them or working in the fields to bring in the crops. Calliope was a lady, yet she did the menial tasks of a serf. She cared for the villagers as if they were her family. He felt like he was a part of that family when he was at her side. Without her, he felt so alone.

As he filled the goblet with wine, his eyes lifted to the painting of the knight on the wall. He'd thought about being a knight every day since he was a child. He dreamed of dressing in chain mail, fighting the enemy, and especially having the chance to joust. These past few days he felt like a knight, even if he was only a bastard in knight's clothing.

He raised the cup to his lips, studying the painting. He'd thrown the goblet and chipped the painting. Now it looked like the knight wore damaged armor. He felt like his armor was chipped as well. He was naught more than a broken man. If Calliope were here, she would probably tell him she could fix him.

After he set the goblet down on the table, he reached out his hand and picked up one of the pieces that hadn't hit the floor. It was the bishop. The broken bishop that Calliope had fixed. He ran his fingers over the piece in thought. Where there was once jagged marble, now there was only a smooth and shiny surface. His eyes wandered back over to the wall. Broken or fixed, it didn't matter. No one could fix his drastic life. Even Calliope couldn't make things the way he wished they would be.

He ran his fingers over the piece again, wondering if there was a way to marry her. The only way he knew of was possibly by making an alliance with the king the way Rowen had done. But to do that, he'd have to betray Reed. He still felt the hurt from when Rowen deserted them. If he left, too, Reed would be all alone. He couldn't do that to his brother.

The cackling of his raven caught his attention, and he looked up at the venting system. Hades was telling him someone was there that didn't belong there. Everad and Wardell had already retired for the evening in the buildings at the other side of the priory. He put the piece down on the table and walked with purpose across the room to collect his sword. Then he headed to the door and pulled the lever to make it open. His bird flew in and, right behind Hades, he saw the glimmer of firelight as someone made their way through the catacombs toward him. His heart almost stopped when he saw Calliope remove the hood of her cloak to reveal her identity.

"Calliope. What are you doing here?" He stepped back into his chamber and hung his sword on a hook. She seemed to float toward him, her golden tresses glimmering in the firelight making her look like an etheric angel.

"Rook, I had to see you."

"Come in," he said, holding out his hand. She reached out for him with no hesitation and entered, slipping her travel bag from her shoulder. He closed the door behind her. "I don't like you wandering around the dark catacombs. It's not proper for a lady." He took the torch from her and fastened it into a holder on the wall.

"Rook, I'm sorry I didn't tell you about the joust. It was just that I –"

He didn't give her a chance to finish. He pulled her into his arms and kissed her hard. "I missed you, Callie."

"I missed you, too. I had to come to tell you how I feel before my uncle returns. Once he does, there will be no chance for me to visit you again."

"You shouldn't be here," he told her. "I'll take you back."

"Nay. Not yet." She wrapped her arms around his waist and rested her head on his bare chest. His hand caressed the top of her head as he rubbed his cheek against her hair. So fresh and sweet. And he was stale and dirty. "I want to spend the night with you, Rook."

He wanted that more than ever, but couldn't agree to it now. "I can't, Callie. It's no good. We are not meant to be together."

"Who says so?" When she looked up, he saw the wetness of her eyes. A small tear escaped and slid down her cheek. He gently brushed it away.

"Your brother says so. And he is right."

"Everad told you he's my brother?"

"He did. I wish you had been the one to tell me, though."

"I made him a promise I'd keep it a secret. It was our deal. He didn't want me connected to him if he was ever caught as the one who gave the Demon Thief information."

"You never told me why you risked your life being our informant," he said.

"I did it because I could," she answered. "It meant something to Everad. He told me you were his friend. I didn't want to disappoint him after . . . what we'd been through."

"He told me, Callie. I'm sorry for what happened."

"Did he also tell you my father was murdered? We've never been able to prove it, but he was stabbed from behind. I know I already told you all this, but we don't think that the attack came from someone outside the castle."

"Who would have wanted your father dead?"

"There is only one person I know of, and it's my Uncle Ovid. He had the most to gain by my father's death. We didn't think much of it at the time, but sending Everad to the monastery gave Ovid the inheritance since my father had died."

"Why didn't you tell someone?" he asked.

"Who would believe a child? There was nothing we could do."

"Callie, you're shivering," he said. "Come, I'll light a fire."

"Nay, I'm not cold. I shake because I feel my life is out of control and I'm about to lose you forever."

"At least have some wine." He took her to the table and seated her in a chair. Then he put the wine in her hand and lit the fire in the hearth anyway.

She took a sip, handing it back to him. But he held the cup to her lips and urged her to have more. "It'll help you relax," he told her.

"I don't want to go back to the castle. I want to stay here with you."

"Nay, you can't," he protested. "You are a lady and must go back to Naward."

"Then you come with me." A tinge of hope filled her sad, green eyes.

He wanted to go with her more than anything in the world, but it wasn't going to happen.

"You know as well as I that as soon as I step foot inside the castle gates, I'll be captured. Do you want me to die?"

"Nay, of course not." She took both his hands in hers. "Marry me, Rook."

His heart skipped a beat. Turning his head, his eyes fell upon the image of the knight in the chipped armor upon the wall. "I . . . can't," he said, pushing the words from his mouth that didn't seem to want to go.

"I love you. Do you love me?" came her next question,

surprising him. Calliope always spoke her mind. That's what he liked about her.

"Please. Don't ask me that." He shook his head, not sure how to answer. Confusion crowded his mind. He no longer knew who he was or what he wanted.

"You don't have to answer," she said, picking up the chess pieces from the table and putting them on the game board. "I understand."

She said she understood, but how could she when he didn't even understand himself?

Bending over, she scooped the pieces up from the floor and arranged them on the board. For the sake of something to do other than to answer her question, he helped her.

"Callie I – I don't know what to say. I'm confused."

"Then don't say anything." She finished lining up the pieces on the board and flashed him a smile. "Just do me one last favor before I'm wed. Let me spend the night with you."

"I'm not sure that's a good idea."

"Not to make love," she said, picking up the broken knight and running a finger in slow, caressing circles over the top of it. Watching the action made him think of his fingers doing the same but on her soft skin. "I just want to spend time with you. We'll play chess and talk, and do whatever you like. When we're tired, we'll sleep in each other's arms. And in the morning I'll leave if that's what you want."

"You know it's not what I want. It's what you need to do."

"Agree to it, Rook. Please. One last night together before I'm forced to marry someone I don't love. After that, I'll never see you again."

His head shouted for him to say no and turn her away,

but his heart cried louder to let her stay. Before he knew what he was doing, he nodded his head and agreed. As soon as he did, she leaned over the chessboard and kissed him, her breasts brushing against his arm in the process.

Then she sat back down and moved a chess piece and smiled. “Your turn.”

He reached for a piece, but his thoughts stayed on Calliope. She had something planned, he was sure of it. He had fallen right into her trap. He didn’t even flinch when three moves later she scooped up his broken bishop and cradled it in her hand. He’d already lost this game to her before he’d even begun to play.

Chapter 19

After one game of chess and losing to Calliope, Rook knew there was no way he'd be able to concentrate on anything while she was staying the night. They'd shared more wine, snuggled by the fire, and they'd eaten some bread and cheese she'd brought with her.

His body ached and he was so tired that all he wanted to do was sleep. But how would he sleep if Calliope were lying in bed with him?

He yawned.

"You're tired," she said. "Let's go to bed."

They were sitting on the floor in front of the fire. She hopped up, full of energy. He pushed up, feeling the burn of the pain in his thigh. She must have seen him wince because her brows furrowed and her smile disappeared.

"Your wound is hurting, isn't it?"

"Just a little. It's nothing." He tried to play it down.

"Take off your breeches. Now."

"Pardon me?" He was no longer thinking about his wound.

"I brought some healing herbs with me. I'll get them

while you disrobe and get on the bed."

"Oh. All right." He did as she ordered while she dug around in her bag, finding what she needed.

Calliope turned back to the bed and almost dropped the ointments when she saw the tent sticking up under Rook's braies. She had stayed, hoping to entice him to want her. She could see now that it had worked a little too well. It excited her and scared her at the same time.

"Let me see that leg." She sat down on the edge of the bed, keeping her eyes directed away from his groin. All she could think about was the night they made love. She wanted to do it again but wasn't sure she should if she was getting married in a few days.

He leaned his head back and closed his eyes as she rubbed the ointment on his wound.

"It's just a little irritated, but doesn't look infected," she told him.

"Probably from all the jousting I've been doing." He sounded tired and his eyes were still closed.

"How is that coming along?" she asked.

"Fine."

"Would you be able to beat someone in a joust?"

He opened his eyes and pushed up on one elbow. "If it's Wardell, then yes. But if you're suggesting I go up against the trained knights that are competing in the tournament, then the answer is no."

"I – didn't mean that." She closed up the jar. It was exactly what she meant and he knew it. "But what if you did try to compete?" she asked. "And what if you somehow were lucky enough to win?"

"That's a lot of ifs," he said, laying back down and

letting out a sigh. "Callie, if there was a way I could marry you, don't you think I would have already thought about it?"

"I don't know." She put the things on the table and wiped her hands with a cloth. "You don't seem as if you want to be married to me."

His bright blue eyes fixated on her and he blinked twice. "I never said that."

"Didn't you?"

"I said we couldn't be married, not that I didn't want to marry you."

"So you do want to marry me then?"

He dragged a hand through his long, dark hair and looked the other way. After letting out a deep breath, he turned back toward her. "I'm confused and tired right now," he told her. "Mayhap we could continue this conversation in the morning."

"Sure, we can." She bit her bottom lip to keep from crying. She had thought for sure she'd be able to make him want her if she came here tonight. But Rook the Ruthless wasn't falling for her antics. He was stubborn and didn't seem to like her suggestions. Or mayhap, he just didn't like a woman telling him what to do. "Perhaps it's better if I go back to the castle and don't spend the night after all."

She started to get up from the bed but was stopped by his hand as it clamped around her wrist.

"Nay, Callie. I want you to stay."

"You certainly don't seem like it."

"That's because I want to make love to you and I know I shouldn't. Don't you understand how hard it's going to be for me to lie with you in my arms all night and not couple with you? It is torture."

"I didn't mean to make things uncomfortable for you,

Rook." She felt the tears dripping down her cheeks. "I just wanted to make you love me. I suppose that is darker than anything I've ever accused you of doing. I am a bad person. Dreadful."

"Love isn't dark. You've shown me that, Callie. Love is the light in the darkest of nights. You have brought so much love and light into my life that I just don't know how to react. I've felt love for my family when I was growing up, but then I was betrayed by those I loved. First Ross and Annalyse betrayed me, and then my brother, Rowen. Not to mention my father who wanted us killed the day we were born. Every time I love, I am cursed over and over again. I was born a cursed triplet on the Feast Day of the Holy Innocents and things will never change. I'm said to be spawned by the devil himself, and I'm starting to think it's true."

"We both know that's not true."

"My father, Edward, has made my life miserable. Yes, he is the devil that sired me. I've been filled with vengeance for a very long time now. It grows with each passing day. I've lived my life in the darkness for the last ten years. To live in the dark and amongst the dead is all I know. I'm not sure I could ever love anyone again after what I've been through. Do you understand?"

Calliope wiped a tear with the back of her hand and nodded. "Yes, Rook, I think I do. I've been calling you the selfish one when I've been selfish and only thinking of myself all along. Forgive me."

"Come here, Sweetheart," he said, holding out his arm. She lay down on the bed next to him and rested her head against his chest. "You are the most selfless person I know, so don't let me hear you calling yourself selfish ever again."

He wrapped his arms around her and kissed the top of her head. Then when she heard the sound of his heart and his breathing slow down, she realized he'd fallen asleep. Calliope smiled to herself and closed her eyes, snuggling up to Rook's body. Even if he never said he loved her, she would love him forever. She felt happy and protected in his arms and didn't want this ever to end.

Her eyes drifted closed as she listened to the snap of the logs in the fire. She would cherish this moment and never forget how it felt for as long as she lived.

Chapter 20

Rook yawned and stretched, having had the best sleep of his life. He awoke today feeling refreshed with a clear mind so decided he would talk to Calliope and see if they could come up with some solution so they could be together.

But when he rolled over to give her a good morning kiss, she was gone.

"Callie?" Rook pushed up to his elbows looking around the darkened room. "Callie, where are you?" He swung his feet to the side of the bed, sitting on something hard in the process. He lit a candle and looked down to see what it was.

The burgundy ribbon she'd worn in her hair the first day he'd met her was wrapped around something. It still had a bloodstain on it from when she'd wrapped his hand after biting him. He'd thrown this to the floor in aggravation and had forgotten all about it.

Picking up the object, he unwrapped it, finding the bishop piece from the chessboard inside. It was the one that had been broken and that she'd fixed.

His heart felt empty without her. He picked up the piece and kissed it, smelling her essence of rosewater upon it. It didn't take him long to realize she had left for good. What was he going to do? He didn't want to think of his life without Calliope in it.

He jumped out of bed, dressing quickly, wondering if he could stop her before she got too far. She'd been so sad yesterday when she asked him if he loved her and he couldn't tell her what she wanted to hear. He'd been confused and still was, but one thing was clear to him this morning. He'd been so guarded that he was going to lose the only woman he wanted in his life if he didn't tell her he loved her soon.

After putting on his breeches and tunic, he hopped on one foot as he donned one boot and then the other. His leg felt so much better this morning, thanks to Calliope's ministrations. He knew she wanted to make love last night and even though he wanted it, too, he didn't do it. It would only make things harder for her with her new husband.

"Husband," he said aloud, feeling his blood boil to think someone else would be taking Calliope to bed soon. He didn't want her kissing anyone or making love to anyone unless it was himself. He had to do something about this, and quickly.

After strapping on his weapon belt, he grabbed his sword from the hook on the wall. Then he opened the wooden door and pulled the lever and listened as the rock slid open much too slowly for his liking. Anxiety filled him, making him want to break through the stone door.

Rushing out of the chamber, he crashed into someone holding a torch in their hand.

"Och, Rook, slow down will ye? Ye almost knocked me on my arse."

"Reed! How did you get here already?"

"What do ye mean?"

"I only just sent the messenger pigeon."

"I came with my men as soon as I read yer missive. Believe it or no', Brody gave us a ride again on the Sea Mirage and dropped us off at the coast. I tried once more to convince him to raid with us, but he wouldna agree."

"Don't worry about it," said Rook. "I've changed my mind. I don't think we should plan a raid right now after all." He looked up and down the catacombs, but it was too dark to see if Calliope was still there. He didn't think she would stay there if she saw Reed and his men, so he guessed she was already headed back to the castle. "Did you see anyone in the catacombs when you entered?" He brushed past his brother and headed outside to the light.

"Nay, I didna see a soul. Whom are ye lookin' for?"

"No one," said Rook, not wanting to reveal to Reed about his intimate time with Calliope. He walked out into the courtyard to see Reed's men eating the food that he'd hunted yesterday in between his practicing. "Nay, what are you doing?" he asked, walking up and pulling a rabbit leg away from one of the Scots.

"We're eatin'," said the Scot. "We need our energy to go up against the king."

"This food isn't for you."

"Who is it for?" asked Reed, taking the rabbit leg from him and gnawing on it.

"I hunted the food for the serfs," Rook answered.

Reed was quiet for a second, as well as his men. Then they all burst out laughing. "Rook, ye are too funny," said Reed. "Ye probably wanted it all for yerself, didna ye?"

"Nay, it's for the villagers," said the monk, coming to join them with Wardell at his side.

"Why would ye hunt for them?" asked Reed, still gnawing on the meat.

"In case you've forgotten, some of the serfs lost their lives helping us on our last raid against the king," Rook pointed out.

"Are ye sure ye're no' just goin' soft on me, Brathair?" asked Reed.

He was going soft and he knew it. If he told Reed too much more, he'd be accused next of acting like their betrayer of a brother, Rowen.

"The villagers help us and we help them in return by hunting or harvesting their fields," Wardell blurted out before Rook could stop him. Rook closed his eyes and waited for his brother to explode.

"What could they possibly do to help us now that most of their men are dead?" asked Reed.

"Wardell, go check on the horses," said Rook, but the boy didn't listen.

"They've been whittling jousting lances for us every day so that Rook can practice," said Wardell.

"Practice what?" asked Reed. Some of the Scots overheard and came strolling over.

"Jousting," answered Wardell. "What else?"

"Who are ye, laddie?" asked Reed. "And why in the clootie's name would my brathair be joustin'? That's only for nobles and knights."

"He's the boy I saved from the dungeon of Naward Castle," said Rook.

"How did ye ken he was there and why did ye save him?" Reed was asking way too many questions and Rook wasn't ready to answer any of them.

"Lady Calliope brought him here," said Everad.

"Lady who?" asked Reed.

"She's a good friend of mine," said Wardell. "She's also Brother Everad's sister and Rook's lover." Wardell smiled, but Rook frowned.

"I've got things to do," growled Rook, heading away.

Reed threw down the bone, wiped his hands in his plaid and hurried after Rook.

"Wait! Dinna leave me afore ye explain all this to me."

Rook stopped in his tracks and turned around. "I don't need to explain a thing."

"If there's a lassie involved, I'm willin' to bet ye're doin' all these crazy things because of her. Please dinna tell me ye're goin' to betray me the way Rowen did to us."

"For your information, I enjoy helping the serfs. It feels good to work out in the sun. It's getting gloomy and stale living in the dark catacombs."

"Since when?"

"Since I decided I like the villagers and the fact they respect me." Rook continued to walk at a brisk pace toward the barn where they kept the horses. Reed kept pace alongside him.

"This isna like ye, Rook. I'm verra concerned."

"Don't be. Everything's fine."

"Why are ye practicin' the joust? Are ye wantin' to be a knight?"

"I've decided the joust is a great advantage to know. It can be used in war."

"How so?"

"I'm going to teach you and your men how to joust. Then we'll be able to attack on horseback and with lances."

"What horses?" asked Reed with a shrug of his shoulders, lifting his palms upward. "Unless ye have some stashed away that I dinna ken about, we're no' goin' to get far with just a couple of horses."

"Well, we had a lot of horses until my mercenaries left. We'll just have to convince them to come back or find new men to hire."

"Ye sent for me, so what did ye have in mind? Did ye get word of the king's next caravan?"

"Nay," he said, not wanting to mention that Calliope was their informer.

Rook walked up to his horse that was hitched outside the barn along with the monk's horse. He realized it was already past midday and that he'd slept very late. His raven landed on a fencepost squawking out a warning. Reed started to talk, but Rook raised his hand to stop him.

"What's the matter?" asked Reed.

"Someone's coming." He looked around but didn't see anyone. Reed's red kite made lazy circles in the sky overhead. "Take Everad's horse and get back to the priory quickly. Hide your men in the catacombs and tell Wardell to get to the village and keep the serfs hidden. Have Everad stay at the ruins in case someone stops there. He can distract them." Rook pulled himself up onto his horse.

"Where will ye be?" asked Reed, mounting the other steed.

"I'm going to find out what's going on."

The sound of a hawk's cry split the air. Rook and Reed looked up to see a hawk flying playfully in the sky with Reed's bird.

"It's Mya," said Reed. "And that means our traitorous brathair is near. I'm goin' to kill him."

"Nay!" shouted Rook. "Be quiet for a moment and listen."

They heard the sound of lots of hoof beats off in the distance. Rook strained his eyes to see an entourage of soldiers and mounted men heading across the land toward Naward Castle.

"I'll be right back," said Rook, heading toward the men with his raven leading the way.

Rook kept to the trees, watching and following, trying to figure out who was going to Naward Castle. Then, when he was close enough, he noticed Edward's banner fluttering from a squire's pole. His stomach clenched and his jaw tightened.

"Edward," he spat.

"That's right, Rook," came a voice from behind him. He turned his horse to see Rowen sitting atop his steed, emerging from the thicket. "Father has returned with Lord Ovid and will be attending the jousting tournament tomorrow."

"Nay!" Rook didn't want to believe it.

"He's sent me to offer you amnesty if you should decide to compete for Lady Calliope's hand in marriage."

"Why would he do that? He doesn't even know that I know her."

"Oh, but he does. You see, I told him all about you and your lover."

"Why did you do that, Rowen? I ought to kill you for that."

"I did it because I could see in your eyes you were in love with the girl."

"I don't love anyone. Everyone who I've ever loved has betrayed me – including you."

"She won't betray you and you know it. If you win the joust, he's even offered to make you a knight."

"He'd like that, wouldn't he?" spat Rook. "Then I'd have to pay fealty to him just like you do."

"It's not that bad," said Rowen. "What you'll gain from the alliance is far better than any satisfaction you will get from harboring revenge. I know that now. It's the right thing to do. We all make mistakes. Forgive Father and make the alliance. Then you'll be that knight you always wanted to be and have a noblewoman for a wife as well."

"Even if I did, Edward will never legitimize us. He said so himself."

"Never say never. People change, Rook, just like you've changed since you've met Lady Calliope."

"It's a trap!" Reed rode out from behind a clump of bushes, drawing his sword. "Rook, we should kill this traitor now for what he's done."

"I won't fight you, Brothers," said Rowen. "I mean you no harm. Now put away your sword."

When Reed didn't listen, Rook rode over and reached out to hit him. "Put away the blade, Reed. We're all brothers."

"Ye sound like ye're turnin' just like Rowen did," snarled Reed. "Is it true? Is there a lassie that ye've fallen in love with that is goin' to talk ye into betrayin' me?"

"That's not it, Reed. You don't understand."

"Mayhap I understand better than ye think, Traitor." Reed turned and raced his horse back to the priory.

"Reed doesn't understand this, but he will in time," said Rowen.

"I don't even understand it," admitted Rook.

"Can I tell the king you're going to join the competition?"

"What if I lose?" asked Rook.

"I'm sure the king would make some other sort of alliance with you if you lost."

"I'm not talking about the alliance, dammit. I'm talking about the fact that if I lose, I'll have to watch as Calliope marries someone else. That would kill me."

"Then don't lose," said Rowen, making it all sound so simple.

"It's jousting, Rowen. I've only just learned to joust within the last week. How can I go up against a seasoned knight and expect to win?"

"I've seen crazier things happen, Brother. Just show up at the competition in the morning. I'll be there with Cordelia. I'll talk to Father in the meantime to make sure you won't be apprehended when you enter the castle's courtyard."

"This is nothing but a trap! Reed is right. Edward is spinning his little web and won't stop until he's tangled us all within it," said Rook, turning away. "And for God's sake, Rowen, stop calling that bastard, Father."

Chapter 21

"I say we raid the king while he's at Naward Castle." Reed moved his rook forward on the chessboard.

"I don't know." Rook grabbed his knight and pulled it back toward his side of the board.

"Why no'?" asked Reed. "We move in quietly and steal from dear old dad while the tournament is takin' place. The castle is open to everyone. My men and I will hide under robes and no one will even notice us." Reed moved another piece, closing in on Rook. He always was the best at chess and nearly unbeatable. Ross had taught him well.

"It's a trap like you said," replied Rook, staring at the chessboard. He saw where Reed was going with this. In another few moves, he'd have Rook's king cornered with no place to go. He haphazardly moved a pawn that Reed spent no time in scooping up off the board.

"Ye're no' goin' to listen to Rowen are ye?"

"How so?" Rook's hand wavered over his queen.

"If ye betray me by marryin' the girl and makin' an alliance with Edward, I'll ne'er forgive ye. Losin' one brother is bad enough."

"Mayhap that would be the better move at this point. After all, we'll never win another raid without Rowen on our side." Rook moved his queen.

"Ye ne'er did ken what the best moves were, Rook. Ye're wrong. Dead wrong. Dinna do it." He slid his bishop across the board and took out Rook's queen.

Rook sighed, feeling stupid that he hadn't seen that coming. But he just couldn't concentrate with so much on his mind. On one side, Rowen was telling him to risk it and join the tournament so he'd have the chance of marrying Calliope. The king even promised to grant him amnesty if he did. If he won, he'd gain not only a wife, but Rowen said that Edward promised to make him a knight. He'd wanted to be a knight for as long as he could remember.

"Take yer move, Brathair. Or are ye afraid?" Reed's head was down, but he looked up with those piercing eyes that challenged and begged Rook at the same time to make the right move.

Rook glanced over at the mural on the wall of the knight jousting. The damaged knight. His hand reached out and his fingers closed around his knight. He moved it forward, taking out one of Reed's pawns. "I'm not afraid of you, Reed, nor will I ever be." He tossed the pawn in the air and caught it with one hand.

"Well, then, mayhap ye're afraid of our faither." He smiled, and then used his castle to take Rook's knight.

"Damn, I didn't see that," Rook mumbled.

"That's just it, Brathair. Ye are thinkin' with yer heart and no' yer head. Ye willna even see what's comin' until Edward has ye in his clutches. Dinna fall for his trap."

"A trap is only detrimental if one doesn't get what he's after." Rook rubbed his fingers over the top of his damaged bishop that Calliope had fixed for him. "What is it that you want in life, Reed?"

"I want to get revenge on Edward for what he's done to us."

"You mean, what he almost did. He didn't succeed in killing us as babies."

"Nor will he succeed now. Hurry up and make your move."

Rook took his hand away from his bishop. "I know things in our lives haven't been good, but mayhap with different choices, our broken lives can be fixed." His gaze fell to the damaged bishop again and Calliope's words keep swirling around in his head.

"We're no' damaged and we dinna need for anyone to fix us."

"Are you sure about that?" asked Rook.

"This is about the lassie, isna it? She's put ideas in yer head. Dinna believe them, Rook. Ye are weakenin'. Ye're thinkin' of joinin' Rowen, are ye no'?"

"I didn't say that." He continued to finger his bishop. "I am just weighing out the consequences. That's all."

"Well, stop it. We need a plan to attack and that's all there is to it. Ye have no choice. It's what we need to do. Now, move yer piece already and stop stallin'."

"We always have a choice, Reed. And don't you ever forget that." He moved his bishop and, in doing so, smiled. "Checkmate."

"Checkmate?" Reed's brow furrowed. "How did ye do that? I didna see it comin'."

"You were so intent on capturing my king that you forgot to watch what you already had," Rook said, standing up and stretching. "I know now that our choices are all that matters. But the question is – how much are we willing to lose in the process, trying to get what we want?"

"Stop talkin' in riddles, ye fool." Reed sprang out of his chair. "What is it ye are tryin' to say? Are ye with us for the raid . . . or are ye against us?"

"How would you like to learn the joust?" asked Rook, heading out of his chamber.

* * *

Calliope sneaked through the dungeon and had just entered the castle's courtyard when her uncle and an entourage came through the gate.

"My lady, where have you been?" asked her handmaid, Amanda, rushing up to greet her. "When I discovered you were missing last night, I went to Lady Joanna right away. She told me not to worry about you, but I did. Are you all right?"

"I had to make one last visit before I got married," she told the woman. "I'm fine. But tell me how Lady Joanna is doing this morning."

"She's still weak and dizzy and hasn't even gotten out of bed. But now that Lord Ovid has returned, he can make sure she's looked after properly."

"I wouldn't hold your breath on that one, Amanda."

The herald sounded the trumpet, announcing Lord Ovid, along with King Edward and his queen, Lady Philippa.

"The king is here?" Calliope asked in amazement. "I wonder what brings him to Naward."

"Mayhap he's here for the tournament and your wedding, Lady Calliope. It's being talked about throughout the land."

"It is?" she asked.

"Lady Calliope, come greet the king and queen," called out her uncle.

"Excuse me," she said, walking forward nervously, not sure she wanted to meet with Edward at this moment. After the story Rook had told her, she saw Edward in a totally different light. Who would order the death of their own innocent babies?

"Your Majesties," she said, curtseying and bowing her head before the king and queen. She had never met them personally before. Since her uncle had kept her locked away in the castle for most of her life, she'd only seen visitors. This was the first time that Edward had visited Naward for as long as she could remember.

"So this is the lucky lady," said the king, holding out his heavily ringed hand. She looked up from her curtsey. "Give me your hand, my lady."

She did as told and he kissed it! His wife stood there watching. "I'm so happy to meet you finally. Your late father, Sir Vance, was one of my favorite knights."

"He was?" she asked, slipping her hand from his. She had never heard this story.

"Didn't he ever tell you that he once saved my life on the battlefield?"

"My father was never one to boast," she remarked.

"My dear, are you ready for the big day tomorrow?" asked Queen Philippa. She was a vision of loveliness dressed in an elegant gown of amber velvet lined with lace. Her dark hair was pulled up atop her head and encircled by a gold crown with jewels. A small, thin veil covered the back of her head.

"The big day?" she repeated, not thinking of anything other than Rook. She wondered what he would do when he woke up to find her gone. Would he come after her or would he let her marry someone else?

"Your wedding day," spat her uncle. "The king has added to the dowry I've offered. Everyone is invited to watch the joust, even the peasants. We will have a huge feast to honor the presence of King Edward and Queen Philippa."

"That's right," said Edward with a chuckle. "Do you see that wagon by the gate? It's filled with riches I'm offering to the winner of the joust."

Her eyes darted over to a wagon covered with a tarp. It looked to be filled with goods. "I am ever so grateful for your generosity, Your Majesty. But if I can be bold enough to ask – why would you do this? You've just met me."

"Calliope, hold your tongue," scolded her uncle.

Edward raised a hand in the air and nodded. "It's quite all right. Lady Calliope has every right to know. As I've told you, your father was once a loyal vassal to me. Now, I'm repaying his good deed by adding to the dowry of his only child."

"Only child?" Her eyes flashed up to his.

"I'm sorry to say I'd never taken the time to know more about Sir Vance's family. But Lord Ovid has told me that your brother died along with his sons in battle."

"He did, did he?" She narrowed her eyes and glared at her uncle.

Her uncle glared back, clearing his throat in a warning for her to stay quiet.

"Is anything the matter?" asked Queen Philippa.

Calliope looked up to the queen, who had a concerned look on her face. "Nay, my Queen," she said, her eyes dropping as she spoke.

"Let us go into the great hall for an ale and to plan the

joust for tomorrow," said Ovid.

As soon as they'd left for the keep, the herald blew the horn again. This time, his announcement surprised her even more.

"Lord Rowen and Lady Cordelia of Whitehaven," announced the herald.

Her eyes darted over to them and her heart almost stopped. This man looked so much like Rook that she wanted to run to him and put her arms around him. But Lord Rowen had bright golden hair, whereas Rook's hair was as dark as midnight. Rowen helped his wife dismount her horse. Calliope noticed Lady Cordelia's hand on her stomach. That was the way Lady Joanna stood as well. Then she remembered talk that Lord Rowen's wife was pregnant. She longed to be pregnant with Rook's baby. If only things could be different – this could be her married to Rook someday.

They glided across the courtyard, looking as regal as the king and queen. It was hard to believe that not that long ago this man was a pirate, raiding the king with his brothers. No one treated him as a bandit now. Nay. They all respected him and bowed to him as he passed by.

"Lady Calliope, I presume?" Lord Rowen held his hand on the small of his wife's back as they came to meet her. Cordelia was a beautiful woman with auburn hair and eyes of emerald green. She wore a green gown covered by a long ermine-lined cloak.

"Lord Rowen, Lady Cordelia, it is so nice to meet you." Calliope curtseyed and paid them the proper respect.

"How exciting that you will be married to the winner of the joust," said Lady Cordelia. "Have you seen how many knights are camped outside the castle, eagerly waiting for a chance to win your hand in marriage?"

"I didn't notice," she said with no excitement in her voice at all.

"You don't sound happy," noticed Lady Cordelia. "Did you want more suitors? With the dowry the king is offering, I'm sure there'll be twice as many wanting to compete on the morrow."

"If you'll pardon me," she said with another curtsey. "I've got much to do to prepare for tomorrow, so I'll leave you now."

She turned and ran back to the keep and up the stairs to her chamber. Once inside her room, she threw herself upon her bed, burying her face in her pillow. She didn't want to marry any of the knights that would show up to claim her as part of their treasure. The only man she wanted for her husband was one she could not have. She would miss Rook and love him with all her heart for the rest of her days.

Chapter 22

The next morning, Rook steadied his lance and urged his horse forward, meeting with Wardell and knocking him from his horse this time. He felt powerful today, as if he could even win the joust and Lady Calliope's hand in marriage if he should decide to compete.

"You have passed up my skills at the joust," said Wardell, getting to his feet and brushing off his clothes. "You are a fast learner, my lord."

"He's no' a lord," grumbled Reed, taking a bite out of an apple as he watched them joust. The rest of the Scots loitered around the courtyard, itching for a raid. He'd yet to give Reed his answer if he would be joining them or not.

"Let's go, Brathair," Reed said. "The competition has already started. If we get there early, there will be a lot of chaos. It will be easy to steal the king's riches and get out before anyone notices we are there."

One of the Scots came running up to join them.

"Reed, I've just come from Naward, like ye told me," he said.

"What did ye find out?" Reed took another bite of an apple.

"The king has a wagon full of riches. It's near the gate and will be easy to pilfer. There is such a large crowd that they barely fit inside the courtyard."

"How many guards are surrounding the wagon?" asked Reed.

"Only two," the man answered. "And they are payin' attention to the joust, not guardin' the riches carefully."

Rook turned his horse a full circle, looking over to his brother. "It's a trap, just like you said, Reed. Edward wants us to come for it. I'm sure it's probably an empty wagon like last time."

"Nay, I lifted the tarp when the guards werena watching," said the Scot. "I saw the barrels and boxes, bolts of fine silk, and even some coins scattered on the bottom. It's real."

"We need to go." Reed tossed his apple core over his shoulder. "Are ye in or no', Rook? We need to ken where ye stand."

Rook felt like he was being pulled in two directions. Rowen wanted him to pay fealty to the king. Reed wanted him to raid the king. Calliope wanted him to marry her, but yet her brother, Everad, wanted him to stay away. What was he to do?

"Did you want to continue jousting?" asked Wardell. "Or were you ready to go to the castle?"

"If we wait much longer, the joust will be o'er and we'll miss our chance," spat Reed. "Without enough men for our army, this will be the only chance we get to raid the king. We need to take it."

"But what if it's just a trap like you said?" asked Wardell. "The king could be putting the dowry out for bait. Once we show up, they'll capture us and throw us in the dungeon." Wardell rubbed his throat. "I don't care to swing from the end of a rope."

"Of course it's a trap," said Rook, dismounting his horse.

"So, ye're sayin' ye willna come with us to Naward?" asked Reed.

"I never said that." Rook ran a hand over his chin in thought. "I'll go with you to Naward Castle, but not without a plan."

"What is yer plan?" asked Reed.

"It is something that I think will work perfectly. And everyone will get what they want in the end."

* * *

Calliope sat in the grandstand, stretching her neck, looking for Rook, but he'd yet to show. The grandstand held raised seats atop a dais, high above the lists and was reserved for the nobles. Spectators watched from the benches set up along the lists or from atop the battlements.

The day dragged on. One after another, men jousted in the tiltyard, vying for the dowry and her hand in marriage. The thought of having to marry any one of these men made her feel ill. She didn't want them. No matter if they had a title, land, money – she didn't care. She only wanted Rook.

She glanced over to Lady Joanna, sitting next to Lord Ovid. Calliope's uncle had dragged the poor woman out of bed and told her she had to attend the tournament today. She looked as white as a ghost and very sickly. Next to them were King Edward and Queen Philippa. At first, the king acted very jolly. But as the day went on, he almost seemed upset. It was probably because his plan of drawing out the

Demon Thief was not working.

Her heart fluttered in her chest. Part of her wanted Rook to stay away so he wouldn't be caught in the king's trap. Yet another part of her wanted him to make an alliance with the king because she selfishly wanted him for herself. He did deserve to be a knight since he was of the king's blood. But then again, he didn't deserve to be forced into doing something he didn't want to do.

"I will be back," she said, standing up, gathering her skirts. She wore a forest-green kirtle made of taffeta with fitchets, or slashes, cut into it with her tan smock peeking out from underneath. Long tippets flowed from her elbows to her ankles. Her hair was coiled around each ear, as was the style of the time. She wore a thin, translucent veil atop her head for the occasion. Her handmaid behind her jumped up as well.

"Calliope, sit down," growled her uncle. "The tournament is nearly over. You can leave once we announce the winner."

"I need to visit the garderobe," she lied, doing all she could to stare at the top of her uncle's head so he wouldn't see she was lying.

"Then hurry up!" spat her uncle. "I'll not announce the winner to an empty chair."

"I feel like I need to go as well," said Joanna, getting out of her chair.

"You'll stay here!" Ovid shoved his wife back down into her chair forcefully.

"I'll take a walk with you," said Lady Cordelia, standing up, being helped by Rowen.

"Hurry back, my love. I'll miss you." Rowen kissed Cordelia on the lips and caressed her cheek. Seeing that only reminded Calliope of Rook, making her feel worse.

Calliope headed down the stairs of the dais with Lady Cordelia. Amanda and Lady Cordelia's lady-in-waiting, Lady Summer, followed behind them.

"You're not really going to the garderobe, are you?" asked Cordelia knowingly.

Calliope shook her head. "Nay, I'm not." She scanned the four or five men left standing in line, waiting for their chance to beat Sir Benton of Suffolk who was winning the joust. He was a large man with a beard so long she was sure it harbored a nest of vermin. He also looked to be at least two decades older than her.

"Is there someone you wish was vying for your hand instead?"

"Nay. Why would you say that?" She continued to scope the grounds.

Lady Cordelia's hand shot out and rested on Calliope's shoulder. They stopped walking and their attendants stopped behind them. "I know you and Rook have made love. Rowen told me."

"He did?" Her head snapped around. "How did he know?"

"He's met with Rook and tried to convince him to come here today to compete for your hand."

"Nay, it's too dangerous," she said shaking her head. "I wouldn't want him to come. He'll be captured."

"Did you know that King Edward has agreed to grant Rook amnesty if he shows up? And if he competes and wins, he can have your hand in marriage and be knighted if he makes an alliance with Edward."

"I didn't know that," she said. "Does Rook know?"

"He does. I'm surprised he hasn't shown up by now."

"Oh, Lady Cordelia, I'm so frightened." She held on to the woman's hands. "I don't want to marry any of these men if Rook doesn't show up. And I'm not sure he will. Even if he does come to compete, what if he loses? What will happen to him then? Or what if he wins and refuses to make an alliance with Edward? He is a complicated man. I never know what he's thinking."

"Rowen did his best to convince him, however, Reed was there trying to stop Rook from taking the deal."

"Reed? The other triplet?" she asked.

"Aye. He is dead set against Edward, so it is uncertain what Rook will do."

"Lady Calliope," came a voice from the crowd. Calliope turned to see the village woman, Ida, holding her baby, with her other children in tow. Two other women from the village were with her.

"Ida, how are you?" She ran to give the woman a hug. "I'm surprised you came to the castle. I know how much you and the other serfs despise and fear my uncle."

"We're here to support you, Lady Calliope. We wanted to be here for you since you have been so kind to all of us."

"Are all the villagers here?" she asked, looking around the crowded area. Nobles and knights roamed the area as well as servants and peasants. Vendors had small carts set up, selling food and ale. The king had also ordered a meal prepared for everyone who had come to the castle today and that food would be served later. A child chased a stray dog through the crowd, darting around one person and then another. And at the entrance of the tiltyard was a long table set up where the competitors registered for the joust.

"We all came," Ida answered with a smile. "We wish you the best with whichever man wins the competition."

Calliope leaned closer and whispered to the woman. "Is Rook here, too?"

"I don't know if he's coming," said Ida. "When we left, he was still practicing the joust."

"Was his other brother, Reed, there as well?"

"He was. And he had a lot of angry Scots with him."

"Oh, no. That can't be good."

"We'd like to enter the contest," came a deep male voice floating on the air. She knew that voice. It was Rook! Calliope spun on her heel to see two men in cloaks standing by the long table.

"You're almost too late," said the man behind the table. "We're down to our last few competitors. You'll need proof of a noble bloodline to show me in order to enter."

"Oh, no," said Calliope as Ida walked away. Lady Cordelia walked up with the attendants right behind her.

"Is something wrong?" she asked.

"It seems Rook has come to the competition after all," said Calliope, her eyes fastened to Rook.

"That's wonderful." Cordelia looked at her and squinted. "Isn't it?"

"It would be, except for the fact they just asked for a patent of nobility and Rook is hiding under a cloak. I'm not sure if he's really here to compete for my hand in marriage . . . or only to steal from the king."

Chapter 23

"Squire, show the man my patents of nobility," Rook said to Wardell who was also half-hidden under a cloak. Wardell put the heavy bag down that held Rook's jousting gear, and patted his pockets, looking for it.

"Try that one," mumbled Rook, hitting Wardell's arm and pointing to the pouch hanging at his side.

"Oh. Right." Wardell fished the parchment out of the bag. It was rolled up and tied with string. Rook had Brother Everad fake the information because he didn't want the king to know he was there. He was only there to create a distraction. He would reveal his identity just before the joust. Everyone would be so shocked to see the Demon Thief there that Reed and his men would easily be able to sneak the dowry out of the castle before anyone noticed. Then Rook would take off before they could catch him.

Rook almost died when he realized the fool had used the opposite side of the bann that announced the contest when he scribed the patents of nobility. He snatched it away from Wardell and quickly unrolled it, so the man behind the table wouldn't notice. Then he slid it over to him.

"Something doesn't look right," said the man, studying the parchment.

Rook groaned and closed his eyes. It was going to be over before it began.

"Sir Rogelio Sebastiano Segundo the fifth of Braviosia?" the man read from the parchment.

Rook's eyes sprang open. Damn. Why hadn't he checked it before coming here? Brother Everad promised him it wasn't going to be questioned.

"And where exactly is Braviosia?" asked the man, leering at Rook.

"Italy," said Rook at the same time Wardell said, "Spain."

"Spain, yes. Si," answered Rook, shooting a sideways glance at Wardell. Perhaps they should have gone over their story a little closer. "I have parents from both places."

"I don't know. Something isn't right." The man shook his head.

"Let him enter," said Calliope, emerging from the crowd. Rook almost called out her name and had to bite his tongue to stay quiet.

"Lady Calliope, with all due respect, I can't let this man enter the contest unless you can vouch that he is of royal blood."

"I can vouch for him. He is a noble," said Calliope looking the man straight in the eye.

"So can I," added Lady Cordelia. "He is a good friend of my husband."

"All right then," said the man, handing the parchment back to Wardell. "Then the only matter we need to handle before you can compete is the entry fee."

"Entry fee?" asked Rook, not knowing about this.

"Yes. It'll be a half-crown," said the man with an outstretched palm.

"But the winner is getting a huge dowry, so why would there be an entry fee?" he grumbled. He didn't have any coins on him and hadn't even thought of bringing any with him. His stolen supply was low and he'd been saving them for food and ale.

"No entry fee, no competing." The man waited with his hand outstretched.

"Give him the money, Squire," Rook said to Wardell.

"Me?" Wardell looked up in confusion.

"Yes, you," he mumbled.

"Are you sure you're Spanish?" asked the man. "You sound English to me."

"Si, si," said Rook, wishing he knew at least another word of the language.

"I'll pay for him," said Calliope, her hand going to the pouch at her side.

"Nay, it's not right for a lady to pay. It's not accepted," protested the man behind the table.

"There you are, Sweetheart." Rowen walked up and put his arm around Cordelia. "I thought, mayhap, the two of you had fallen into the gong pit since you weren't returning."

Rook fixed his hood and looked downward. Why did Rowen have to show up right now? He was going to ruin all the plans. With his head down, he glanced back over his shoulder. Reed was waiting, dressed in a hooded monk's dark cloak by the front gate. His weapons were hidden underneath the garment. The rest of the Scots were also clothed like monks, wandering through the crowd. Brother Everad stood in the shadows.

"Rowen, do you have a half-crown you can give the man to pay for our friend's entrant fee so he can joust and compete for Lady Calliope's hand?" asked Lady Cordelia.

"Our friend?" Rowen looked up in confusion.

"I'm sure you remember Sir Rogelio Sebastiano Segundo the fifth from Braviosia in Spain?"

"Who?" Rowen looked at him closer. Rook knew it was no use. He raised his face, his eyes interlocking with his brother's.

Rowen chuckled and pulled the coin from his pouch and plunked it down on the table. "Aye, I remember our good friend now. Ladies, go back to the grandstand and wait for me there."

"But I'd like to stay," said Calliope.

"Ladies?" Rowen splayed out his hand. "I'll be right with you. I'd just like to make sure our 'friend' knows the rules of the game."

"Come along, Lady Calliope," said Cordelia, pulling Calliope along with her. "I'm sure Rowen will handle everything."

Rook's eyes met with Calliope's as she looked over her shoulder, being all but dragged to the grandstand. He saw the despair in her eyes and wanted to take her in his arms and comfort her, but he couldn't. What would he even say? That he wasn't here to marry her and make an alliance with the king? That he was only here to save Reed's ass because the fool was hell-bent on raiding the king today of all days although Rook was against it? Nay. That would only break her heart. He didn't ever want to hurt Calliope. She was much too special.

"Lady Summer, come along," called out Lady Cordelia.

"Summer?" he mumbled, looking over to see his sister sniffing a flower that she had just gotten from a passing merchant. As she turned, her eyes interlocked with Rook's and she stopped in her tracks. Her mouth fell open and he was sure she was about to cry out his name. He lowered his head quickly. "Come along, Squire." He stepped around the table and walked away from Summer, although he wanted to look at her longer. He'd seen her briefly from a distance at Rowen's wedding, but now that he saw her close up, memories filled his head.

Memories of the times he'd take her riding with him when she was just a child. He'd teased her about the freckles on her nose and pretended to snip her nose off with his hand, showing her his thumb and making her think he'd actually taken it. He'd made her cry more than once in her lifetime. Now he just wanted to tell her that he was sorry.

"Go back to the grandstand while I talk to Lord Bravo," he heard Rowen tell Summer from behind him.

"Braviosia," the man behind the table corrected him.

"Aye, wait up my good . . . friend." Rowen ran up behind him and grabbed him by the elbow. "What the hell are you doing?" he mumbled in his ear.

"Leave me alone." Rook shook out of his hold.

"I told you, the king has said you could compete and he would grant you amnesty," he said in a low voice. "You don't need to pretend to be Lord Sigmund Bravo."

"Sir Rogelio Sebastiano Segundo the fifth," Wardell corrected him. "From Braviosia. That's Spain, not Italy."

"Wardell, enough," growled Rook. "This is my brother, and he knows who I am."

"Oh, yes. I see the resemblance now. So glad to meet you." Wardell raised his chin to look at Rowen. When he did, he saw the competitors and gasped.

"What's the matter?" asked Rook.

"That's Sir Benton," said Wardell, pointing toward the lists.

Rowen nodded. "That's right. Sir Benton is jousting with the last competitor. He's been beating everyone and is about to win the competition."

"Sir Benton?" asked Rook, looking up, wondering who the man was.

"I used to serve as that knight's squire," said Wardell. "You know who I mean. The king's best knight."

"Him?" Rook took a better look. Sir Benton didn't seem that threatening. "He's old. And look at that ungodly long, wiry beard."

"He's going to be Lady Calliope's husband in a few minutes unless you do something about it," Rowen reminded him. "That is why you're here, isn't it? You've decided to fight for the woman you love?"

Rook swallowed deeply, looking over his shoulder at Reed and his men again. He had come here only to create a distraction, but now he wasn't so sure. He needed time to think about all this and now there wasn't any time left. Could it be love he felt for Calliope? And what if it was? What would it matter? He would always be a bastard and not worthy of her. He also would never forgive his father for what he'd done.

"Sir Benton is too good at the joust," said Wardell. "My lord, you need to leave here now. You'll never beat him."

"Father is expecting you to compete," said Rowen. "We were all surprised you hadn't shown up by now."

"Dammit, I don't want to fall into his trap just like you did, Rowen." Rook noticed Edward and Philippa sitting atop the dais.

"You'll be knighted. You've dreamed of that since we were boys."

Rook clenched his teeth and watched as Sir Benton's

lance broke on the competitor's chest. Cheers went up from the crowd. The smell of cherry tarts drifted on the breeze as a pie vendor passed by carrying a tray high in the air. The courtyard was bustling with people of every status, yet everyone was happy. Knights drank ale from large tankards, laughing and slapping each other on the back.

Once more, the competitors met. This time, the sound of the horses' hooves pounding the earth and the exciting shattering of the wooden lances made Rook's passion push anxiously through his veins. He did want to live the life of a knight. Rowen was right. He couldn't deny it.

"Nay! I'll always be a bastard, even with a title," he spat. "You know as well as I that Edward will never legitimize us."

"I've learned to live with that decision," said Rowen.

"Well, I can't." He tried not to let his surroundings affect him. He needed to keep his mind on the reason he was here.

"Can you live with the decision that Calliope is about to marry Sir Benton instead of you?" asked Rowen, driving the notion home. It hurt him deeply, but he needed to stay strong. Just like Brother Everad said, he was no good for Calliope. Sir Benton could give her more than he ever could.

"I'm sure Sir Benton is an excellent knight and will make a good husband to her."

"Aye, I suppose you're right." Rowen turned to look at Sir Benton. The knight was parading around the tiltyard on his horse, waving his hands in the air. "That is, if you don't mind that he likes to beat his women."

"What?" Rook's head snapped around.

"Tell her, Wardell. You were his squire. Tell my brother how Sir Benton beats his women day and night."

"Huh?" Wardell looked up in surprise. He hesitated and

then grinned. "That's right," he agreed. "Sir Benton has a whip, too. He uses it on his women in the bedchamber during coupling. I know, because – because I used to be his squire."

"And that was the last competitor of the day," shouted the knight marshal who announced the joust. "Sir Benton has managed to beat them all."

"You'd better hurry if you're going to save her from a life of doom," said Rowen.

"Callie," whispered Rook, seeing her sitting in the lists, looking around for him. She wore a worried expression on her face and did not look at all happy. He did love her, he decided. It must be love. Because if not, what else would drive him to do what he was about to do?

The marshal called out once more. "I hereby announce the winner of Lady Calliope's hand in marriage to be –"

"Stop!" shouted Rook, pushing his way through the crowd to get to the jousting area. Wardell and Rowen followed at his heels. "Stop, I tell you. I am going to compete for her hand in marriage. Do you hear me?"

"Another competitor has arrived at the last moment," said the marshal. "Come out onto the field and tell us your name."

Wardell rushed out in front of him. "I give you Sir Rogelio Sebastiano Segundo the fifth of Braviosia in -"

"Enough, Wardell," said Rook lowering the hood of his cloak to make his presence known. The crowd quieted. Then he heard a child call out.

"Is that the Demon Thief?"

"The Demon Thief?" asked the marshal, causing a commotion amongst the crowd.

"Nay, I'm not the Demon Thief," Rook shouted to the

crowd. His eyes remained fastened on Calliope as he spoke. Her eyes were filled with fear and she held her hand to her mouth. “My name is Rook. I am the bastard son of King Edward and I am here to claim the title of husband to Lady Calliope of Naward. Aye, I am here to fight for the woman I love.”

Chapter 24

Calliope's heart soared when she heard Rook proudly telling the world who he was and why he was there. He said he loved her! He'd said it aloud. This was more than she could ever have hoped for. She hadn't been sure of his motives when she saw him posing as someone else. But now he had nothing to hide and she couldn't be prouder of him than she was right now.

"Son," said King Edward, standing up and looking over the rail.

"Get him out of here," shouted Lord Ovid, waving his hands in the air.

"Nay, let him compete. Please," Calliope begged, not wanting anyone to send him away.

"Let him pass," said the king with a nod of his head. Calliope didn't miss the small smile Edward tried to hide.

"But he's a bandit who has been raiding you, Your Majesty, if you don't mind me pointing out the fact," complained Ovid.

"I do mind," said Edward in his low, gravelly voice. "This is why I'm here. I'm here to make an alliance with another of my bastard sons."

"You are?" asked Calliope's uncle. "You said you were here because you were close to my half-brother and wanted to see that his daughter married well."

"That is partially correct," said the king. "But did you think I would give such a grand dowry without getting something in return?"

"You knew he was coming," spat Ovid.

"I had hoped so. That's why I lured him here with the dowry. Now, he needs to win the joust so he can make the alliance with me."

"He can't joust. He's a cutthroat, not a noble."

"Rook can joust," said Calliope. "I've seen him do it. I've even given him lances to use for practice while you were away."

"You did what?" Ovid turned and glared at his wife. "You knew about this, didn't you? Why didn't you stop her?"

"Because she is in love, Ovid," said Lady Joanna, still seated, rubbing her stomach. "Leave her alone."

"Don't tell me what to do!" He swung his fist and knocked Lady Joanna off the chair.

"Nay!" Calliope ran over to help her to her feet. "Uncle, how could you hurt your wife? She's carrying your child."

"You're right," spat Ovid. "You are the only one to blame, Calliope." His fist came down toward her next, and she turned her head and closed her eyes, waiting for the contact.

"Don't even think of hurting another woman." Her eyes opened to see Rowen standing there, grasping Ovid's arm, stopping him from hitting her.

"You'll pay for this, bastard!" said Ovid, pushing away from Rowen and going for his sword.

"Stop it, Lord Ovid, or I'll take you down with my sword," said the king. "And God's eyes, learn how to treat women."

"Lady Joanna," said the queen, getting up from her chair to look over to the women. Calliope helped her friend to stand.

"Everyone sit down," said the king. "My son is going to joust now and you will all watch him."

* * *

Sitting atop the horse Rowen had lent him, Rook held his helm in two hands, glancing over his shoulder toward the gate. The crowd had moved closer to watch the Demon Thief joust. He could no longer see Reed or the Scots.

He hoped they hurried, took the dowry and left by now. He didn't want Reed to see him betray him by actually going through with the joust to try to win Calliope's hand. He hadn't planned on doing this when he'd entered the courtyard, but something snapped within him when he realized that Sir Benton, the woman-beating knight, was about to become Calliope's husband.

That made him realize that, although he was only a bastard and far from worthy to have someone as wonderful as Calliope for his wife, at least he would never physically hurt her. He only hoped he hadn't hurt her emotionally by not being able to tell her before now that he loved her. But love wasn't something that came easily to Rook. It took him a while to realize it, but he'd finally come to terms with his feelings.

"Are you ready?" asked Wardell, standing next to the horse with a lance in his hand. The horse was covered by chamfron, or a leather armor protecting its face. Brother Everad stood at the lists, watching intently.

"I'm not sure I'll ever be ready for this," said Rook. "But what choice do I have?"

"You can do it, my lord," said Wardell a little too enthusiastically.

"You don't honestly believe I can beat a seasoned knight that has just won all the other jousts, do you?"

Wardell made a face and shrugged his shoulders. "Like you said, my lord. What other choice do you have at this point?"

"Thanks for the vote of confidence." He covered his head with the helm and slammed down the visor. "Give me the lance, Wardell, and get the hell out of my way. I'm not at all sure what's going to happen."

"Just remember to angle the lance so it breaks. And lean forward a little when you strike so you don't fall off the horse," said Wardell. "Do it just like you have in practice."

"Remind me again why I'm doing this," mumbled Rook, feeling his heart in his throat. This wasn't practice. This was the real thing. He was competing like a knight in a real joust and there was no turning back now. He could end up getting killed if he wasn't careful.

"You're doing it for Lady Calliope," said Wardell, as the marshal counted off. "You're doing it for love. Now, go and win her hand in marriage. Nothing else matters." He slapped the horse on the rear and Rook shot forward.

"Love," he said, as he charged toward his opponent at the lists. The word tasted bittersweet on his tongue. If he won, he'd save Calliope from Sir Benton and have a chance to marry her himself. But he knew in order to do that he would have to pay allegiance to Edward. That is something that still boiled his blood.

His heartbeat pounded in his ears as the destrier beneath him raced forward, its hooves beating the hard earth. He held the lance in a vertical position, clinging to his shield in his left hand. It still felt unnatural to fight right-handed since his dominant hand was his left one. Just one more thing that tagged him as being cursed.

The weight of the metal helm seemed heavier than usual. The visor blocked from his view anything except what was directly in front of him. He could do this, he told himself, getting closer to the ominous Sir Benton.

Barreling toward him was the horrific vision of a man wearing heavy plate armor that covered more of his body than Rook's. A feathered plume sprouted up from the man's helm. His lance looked solid and steady. And his shield boasted the crest of a man with a true title.

"Turn your lance," he heard Wardell call out, jerking him from his thoughts. He suddenly realized that he still carried his lance in a vertical position. He flipped it horizontally, but it was seconds too late. Sir Benton's lance plowed into him, hitting his helm. He fell back on his horse and dropped his lance, hearing and seeing wood splintering in the air from Sir Benton's blow.

The crowd cheered loudly and Rook felt as if he could barely breathe. The impact to his head made his ears ring and he saw stars. Still, he held on to the horse and wasn't unseated.

"Two points awarded to Sir Benton," called out the marshal.

"Two points?" complained Rook, heading back to his starting point where Wardell and Everad ran out to join him.

"My lord, I need to talk with you," said Everad, taking

hold of the horse's reins.

"Not now, Monk. Or haven't you noticed, I'm a little busy?" Rook adjusted his helm, not liking the way it felt. It was heavy and suffocating him. He only had a small area from which to look, and it made him feel boxed in and trapped. He turned and looked back at the grandstand. Calliope was standing there gripping the rail, watching intently. The king was on the edge of his seat, seeming concerned as well.

"I want you to marry my sister," said the monk.

"What?" Rook turned his horse around so he could face Everad. "You told me I wasn't worthy of her and that she needed to marry a real knight."

"I've changed my mind," he said. "I can see how much you love each other. I want you two to be together. Please, win the joust. I don't want her to marry Sir Benton."

"You and me both," he said, taking the lance from Wardell.

"Try to hold on to the lance this time," instructed Wardell. "The idea is to use it to hit your opponent."

"Don't you think I'm trying to do that, you fool? This isn't as easy as jousting against you."

"Sir Benton is one of the best," said Wardell, nodding his head. "He's been unbeaten in every competition for the last two years."

"Now you tell me." Rook slammed down his visor. When the flag was waved, he shot forward on his horse. This time, his grip on the lance was secure. He wouldn't be taken by surprise again. Between his vision being impaired by the helm and his lack of air to breathe, he felt suddenly lightheaded. He charged forward anyway. This pass was better than the first. He managed to strike his opponent, but for some reason, his lance didn't break. Sir Benton's lance hit his chest hard and, once again, almost knocked Rook off his horse. The crowd squealed and shouted, and he came away feeling like a fool again.

"Sir Benton receives two more points," shouted the marshal. "There is only one more pass and the winner of Lady Calliope's hand in marriage will be chosen."

"Nay," he said tearing off his helm and throwing it to the ground. His eyes met Calliope's and he felt like a failure. He wanted to win more than anything. And this time, it had nothing to do with being a knight. He directed his horse over to the grandstand, stopping in front of the woman he loved. "Calliope, I want more than anything to win this competition, but we both know it's impossible for me to beat a trained knight."

"Nay, Rook. You can do it." She removed the veil from her head. "Hold out your hand."

"Why?" he asked.

"Please, just do it. I want you to wear my favor for good luck."

He held out his hand. She tied the veil around it, much like she'd done the first day he met her when she'd bound up his wound with her hair ribbon.

"You win this and I'll knight you, Son," promised the king, causing Rook to turn and look eye to eye at his father.

"He's a bastard," complained Lord Ovid. "He shouldn't even be competing."

"He's my son," said the king. "He's of noble blood, even if he's not legitimized. I'll not hear another word from you, Lord Ovid."

"Yes, Your Majesty," mumbled Ovid, dropping back into his chair.

"You love Lady Calliope, don't you?" asked the queen. She'd been so silent that he'd almost forgotten she was there.

Rook's attention trailed back to Calliope's bright green eyes. She held her chin high and smiled, but he knew she felt scared right now. "I do love her, with all my heart," he said, watching her face light up. "I didn't realize it before, but I do now. And I would do anything at all to make her my wife."

"Even enter into an alliance with me?" asked the king, snapping him out of his lovelorn gaze.

"If I win this competition, will I still be able to claim Lady Calliope as my wife if I don't pay allegiance to you?" he asked.

"Nay!" shouted Ovid, springing out of his chair. "My niece won't marry a bandit."

The king held up his hand to still him. "Finish your joust, Son, and we'll talk."

Rook didn't know what that meant. But at this point, he didn't have a choice. He had to finish what he'd started.

"Win for me, Rook. Please. I don't want to marry Sir Benton." The fear in Calliope's eyes was all he needed to see. He would win this joust or die trying.

"Yah!" he shouted, directing his horse back to Wardell where he would receive one more lance – the last lance that would shape his destiny, as well as Calliope's.

"Hurry," said Wardell. "They're about to raise the flag."

"This is it," said Rook taking the lance. "Any words of wisdom on how to beat your former lord?"

"I wish it were as easy to beat Sir Benton in the joust as it is to beat him in a game of chess," said Wardell. "He can't play chess to save his life."

"I don't care about chess. I'm talking about the joust, dammit. Doesn't the man have any weaknesses?"

"The only weakness he has is that he holds his lance too high and his entire right side is exposed under his ribs."

"You first tell me this now?" growled Rook.

"I didn't mention it because it won't make a difference. His lance will hit with yours before you can ever get it into position."

"Mayhap not," said Rook, changing the hand with which he held the jousting lance. He tested his grip and realized it was much stronger. He'd been jousting right-handed since Wardell had told him that was the only way to do it. But now, with his lance in his dominant hand, he felt as if he were in control.

"What are you doing?" cried Everad.

"I'm using my strength against Sir Benton's weakness."

"You're exposing too much of your body this way. It's not safe," said Wardell. "With the lance in that hand, you'll never get the right angle for it to break at all."

"And where is your helm?" questioned the monk.

"I don't want to wear the helm. I can't see my target well enough with it on and it's hard to breathe. We all know for me even to have a chance of winning, I need to unhorse my opponent."

"You won't need to worry about breathing since you're going to be killed on this pass if you don't protect yourself," scolded the monk.

"I'm trying to protect Calliope. Now leave me be."

The flag was waved and the last pass of the joust began. Rook felt alive and powerful as the wind whipped through his hair. He could see everything now, as well as hear the crowd cheering. Calliope's voice rang out, urging him to win.

As the horses came closer, his life passed before his

eyes. He saw his days as a child, growing up in Scotland with his family, and the horrible day of Burnt Candlemas when he'd lost everything. Then he thought of holding Calliope and kissing her lips – and making love. He wouldn't let another man win her hand in marriage. He would win this joust if it were the last thing he ever did.

His lance being in his left hand didn't cross over his body, nor was he protected at all from the angry knight barreling toward him. Still, Rook felt like a knight as he met his competitor at the list. It was the most powerful feeling he'd ever had in his life.

"Aaaaaaah," he cried out, leaning forward in the saddle, focused on knocking Sir Benton's ass to the ground. Sure enough, the knight held his lance high just like Wardell said. With Rook holding his lance in his left hand it was closer to the center list, and he was able to sneak it under Sir Benton's, hitting him in the exposed ribs. At the same time, Sir Benton's lance grazed Rook's injured leg. He cried out in pain, closing his eyes as the sound of his splintering lance filled the air.

Then he heard cheering, lots of cheering. Rook opened his eyes to see Calliope smiling with her hands on her head. He turned his horse and shouted again when he realized he'd manage to knock Sir Benton to the ground.

"That's three points to Rook the Ruthless," said the marshal, making Rook feel uncomfortable that he hadn't been able to be called "Sir". However, he wouldn't let that bother him because he just knocked a trained knight off his horse. He cheered again and headed his horse back to Wardell and Everad, who didn't look as happy as he felt.

"Did you see that? I unseated him," said Rook excitedly. "My left-handed trick worked. It took him by surprise and I was able to knock him to the ground."

"Aye, my lord," said Wardell. "But you still haven't won."

"I haven't?" he asked, turning back to look at the marshal. "Why not? I knocked him from the horse to the ground. I should have won."

"If you'd taken the time to let me teach you the rules of jousting, you'd realize that your score of three matches Sir Benton's score and now you are tied," explained Wardell.

"Tied?" Rook groaned. His wound had reopened and he was bleeding. Every part of his body ached. How could he ever do another pass to break the tie?

Chapter 25

Calliope screamed and jumped up from her chair, holding her hands to her head. Rook had done it. He'd knocked Sir Benton to the ground and now the score was tied. She'd been so frightened when he hadn't worn his helm. And when he jousted left-handed, she thought that would be the end of him.

"The score is tied," announced the grand marshal. "We will take a short break and then there will be the tie-breaking pass. Whoever wins, will be awarded the Lady Calliope's hand in marriage."

"I'm so frightened," Calliope said to Lady Cordelia. "I don't know if Rook can go another round. He's not used to this."

"I'm sure he can do it," Cordelia tried to reassure her.

"Nay." She shook her head. "I saw blood on him. I think the wound on his leg has broken open. And now that Sir Benton knows Rook's trick, he's going to be prepared. Oh, Lady Cordelia, I don't want to lose him."

She noticed the queen lean over in her chair to whisper something to her husband. Edward nodded and stood, raising his hand in the air to get everyone's attention.

The crowd quieted instantly, waiting to hear the king's announcement.

"For the tie-breaking round, I have decided, by the request of my dear wife, to change the competition."

"Change it?" Calliope looked up. "What could he possibly change it to?" she asked Cordelia. "Rook's hurt. He might not be able to sword fight either. I don't even know if he can stand."

"Shhh," Cordelia told her. "Just listen."

Rowen looked over and nodded to her. "Edward knows what he's doing."

Calliope held her hand to her mouth, wanting to cry out that it wasn't fair. Rook wasn't trained like the rest of the knights. He was a good fighter and a fast learner, but she knew he needed more time to hone his skills.

"The final competition will not be the sport of jousting," announced the king.

"Is it the swords?" asked Calliope's uncle. "Sir Benton will take him down with no trouble if so."

"Nay, it isn't the swords, nor is it anything that involves a weapon," said the king.

The confused conversation of the crowd grew louder.

"What do you mean, no weapon?" growled Ovid.

"Silence!" Edward shot Ovid an angry glare. "The last competition will be held right here in the tiltyard, but it will be a game of chess."

"Chess?" complained Ovid. "What kind of nonsense is this?"

"Ovid, please, sit down," begged his wife, reaching out for his arm.

"Do not touch me or tell me what to do!" He slapped Joanna's face.

"Lord Ovid, you'd better sit because you are angering me," said Edward. "And if you so much as touch your wife harshly again, you will pay for your actions."

Calliope's heart went out to Joanna. She wanted to run to her, but couldn't interrupt the king.

"Sir Benton. Rook," said the king. "Come to the grandstand. Someone bring a table and a chessboard and make it quick."

* * *

"A game of chess?" Rook tried to gain his breath as he removed his gauntlets.

"That's good news, my lord," said Wardell. "I happen to know Sir Benton is horrible at chess."

"Mayhap I'll still have a shot at winning then," said Rook with a nod.

"What the hell are ye doin'?" came Reed's voice in his ear. He turned around to come face to face with his angry, reckless brother.

"Reed, you're supposed to be waiting at the gate with your men." Rook's eyes darted back and forth, making sure no one saw them talking. Reed was still covered by the hooded robe of a monk and, thankfully, his green plaid was hidden for now.

"Ye were only supposed to come in here to make a distraction. I thought the plan was as soon as ye revealed yer identity, ye were goin' to give the signal and we would steal away with the king's goods."

"Plans changed," Rook said, rubbing his hand over his bloodied leg.

"Ye had this planned all along, didna ye? Ye kent ye were goin' to marry Calliope. I'm sure ye're goin' to backstab me just like Rowen did and make an alliance with Edward."

"Calm down," he said under his breath, noticing a few people in the crowd looking in their direction. Rook's raven sat nearby, atop a wagon filled with hay. Rowen's sea hawk was sitting on a perch up at the grandstand and, thankfully, Reed's red kite was nowhere in sight. "You're going to alert Edward that you're here."

"I'll alert him all right. With my sword to his bluidy throat."

"Let me finish the competition. Don't do anything until I tell you."

"Why should I let ye do that? Then ye'll marry the girl and do the king's biddin'. Dammit, Rook, ye are no better than Rowen."

"Yes, I want to marry Calliope because I love her," admitted Rook. "But I haven't decided yet if I will make an alliance with our father."

"Our faither? I've ne'er heard ye call him that. Ye are goin' to betray me, Rook, and I dinna like it."

Rook felt his brother's pain deep in his own chest. He knew it because he had felt the same pain when Rowen turned his back on them. He never thought he'd be in this position, but he was starting to understand why Rowen did it now. "I don't know what I'll do yet, Reed. But whatever it is, I swear it won't be to betray you. I love Calliope. I want her for my wife. And if getting knighted and paying fealty to Edward is what I have to do to give Calliope the life she deserves, then mayhap it isn't as bad as we thought."

"Ye bluidy bastard!" spat Reed. His blue eyes turned

murky with the hatred and anger he held inside. "I should kill ye right now for even havin' a thought like that. Ye are no longer my brathair." He turned sharply on his heel. Rook's hand shot out to clamp around his wrist to keep him from going.

"Reed, listen to me. No matter what I decide, I swear I won't let you down."

"Ye already have."

"I'll cause the distraction as soon as I feel the time is right after I win the competition. That's when you and your men will steal the goods and get the hell out of here."

"Ye no longer call the shots, Traitor. I do, now. So dinna ye worry about me. I dinna need brathairs."

Rook's fingers slowly released Reed's wrist. He watched his brother walk away and disappear into the crowd. Once again, he was torn. But this time, he knew what he had to do.

Chapter 26

Rook limped over to the competition table, seeing that a chess game had been set up in front of the grandstand where the nobles would be able to watch the progress. He felt confident that he'd win now. He almost chuckled aloud when he saw the disturbed look upon Sir Benton's face.

"All right," said the king from his chair. "The competitors will sit and play the game. The winner will have Lady Calliope as his wife."

"I'd like to call in my champion to play for me," announced Sir Benton, surprising Rook.

"Your champion?" asked the king, grabbing on to the arms of his makeshift throne.

"Your Majesty, I have competed and fought in your place on more than one occasion as your champion, have I not?" Sir Benton spoke loudly and played to the crowd.

"Why . . . yes," said the king. "But how does that relate to this?"

"I think you, as well as anyone, knows that the joust is very . . . shall I say, tiring for someone of my age."

"Make your point, Sir Benton," snapped the king.

"I'd like to call in my champion in my place since I don't feel my mind will be able to focus right now. That would not be a fair competition. Unless, for some reason, you are favoring Rook since he is your bastard?"

Rook refrained himself from shouting out that the joust hadn't been fair for him. But since he felt confident in his ability to play chess and win, he said nothing. The crowd became dead silent as they waited for the king's answer.

"Of course I'm not favoring Rook. You've been a good and loyal knight to me, Sir Benton. Go ahead and call in your replacement."

"Thank you, Your Majesty." The man bowed. "I noticed today someone in the crowd I haven't seen in some time now. I'd like to call in as my replacement, my former squire, Wardell."

Rook could do nothing but groan when he heard the announcement. Wardell stepped forward, removing his hood and making his presence known. The crowd gasped and mumbled their shock.

"This is my messenger," said the king.

"He's also the criminal who escaped my dungeon," shouted Ovid, jumping out of his chair. "He's the informant to the Demon Thief, Your Majesty. He was scheduled for execution and needs to die."

Edward nodded his head slowly. "I suppose you are right, Lord Ovid. That is treason, and I can't let him get away with it. Wardell can play in Sir Benton's place and, afterward, he will be executed."

"You can't do that. He's innocent. I won't play against him," protested Rook.

"Did you want to call in a champion in your stead as well, Rook?" asked Edward.

"I didn't think this was a fight to the death," said Rook. His eyes met with Calliope's and he could see that she was crying.

"It's not," said the king. "But I can't let escaped prisoners go free either."

"Then make a deal," said Rook. "If he wins the game for Sir Benton, his life will be spared."

"Nay!" shouted Ovid, pounding his fist against the wooden rail.

"I will grant that request," said the king, seeming irritated by Lord Ovid's outbursts. "The only one who will die is the escaped prisoner should he lose. Now, are you calling in a replacement for you as well, Rook?"

Rook's head spun. He felt so confused. He didn't know what to do. If he won the game, he'd win Calliope and save her from Sir Benton. But in doing so, Wardell would lose his life. He'd grown fond of the boy lately. Wardell had gone out of his way to help Rook. Rook also knew that Wardell wasn't the informant – Calliope filled that position.

He was doomed either way. He couldn't let the boy die, but neither could he expose the truth that Calliope was the informant. If he purposely lost to save the boy's life, Calliope would think he didn't love her. Then his dreams of living with her at his side would be over.

"I choose not to call in a replacement, and I urge Sir Benton to reconsider as well," announced Rook.

"Nay. I will not reconsider, nor will I lose," said Sir Benton. "I know Wardell's talent with the game and have never seen him lose. I have nothing to worry about and neither should he."

"So it seems I'm the only one who loses," grumbled Rook.

Edward sank back atop his cushioned chair. "Competitors take your seats, as the game has begun."

As they both sat at the table, Wardell leaned over and whispered to Rook. "I know how much you and Lady Calliope love each other. I won't do anything that will stop you two from being together."

"Nay," Rook whispered back. "You will not give your life because I won't let you."

"The game has begun," the king reminded them. "The boy will make the first move."

Wardell pushed a pawn forward and Rook reluctantly matched him. The courtyard was silent as everyone watched to see what would happen. After a few moves, Rook could tell Wardell was purposely trying to lose. He'd moved his queen right in the line of Rook's bishop. He had no other choice than to take it. His fingers touched the top of the bishop, but he stopped and pulled back his hand. Pushing up from his seat, he reluctantly looked up to Calliope and shook his head.

"I'm sorry, Callie, but I can't let the boy die." Then he made his announcement. "I reluctantly withdraw from the competition."

The crowd went wild, cheering and booing all at the same time. Then Calliope shouted out, "Nay, you don't need to withdraw, Rook."

"Lady Calliope, please," said Cordelia, reaching for her, but Calliope pushed her hands away.

Rook's eyes met hers. His heart stood still as he heard words he didn't want her to say.

"Rook doesn't need to withdraw from the competition and Wardell doesn't need to die. Wardell isn't the informant, but I know who is."

Chapter 27

Releasing her breath, Calliope felt she was doing the only thing she could. She'd seen what a predicament Rook was in and her heart broke that he'd have to make such a decision. He was an honorable man to give up everything he wanted in order to save Wardell's life. She respected him for that. Still, it wasn't right. Wardell wasn't guilty.

She didn't care what happened to her now. Her confession would save Wardell and show Rook that she loved him.

"Callie, no," said Rook, making his way to the grandstand.

"I have to, Rook. I can't let Wardell die."

"He won't die. I withdrew from the competition," Rook explained.

"I know you love me and I love you. I understand what you did. And I hope you understand that I can't live with this secret while you battle your own decisions. You are too good of a man to have to go through that."

"Lady Calliope, what is it you're trying to say?" asked the king.

She would hesitate no longer. She looked King Edward in the eyes and said, "I am the informant to the Demon Thief."

Gasps went up from the crowd. Even the king looked very surprised.

"Really?" He nodded his head with his eyes sparkling. "Well done. When I sent Wardell to Naward, I had a feeling it would lead me to the true informant. And when I just agreed to take his life if he should lose, I had hoped the real culprit would come forward. But never would I have guessed it was a woman!"

"You set this whole thing up," Rook growled at his father. "I should have figured you had your fingers in the pie as you always do. You laid a trap for the informant just like you did - and are still doing to my brothers and me."

"It's all part of the game, Rook, now calm down," said Edward.

"How can I? You've put Lady Calliope in a horrible situation."

"I'd say she did that herself the minute she decided to work against me," said the king.

"Oh, stop all the idle chatter." Lord Ovid rose from his chair. "Put them both in the dungeon to be executed," he cried out. "As well as the Demon Thief. None of them deserve to live."

"Ovid, stop being so cruel." Lady Joanna got out of her chair, ducking as her husband swiped at her again. "Calliope is your niece."

"She's also an informant and needs to die," he said with no pity at all.

"I thought we would be happy together and that you'd love my baby and me," said Joanna with tears streaming from her eyes. "I lied for you, you bastard." She reached out and pushed him. "I never told a soul your secret that you revealed to me in your sleep."

"Sit down and shut up, Joanna," snarled Ovid.

"I will not!"

Calliope had never seen Joanna so angry. Nor had she seen her stand up to her abusive husband before.

"Another secret?" asked the king. "My, this is some day."

"Don't say a word," Ovid warned her.

"This horrible man killed his own brother in order to gain his inheritance," she announced with tears streaming from her eyes.

"That's not true. My brother died in battle." Ovid glared at her.

"He died from a stab in the back, from you, you coward," cried Joanna. "You also sent your nephew away to become a monk so you could claim everything and give it to your heirs upon your death."

"That's outrageous!" The king got to his feet, his hand on his sword. "Is this the truth, Lord Ovid?"

"It's all a lie," said the man.

"Nay, it's not." Everad stepped forward. "I had my suspicions my father was murdered and even more so when my uncle sent me away to the priory right afterward. I could never prove it, but the fact he'd banned me from ever returning to Naward makes sense now."

"You bitch! Why couldn't you keep your big mouth closed?" Ovid hit Joanna hard and she stumbled backward. She couldn't regain her balance and fell head first down the stairs of the grandstand.

"Joanna!" screamed Calliope, running down the opposite

side and coming around the front to try to make it over to help her friend. Rowen rushed down the stairs after her.

"Calliope, nay," said Rook, reaching out to stop her.

Rowen ran over and bent down to feel the woman's neck. Then he stood up shaking his head. "She's dead," he announced.

The crowd went wild.

"Nay!" Calliope screamed and cried as she fought against Rook's tight hold. The sound of a hawk in the sky made her look upward to see a red kite circling above them. Rowen and Rook noticed it as well.

"Reed," said Rowen

"The Demon Thief has stolen the king's dowry," shouted a guard.

"What the hell is he doing?" Rook let go of Calliope, turning around to look for his brother. Calliope noticed the Scots throwing off their disguises, their robes, to the ground and heading out the gate with barrels over their shoulders and trunks in their arms. She saw someone who looked like Rook but with red hair throw off his robe and draw his sword. It was Rook's brother, Reed.

"Go!" Reed shouted to his men. "I'll hold them off."

"As will we." A good dozen of the Scots fought the guards, trying to give the rest of the men time to escape with the king's riches.

"Kill them. Kill them all," shouted Ovid, drawing his sword and running down the stairs.

The crowd went crazy. With so many people pushing and shoving, trying to get to safety, Calliope was quickly separated from Rook and swept away into the crowd. She tried to make her way back to the grandstand but kept being pushed further away by the frenzied people.

The sound of swords clashing echoed through the courtyard. She feared for Rook and his brothers, as well as for every woman and child there.

"Lady Calliope, I can't find Matthew," screamed the villager, Ida. She clutched her baby to her chest and held the hand of her young daughter, Mary. Her oldest son and daughter stayed close to her side.

"Get to the keep, you'll be safe there," said Calliope, shuffling the woman and her children in the right direction. "I'll find Matthew, don't you worry."

Rook didn't want to fight Reed and the Scots. Neither did he want to fight the English soldiers. All he wanted to do was grab Calliope and get the hell out of there. This had been the worst day of his life. He longed for the silence and comfort of his catacomb chamber, wishing more than anything that he had Calliope safe in his arms. But he didn't. And now she was wanted for her betrayal to the king, just like himself.

"How could you have led Reed and his men in here?" shouted Rowen, fighting with a Scot as he made his way to Rook's side.

"He was being reckless again and strayed from the plan." Rook turned and lifted his sword, clashing with one of Lord Ovid's men.

The crowd continued to be out of control, screaming and pushing as they made their way to the front gate.

"What the hell kind of plan was it?" growled Rowen. "Were you planning a melee that involved women and children?"

"Nay, don't be silly." He hit the guard over the head with the hilt of his sword and pushed him to the ground. "I was supposed to create a distraction so he and the Scots could sneak the dowry out of here while no one was watching."

"Good job," answered Rowen sarcastically. "I need to find my wife and protect her and my unborn child. Why don't you figure out a way to remedy this situation quickly?"

"If only I could," mumbled Rook, punching a Scot so he wouldn't have to kill him.

Rook no longer knew who he was or what side he was fighting for. He'd made some mistakes today and, because of it, he was the cause of all this chaos. He'd never forgive himself if anything happened to Calliope.

"Callie, where are you?" he called out, not seeing her anywhere in the crowd.

"Matthew, come here." That was her voice. He turned to see her by the well, holding on to the hand of one of Ida's children. He quickly made his way over to them.

"Callie, take the boy and get to safety in the keep. Hurry."

"What about you, Rook?"

"Don't worry about me. I can take care of myself, now go!"

She had just left when he turned around to meet with Ovid's fist to his face. Caught by surprise, he fell to the ground and his sword went sliding across the cobblestones.

"This is all your fault. If you hadn't come around, none of this would have happened." Ovid had malice in his eyes. Rook knew he was there to finish him off.

But before Rook could sit up and look for his sword, Ovid's blade came down at him like the hammer of Thor.

"Nay!" he shouted, rolling out of the way just as Ovid's body came crashing down next to him. He grabbed his sword and turned back to see King Edward putting his foot on Ovid's backside as he retrieved his sword from the man's body. Ovid was dead.

"I didn't see any problem stabbing him in the back since that's what he did to one of my good friends." Edward extended his hand to Rook and smiled. "Come on, Son. Let's stop this nonsense before anyone else gets killed. We're here for a wedding, not a funeral."

All thoughts of hatred and revenge toward his father left him at that moment. His father – the king – had just saved his life when he was sure the man was out to take it. He stared at Edward's proffered hand. All he had to do was accept it and everything would be different. This time, Rook didn't hear that voice warning him not to do it. With Edward's kind gesture, not to mention the fact he'd just saved Rook's life as well as called him 'Son', something deep inside Rook was released. He no longer wanted to be mad at his father and felt as if they should be friends.

Perhaps it was the man's past decisions and actions he had hated and not really Edward himself. Edward had made some decisions he now regretted. Rook had done the same. He wanted more than anything to reach out and take his father's hand. It felt good. It felt like the right thing to do.

It felt like family and it felt like home.

With one shaky hand, he reached up and pressed his hand into his father's. Edward's fingers curled around, gripping Rook's hand tightly as he pulled him to his feet. Then he chuckled.

"I knew you boys would be trouble from the day you were born," said Edward. "However, I didn't know how much trouble."

Rook didn't say a word. His tongue felt three sizes too

big for his mouth. He couldn't find the words to speak.

"I know you hate me, Rook. I would, too, if I were in your place. We've all made mistakes in the past and made decisions that we wish we could go back and change. I no longer hold it against you and your brothers that you fought against me as the Demon Thief. It was an infamous legend while it lasted, but it needs to be over now. I want things to be different between us from now on. I hope you do, too."

"I – I guess so."

"Dammit, Son, don't sound like a milksop. Either you want Calliope for your wife or you don't."

Rook smiled and nodded to his father. "Yes, Sir, I do," he answered, feeling more confident than he'd ever been in his life.

Chapter 28

Two days later, Rook waited nervously in the castle's chapel with his brother, Rowen, at his side. The priest bowed his head, pretending to look at the prayer book rather than to look in the Demon Thief's eyes. Today was the day Rook would marry Calliope. The last few days had been bedlam. They'd spent time helping the wounded and burying the dead.

Once Ovid was killed, the king called back the guards, allowing Reed and the Scots a head start before he sent his men out to look for them again and collect the stolen goods. Rook wasn't sure if it was part of Edward's cat and mouse game or an actual act of compassion toward the only one of his bastard sons who he hadn't been able to bring over to his side.

Either way, it didn't matter. With Ovid gone, Edward had taken control of what went on at Naward Castle.

"Stop with the fidgeting, Rook. You've made the right decision," whispered Rowen.

"I'm worried about Reed," he said. "I've never seen him so angry or acting so reckless. The damned fool could have gotten himself killed."

The priest cleared his throat and looked up at them from the corner of his eye. Rook lowered his voice and continued to talk.

"I didn't want to betray him, Rowen. But I understand now why you did the things you did and made those decisions."

"I knew you would in time." Rowen put his hand on Rook's shoulder. "You won't regret it. Calliope is a wonderful girl and you two will make a good couple."

"I still don't feel like I deserve her."

"Try to forget about all that and enjoy yourself, Brother. This is your wedding day."

A musician started playing soft music on a lute that helped Rook to feel at ease. Inside the chapel, in the front row, sat Edward and the queen with the nobles filling up the rest of the room. He turned around to see a vision of loveliness that walked down the aisle.

First came Ida's young daughter, Mary, carrying a basket and sprinkling wildflowers along the path. The chapel was small and crowded, with most of the villagers and serfs standing out in the corridor, peeking in at the ceremony.

Behind the young girl was Rowen's wife, Lady Cordelia, dressed in a beautiful, burgundy gown and carrying a small bouquet of autumn flowers. Behind her was the biggest surprise. His eldest sister, Summer, looking radiant and beautiful, smiled at him, leading the way for the bride.

"Summer," he whispered, so happy to see her again after so many years. When Rook and his brothers left them the night of Burnt Candlemas, their sisters were only toddlers. He never thought he'd see them again. They were actually cousins, since their mother, Annalyse, had been his mother's twin sister, but he'd always consider them his sisters.

"I sent a missive to Whitehaven," said Rowen. "Annalyse, Autumn and Winter have come for your wedding as well." Sure enough, Rook spotted his other two sisters and the woman he'd known as his mother at the back of the room. His heart was filled with gladness. This brought back memories of his childhood, bringing a tear to his eyes.

With hair of black, blond, and red, his sisters were so much like Rook, Rowen, and Reed. He smiled at Annalyse and nodded as he caught her eye. She blew him a kiss. That's when he realized he missed her most of all. He would never stop wondering his entire life what it would have felt like to have known his birth mother.

How could a man feel so empty and so fulfilled at the same time? He'd convinced himself he didn't need family. But Calliope had made him realize that mayhap he did.

"Callie," he said, his eyes fastening to the golden goddess that emerged next, wearing a long, blue velvet gown with gold brocade and long tippets. Her green eyes twinkled in the firelight of the candles. Her skin looked like snow and her lips like a red berry in winter.

Her brother, Everad, walked her down the aisle, dressed in one of his best robes.

Rook took Calliope's hand as she approached, feeling so lucky and wealthy to be with the woman he loved.

As if in a dream, the wedding went by quickly. Rook barely remembered saying his vows. Before he knew it, they were kissing and everyone applauded.

"We are finally married," said Calliope, looking at the ring on her finger. Rook had bought it from a traveling vendor yesterday, not wanting Calliope to be married without a ring.

"I'll buy you a better ring as soon as I have more money," he said, lifting her hand and kissing her fingers. It was a simple ring and not very expensive, but she didn't seem to mind.

"I don't need fancy baubles, as long as I have you. This is my dream come true."

The king had pardoned both Calliope and Everad for their deceit of being informants. And, of course, Wardell was free as well since the boy was innocent and only a pawn in the king's game.

Edward cleared his throat and stood, making his way to the altar.

"Now that you're married, Rook, I'd like to make you a knight."

"A knight," he repeated, thinking of the painting on his wall in his catacomb room. He'd stared at it for years, always wishing and dreaming to be in that position. Then he thought of the chess piece that had been broken and how Calliope had fixed it. He had been broken as well. But because of Calliope's love and faith in him, he felt like a knight already even if he wasn't titled.

"You're not changing your mind, are you, Son?" asked Edward.

Calliope looked up and bit her lip, waiting for his answer. "Rook. You will be knighted and pay fealty to King Edward now that we're married, won't you?" she asked.

Rook had gone through so much turmoil in his head, weighing out the consequences over and over again in the past few days. He had, at one time, thought he would never forgive Edward for wanting them killed at birth. Then again, he had never thought he'd find someone like Calliope who would turn his life around and help him to forget about his dark ways and vengeance.

"I'm sure of this," said Rook, staring into his new wife's eyes. "I've had a very special person help me to realize that I've been wrong in my thinking and have missed out on so much in life because of it."

"Then let's proceed." The king held out his hands and Rook gave him his sword. Then Rook got down on one knee and bowed before his king, making a second vow that day. He closed his eyes as Edward tapped him on each shoulder while Rook repeated the vows of a knight. His head dizzied and his heart beat faster when he heard Edward's next words.

"I dub thee, Sir Rook."

Rook opened his eyes and stood up, bowing to his father. After replacing his sword, he turned to the sea of onlookers smiling at him and applauding.

"You're a knight now, but you'll need a squire," said Rowen.

"Did you have one in mind?" asked the king. "If not, I can assign one to you."

"Thank you, but there is only one person for the job," said Rook with a smile. "Wardell, will you be my squire? You have already acted like my squire in training me for the joust amongst many other things. I would want no one but you at my side to cover my back when I went to battle."

Wardell walked up slowly, bowing when he got in front of Rook. "It would be my honor to serve you, Lord Rook."

"Then it's settled," said Rook, reaching out and embracing Wardell with a slap to the back.

"There is still one more issue of concern," said the king. "I'd like my wife, Queen Philippa, to come up here and tell you what it is."

A guard escorted the queen to the dais. Queen Philippa was breathtaking with the royal jewels around her neck and wearing a purple silk gown. She smiled, having the kindest expression upon her milky white face. Rook had known it was Philippa's idea to have the chess game at the competition. He also knew that she was a strong woman and wanted him to win so he could marry Calliope.

"Sir Rook, since Lord Ovid's passing, you will now inherit Naward Castle and the lands that go with it. With Lady Calliope at your side, you will rule as Lord of Naward."

This was more than Rook could ask for and a dream come true. But when he looked over at the monk, he knew he couldn't accept such an offer. He shook his head. "Nay, it should be Brother Everad, not me. He is the first male heir of the late Lord Vance Duval of Naward."

"It's all right, Rook." Everad smiled and pressed his hands together as if in prayer. "You see, I've decided to stay a monk. I am going to go through my training again. This time, I won't stray from my vows. So, I'm sorry to say I won't be fighting at your side anymore, Sir Rook.

The crowd laughed at his announcement.

"I respect your decision, Brother Everad." Rook reached out and shook the man's hand. Then he looked back to the king and queen. "I am happy to say that I accept the position as Lord of Naward. And Everad and Calliope, I swear I will do your late father justice in his stead."

"You will be a respected and fair lord," said Calliope, reaching up to kiss him. "The villagers are excited that they will be under your rule now instead of my uncle's. I already told them that you would make things right again."

"You have a lot of confidence in me, Callie. I'm not sure

I'll even make a good knight."

"I'm sure you will. I've seen that spark within you growing to a flame lately."

"Aye, with your help to fan it," he answered with a chuckle. "Seriously, though, I feel the change as well. It is so good to come out of the darkness. I promise you, Callie, as well as all the occupants of this castle, the nobles, the servants, the villagers, and my father – my king, that I will be a loyal and fair knight and uphold my vows. Never again will you see the selfish man who lives in the dark amongst the dead. I feel as if I've been offered another chance at my life and I plan to make the best of it. Thanks to your love, Callie, I've moved toward the light and will continue to do so more and more each day. I have put to rest not only an old legend based on hatred and vengeance, but I've also laid to rest my reputation of being ruthless. No one will ever be able to call me a ***Ruthless Knight!***"

From the Author:

I hope you enjoyed ***Ruthless Knight*** – Book 2 in my **Legendary Bastards of the Crown Series**. If so, I'd love for you to leave a review for me on Amazon.

Rook was more or less my "middle child" of the triplets. Being pulled in both directions, it was very hard for him to know if he should follow Rowen or Reed. He was torn between the dark and light. Of course, a good woman like Calliope was there to show him the way out of the darkness and back to the light.

He had to be one of my most mentally tortured heroes with all the choices he had to make. Be sure to watch for Reed's story, ***Reckless Highlander*** coming this spring.

If you happened to miss the prequel for this series, it is called ***Destiny's Kiss*** and is the backstory of Annalyse and Ross and the boys as children. In the last book of the series, Annalyse and Ross will tie up their loose ends as well.

And if you haven't read Rowen's story, be sure to do so in ***Restless Sea Lord***!

Please be sure to stop by and visit my website at **http://elizabethrosenovels.com** to find out more about my books. You can also follow me on Twitter **@ElizRoseNovels**, or Facebook, **Elizabeth Rose – Author**, (don't forget the dash.)

Elizabeth Rose

Made in the USA
San Bernardino, CA
21 February 2017